entertaining disasters

a novel (with recipes)

entertaining disasters

a novel (with recipes)

NANCY SPILLER

COUNTERPOINT

BERKELEY

Refugee Stew recipe courtesy of San Francisco History Center,
San Francisco Public Library

Library of Congress Cataloging-in-Publication Data

Spiller, Nancy.
Entertaining disasters : a novel (with recipes) / Nancy Spiller.
p. cm.
ISBN-13: 978-1-58243-451-3
ISBN-10: 1-58243-451-4
1. Food writers—Fiction. 2. Parties—Fiction. 3. Dinners and dining—Fiction. I.
Title.

PS3619.P547E58 2009
813'.6—dc22

2008034649

Cover design by Gerilyn Attebery
Interior design by Tabitha Lahr
Printed in the United States of America

COUNTERPOINT
2117 Fourth Street
Suite D
Berkeley, CA 94710

www.counterpointpress.com

Distributed by Publishers Group West

10 9 8 7 6 5 4 3 2 1

For Marguerite
(1918–2007)

"I have finally arrived at an age where the things I remember most clearly, never happened at all."

—Mark Twain

• •

"No amount of fire or freshness can challenge what a man will store up in his ghostly heart."

—F. Scott Fitzgerald, *The Great Gatsby*

CONTENTS

....

Chapter 1

GRAINS OF PARADISE 1

Chapter 2

CHRONIC CULINARY FATIGUE SYNDROME 13

Chapter 3

BONUS TIME 21

Chapter 4

OPERA CAKE 35

Chapter 5

ZERO POPULATION COLESLAW 49

Chapter 6

COMMANDER AND CHEF 59

Chapter 7

WHERE THE THISTLE GROWS 71

Chapter 8

HORSE AND CARRIAGE 81

Chapter 9

THE SICK ROOM 103

Chapter 10

YELLOW WALLPAPER 123

Chapter 11

GARLIC MAKES US INTERESTING 137

Chapter 12

THE BEE MAN 153

Chapter 13

WELCOME TORTURES 167

Chapter 14

TRAIL'S END CAFE 187

Chapter 15

REFUGEES' COOK BOOK 203

Chapter 16

SARGASSO SEA 221

Chapter 17
AN ARMY OF GINGERBREAD MEN 239

Chapter 18
FROG STEW 253

Chapter 19
REDEMPTION CENTER 267

Chapter 20
HOW TO MAKE A PIE 281

Chapter 21
HANDS FRAGRANT WITH ROSEMARY 297

Chapter 1

GRAINS OF PARADISE

I paw through the kitchen cupboard for my Grains of Paradise, the seeds of a flowering West African plant used in medieval Europe as an inexpensive alternative to the precious black pepper of South India's Malabar region. Grains of Paradise look like peppercorns, only they're smaller and, when bitten into, have a floral essence with a hot aftertaste. Few people in modern times have ever heard of them; thus the necessity of finding the small plastic pouch, ordered online and delivered by U.S. mail, for my dinner party Saturday night. I'll sprinkle the cracked seeds on the squab before grilling. The novelty will provide a few moments of energetic conversation as guests exclaim and inquire as to its history and use.

If I can find it. If I can't, I'll have to find something else to talk about.

Like the fact that I haven't given an actual dinner party in nearly ten years. This despite my having written about them for countless magazines and newspapers during that same period, as if I had been graciously throwing them on a regular basis as effortlessly as others breathe.

The truth is, I am a food writer giving my first dinner party in a decade after inventing them for the page all that time. In print you'd think I slept in a hostess apron and oven mitts alongside a rumaki tray. In truth, just the thought of having people over left me paralyzed with fear. Despite doing it most all my life before I started writing about it, I considered each and every event an unmitigated disaster voided only by launching plans for the next dinner party or Sunday brunch or ladies' luncheon. I believed with the hope of the blind, naïve, and foolish that every new undertaking would be better than the last.

I don't want to talk about that during the course of the evening's festivities; hence I must find the Grains of Paradise, a more suitable, less volatile subject. Especially since the reason for the evening is Richard Cronenberg, an editor for a major food magazine who believes in my fantasy-hostess life and who I hope will ask me to write about more such mythical events for his publication.

The grains are here somewhere, buried deep, past the truffle oil I consider too expensive to use anytime I remember its existence, and the can of baking powder untouched since my last biscuit foray, about a decade ago, when carbohydrates were still cool, past the hundred and one different kinds of tea we keep even though my husband and I only drink it when we're out of coffee, a condition we're so paranoid about facing it will never happen, not in this house, not in our lifetime—still, I can't resist a good-looking box of tea, getting all the alleged soothing and inspirational benefits of the beverage just from the packaging art—past the balsamic vinegar, the real thing, the good stuff from Modena, a bottle hand-carried back from Italy, boasting the official D.O.P. stamp assuring its twenty-five years of age and meeting traditional standards currently maintained by the *Consorzio Produttori*. This isn't the same stuff that they pour onto the plate along with olive oil for dipping bread, or use by the bucket for salad dressing at every Italian restaurant. This is the sumptuous distillation of the unfermented musts of trebbiano, lambrusco, and sauvignon grapes boiled in an open copper pot over a direct flame down to a syrupy thickness, then aged in a succession of various wood barrels, including chestnut, cherry, oak, juniper, mulberry, each imparting its own perfume and hint of flavor—a method dating back to the early Middle Ages and perfected during the Renaissance by the Ducal family of Este, who kept a special room in their palace in Modena for the aging that would span generations, the precious end product being of prime interest in many Modenese wills. When Modena was threatened with bombing by Allied planes in World War II, evacuees were seen taking the family cask of vinegar along as one of their most precious possessions. This balsamic vinegar is so potent it is used in droplets, for centuries was considered medicinal, enjoyed by the sip like a cordial. Rossini is said to have cured scurvy with it (and what, might one ask, was Rossini doing with scurvy?). It is a phenomenon from a slower, more intensely flavored and authentic world that is difficult to secure and comes, always, at a steep price. *Troppo caro*, as the Italians say. Too dear.

I'll leave the good bottle out on the counter, even though I'll use only a few drops in the vinaigrette, mixing it in with a large measure of the less expensive supermarket ringer, the industrial version of balsamic, that has caramel additives to fake the real thing's aged mellow sweetness. The authentic item in the eccentric bottle is part of the set dressing for the party, six days from today, my panic regarding the evening's conversation content having set in particularly early, and I can't settle down to the other, more substantive tasks until I've found a potential icebreaker.

"Why do they call it balsamic?" an unsuspecting guest will ask. It's all the flick of a riding crop I need. "For its alleged health-giving properties," I'll respond, galloping off from there down my usual garrulous path. I'll try to rein myself in, but sometimes it's hard; sometimes I suspect I know far too much about food, and nothing about so many much more important things. Not that food isn't the stuff of life. It's just that at times I wonder if there isn't more to life than this stuff. Anyway, it's what I do, and my incessant talking and thinking and writing about it is a professional hazard, so, my apologies in advance to all my evening's victims.

I grab the step stool, which hoists me up another foot and a half, and there they are, the Grains of Paradise, lurking behind a stack of toothpick boxes. Hostess Tip #3,112: One can never have too many toothpicks, but do try to use them sometime. I set a box on the counter and resolve to find something to stab them into during the evening's merriment. I set the Ziploc bag of Grains of Paradise next to the balsamic vinegar—a dress rehearsal for Saturday's program.

Okay, that's good for one chatty stretch. What else will we talk about?

*A*t my invented dinner parties, conversation flows like vintage Dom Pérignon. Every one of my highly culti-vated, well-traveled, and gastronomically sophisticated guests is at ease, witty, and bright, while I enlighten and entertain a deliciously captive audience with well-crafted bits of culinary esoterica. In truth, I've always had to dig desperately and deep to whip a brief moment of banter into bubbly blocks of time and pray that my tongue won't be tied and my brain frozen by the end of the first hour, knowing there will be, if I am both blessed and cursed by the presence of actual guests, several more hours to fill.

I realize full well that I play a large part in my misery. I am a writer working at home. I have nothing to say, but a greater need than most to say it. I am also married and, contrary to popular myth, this arrangement of a second, known entity cohabiting under the same roof does not provide some measure of company. An Episcopal priest once referred to marriage, of which he had performed many, as "the end of loneliness." I trust he was being ironic. Marriage isn't the end of loneliness; if anything, it's a final confirmation of just how lonely two people can be. I married that outgoing Other with the dashing smile and ebullient manner only to discover that, like the tool box he owned but didn't know how to use, he was as uncomfortable in the larger world as I.

Now long conjoined, our daily tête-à-têtes involve tracking dull household details and mapping nonevents. "Ja eat?" is couples' French for "I'm hungry, and all else at this moment will remain unspoken." Guests, on the other hand, force you to say something fresh and engaging in the quotidian setting of your own home. They are like good art in the sense that they *re*-present the world. Toss a few around the living room, and suddenly you will see yourself in a new light—even if it is the ashy glare of burning adrenalin.

When desperately seeking topics of discussion, know that under no circumstances is television considered suitable, lest one be labeled a Television Watcher. This is a challenge for me, considering that as a child I was raised by the *Idiot Box* or *Boob Tube*, as my father dubbed it—growing up in the suburbs of Northern California. I still have a fondness for it today, on a strict anthropological basis, of course. During my previous Dinner Party Throwing Era (DPTE), my rule was no television for two weeks leading up to the date. Like a snail dining on lettuce prior to becoming someone's feast, I would cleanse myself of all tainted televised stimuli so that more subtle and civilized discussions could evolve, prompted by a recent *New Yorker* article or a fascinating book finally finished.

This was because no one watched television anymore, or at least admitted watching it. And if they did confess to a few brief moments of attention blown on the déclassé box, it was only because they were busting a gut to tell you about some special they'd caught on a premium cable channel (during a week when it was free, as they would never dream of paying for it) or the decline of civilization they'd witnessed on one of the increasingly desperate broadcast networks' shows.

And whatever it was they'd watched, I no doubt hadn't seen it. There were no "must see" shows, because no one watched television anymore, so there was no way to anticipate potential common ground, know what you should try to watch in an effort to participate in an exchange. I was left no choice but to listen and nod at their monologue, just as they might have to suffer in silence if I seized the pulpit with a food foray.

TV is considered a waste of time, a distraction from work or exercise, which are good for you, but a solo pursuit, not a shared culture. Movies used to be a shared culture, but good ones and the time to see them and the likelihood that whoever you were talking to had seen the same film were becoming as rare a treat as a four-leaf clover found on the 405 freeway during rush hour. Shared popular culture of an intelligent nature is increasingly difficult to come by. We are all islands, or maybe glacier pups, bumping into each other in arctic waters in the middle of the night.

*B*ut I didn't have two weeks this time around for my TV fast. By Thursday last, ten days before the big day, my mind was too wobbly for words on the page. I needed a comalike calm achieved only by watching something that moved across a screen and spoke to me, however low the level of discourse, and despite the fact that it was a piece of furniture.

It didn't matter what I watched, since gabbing about it wasn't going to be an option. Thursday night's TV listing featured a promising distraction: an episode of a three-part BBC documentary on PBS about a house built in London to re-create life for the British middle class in the year 1900. Its talking stock potential rose because it was on PBS, with bonus points earned for originating with the BBC. Maybe I'd cull an entertaining three-sentence critique from an hour or two spent.

I sat, I watched, I saw a British family from the end of the twentieth century living in the 1900 house for a period of months while camera crews captured the time travelers' challenges. The entire episode was filled with the wife's complaints about dust. Her days were devoted to chasing dust balls across floors, lodged beneath furniture, and settled on every surface. It was driving her mad, she said, absolutely bonkers, and her solution was to hire a lower-class female to dust. This woman was as desperately dull as I feared I was becoming. Mention this to anyone, and they'd start acting like dust bunnies, drifting toward the door.

I grabbed my volume of *A Brief History of Time*, which I'd begun to read dozens of times before, pulled on my sweats, and headed for the gym. Walking helped me focus when I was too frazzled to sit and read. I mounted the treadmill, marched an hour with Stephen Hawking, exercised my brain and body, burned a few calories, and finally got past page twenty-two, a few stomps closer to understanding the theory of relativity, yet miles away from anything interesting to say while staring deep into the gaze of a living guest.

The reason I go to such great lengths to salt the kitchen with conversation pieces, like the bottle of twenty-five-year-old *aceto balsamico* and the Grains of Paradise, and read books that I won't finish, barely understand, and won't retain a week after I shut the cover, is that I have no family to speak of. I am reminded of this when I pull the balsamic bottle from the cupboard only to reveal a box of fruit jellies. These dusty-looking squares of brightly colored jelly, each artificially flavored to match a cartoon concept of fruit, i.e., red for strawberry, green for apple, and so on, are too suspect to eat and too emotionally charged to throw away. They were a gift from my brother Hailey countless Christmases ago.

They are a physical manifestation of my ghost family, the family that exists beyond my reach. They haunt me with their distance, and because of this distance I can't go a day without thinking of them.

They are ever present in my thoughts, yet I don't speak of them to anyone, as if their distance, which I've never understood, were my personal failing. They are my dark obsession, thoughts of them gnawing at me constantly, like a pack of mice tunneling into a loaf of bread.

Talk of television with my guests would reveal the bare horizon of my days. A glimpse of my ghost family would hint at the blank landscape of my life.

Hailey's jelly squares came with no return address. Most years it's just a card. Because there is never a return address, I am unable to reciprocate. My father gives me phone numbers to call, and I get disconnected lines. The addresses he finds when asked come back RETURN TO SENDER. Because of this, I can't stop thinking about Hailey. I wonder what could I do or say that would make him want me in his life? Or get him to leave me permanently alone? I rehearse the speeches in my head. I know this is ridiculous, yet I am unable to abandon the idea that he is my family and family is all I've got. I feel helpless to keep this chronic Hailey invasion from my mind.

There are no calls or cards coming from my younger brother, Howard. I know well where he can be found, but consider him an untouchable. His anger has metastasized to such an alarming degree, I've stopped visiting for fear of my safety. He lives in an old farmhouse on a few acres east of Livermore, in Northern California, where he stores earthmoving equipment and keeps a pack of vicious rescued dogs, dogs that bark and threaten in a way he can only dream of doing himself. Last time I paid a call, I left shaking and never went back. It has been surprisingly easy not to act on the urge to contact him when I'm in the area, but painful all the same. He makes no effort at communication, and that makes me worry about him, still. Why? Because the thought of him breaks my heart. Proof, I suppose, that I still have one.

I don't know if my sister, Hunter, is alive or dead. The last I heard from her was a message left on my cell phone, which I rarely use or retrieve messages from, so it's a safe number to call if someone doesn't want to talk to me. She said she had uterine cancer and just wanted me to know "so you can keep an eye on yourself." My father assured me she was fine, though he said he couldn't find her phone number when I asked, or that he'd temporarily misplaced her new address and he'd get back to me with it, but he never did. He would never say she asked him not to give me the information; he preferred to distract, as is his nature, with amusing feints and quips and was expert at changing the subject.

If Hunter were dead he probably wouldn't tell me that, either. He doesn't like to upset.

My father takes my phone calls, returns them when required. He accepts my visits but makes none of his own. We talk of the weather and real estate prices and the mysteries surrounding my ancestors several generations back. We don't talk of the living or of our family's dissolution or of my mother, who is living, but not in our world and hasn't been fully since before I was born.

All of this gets a fresh stir when grieving families who have lost loved ones are reported on the news. My family remains in corporeal existence in the form of six people, yet died in spirit sometime long ago in a tragedy no one has ever discussed. They are like an exploding cloud of space dust, particulate matter racing farther apart with time's passage. If a microphone were shoved into their faces in search of a reaction to our clan's demise, the response would be a blank stare or no comment.

No one, as far as I know, has ever reported on a family's grieving at its own death. That would take too much newsprint and airtime.

There isn't a place for a family like ours in the grand scheme of American dreams, and no one, least of all us, knows how to respond to it.

Sometimes I fear that if I stop mourning its loss, this family will cease to exist altogether. That my sorrow is the only thing keeping it alive. Or possibly that this family never existed at all.

I don't feel comfortable mentioning any of this in polite company, yet it is the prime reason I seek the solace of polite company. Thus the set dressing, the bottle of balsamic, my modest affectations in an effort to keep things rolling along.

Parmigiano-Reggiano and Aceto Balsamico

. . . .

1 chunk Parmigiano-Reggiano, aged at least 24 months (36 is better)

1 bottle aceto balsamico, at least 25 years old, with authentic D.O.P. stamp

Arrange chunk of cheese on a board, let come to room temperature, and slice into thin slivers or sticks. Pour small amount of *aceto balsamico* into attractive, appropriate-size dish. Dip cheese slivers into vinegar; nibble and savor; count blessings.

Chapter 2

CHRONIC CULINARY
FATIGUE SYNDROME

*I*n my previous life as a hostess I did dinner parties on a
regular basis, despite the fact that each episode left me a
shredded wreck. For months afterward I suffered facial tics and
blurred vision and felt stupid, my mind gooey as marmalade,
with a shocking loss of energy requiring extended bedrest and
daily afternoon naps. It was as if the effort had induced a chronic
culinary fatigue syndrome.

While my guests were on the premises I felt occupied, infected
by their presence, resenting them as if they were an invading army.
Once they came through my door, I couldn't remember why I'd
invited them and couldn't wait until they'd left. All I could think of
from the moment they were crowding me in my kitchen, a glass of
freshly poured, properly chilled Domaine Chandon in their hands,

smiling meekly as they struggled to relax, trying to act interested in the mess I was making of the stove, the countertops, my life, until the moment they were sitting at my table, ingesting whatever it was I'd thrown at them in my panic—all I could think of as I watched them chew, swallow, and attempt to keep the conversational flow going—was *How can I get them out of here? Sooner rather than later?*

And no one ever reciprocated. Despite what the etiquette books say. Either they didn't read them or they didn't care or they felt the discomfort behind my hard, frozen smile and chose not to invite it onto their own turf.

I justified this damage, launched a new undertaking, when my hunger for human encounters hit the crisis point. I'd wake suddenly from a long spell of total isolation, feverishly in need of social contact. I was like a hiker crossing the desert who forgets to drink until she's collapsed in a dehydrated stupor: My tongue was thick for lack of use, unable to concentrate on anything other than lingual communion; my mind was like an enraged beast. I had no choice but to cut it loose from whatever writing assignment it might be lashed to, and watch as it circled the room like a lonely child frantically wondering whom it might get to come over and play. By the time I actually gathered a group—something that can take months in the challenging minefield of Southern California's urban sprawl, murky social hierarchies, unpredictable work, vacation and baby-sitter schedules—I invariably overdid it. I didn't know how to act. I couldn't find the balance between caring and sharing and wanting to throw my guests off the deck.

The deck I refer to is two stories above the front garden. We used to dine there during the summer, before we found workers[1]

---

1 Third World economic refugees who risked their lives illegally crossing the border, lured by the dream of a "better life." Little did they know their cheap and desperate labor would be providing that better life for us while they slept in converted garages in Compton and committed slow suicide with a steady diet of McDonald's.

willing to install a garden in the steeply sloping, multi-terraced backyard. I imagined more than one guest impaled on a wrought-iron trellis for failing to eat the last bite of hand-stuffed pumpkin ravioli or homemade saffron and anise ice cream.

Who the hell were they to push aside my passionate labors after what I'd gone through to get them and a pile of lovingly crafted food to my table? What would they think of my cooking if, once they were trapped by the trellis like specimen insects pinned to a display board, I scraped the remainders into their gaping, groaning mouths? Satisfied that they'd swallowed every last bite, I'd wash it down with a glass of arsenic-laced, entrée-appropriate wine and dessert them with brandy and an exploding cigar.

This was the vision that, with each event, began to unspool in my mind, replaying on my psychic big screen for days, weeks, even months afterward. I started to fear for my sanity and my guests' safety. Doubting my ability to curb this criminal intent, I stopped giving dinner parties.

*U*nfortunately, that activity ceased before I fully contained my need to plan events. I'd get a lively idea in my head—a fussy ladies' tea to celebrate the blooming garden, or a sudden urge to make cioppino for twenty—and I'd start collecting recipes and rounding up guests, reaping all the benefits of that animating exercise. Then, a few days short of the designated date, before I'd actually bothered with shopping and cleaning, the more mundane chores involved in the undertaking, I'd latch on to some perfectly plausible excuse to cancel everything last-minute. They all understood, rainchecks were graciously accepted, best wishes given for my mother's speedy recovery from what toward the end had become a staggering list of maladies, including two pacemaker operations and an angioplasty with a bonus brain shunt (only one of which actually ever took place), that would have permanently felled a woman half her age and in far better health.

After too many rounds of baiting a withering list of sporting guests, even I grew tired of this game of catch and release. It was then I decided to abandon the mess and nonsense of the actual to invent perfect gatherings for the page.

As a writer I could reshape reality with the clay of language. Who needed the tangible world when there were words? Food and entertaining was an area in which I could sound authoritative, intimate, and truthful while perpetrating pure fiction. No one checked. Everyone took my word for it. Why would I lie about anything as sacred as the pleasures of the table?

In print I could correct my mistakes, make it sound as if I were a successful, gracious hostess. I seduced my readers with lies, let them make what I considered miserable fun. If I couldn't do it anymore, let them fall for the promise of my spring supper–on–a–terrace fantasy, let them suffer the same hangovers of anger, physical ailments, and mental dissolution I had when I believed in such blather.

In writing about instead of doing dinner parties, I hoped to understand the love/hate relationship with entertaining that ruled my life. That was ten years ago. While I still wait on that order of enlightenment, no one has ever questioned the truth of my entertaining tales.

I was confident that amongst those friends and acquaintances who might suspect I'd given up hosting, people who had experienced one of my events firsthand, none were ever going to write my editor to set the record straight. Everyone I knew was too busy to do anything as mundane as write a letter to the editor and/or read my articles in the first place.

My husband was thrilled with my decision. He loathes home entertaining. After an excruciating workweek, he welcomes the empty quiet of an uncelebrated weekend. He sees dinner parties as an uncomfortable extension of the itch-inducing office politics he endures during the week. As far as he is concerned, people bring their agendas along with a decent bottle of wine. No one ever accepts an invitation until they know who else is coming, and then they arrive with excuses for why they are late and have to leave early.

Once they were here, within the privacy of our home, sitting at our table, eating our food, sharing our oxygen, they seemed so un-available to us that I might forget everyone's name mid-meal and suddenly find myself grazing in a herd of "dear." Everyone became "dear" this and "dear" that, though there were a number of more pi-quant, less polite terms I would assign when replaying the event in my mind.

As for my dear husband, he claimed immediately after such events to develop a sourness in his throat that lingered for days, weeks, sometimes even months, a bitter reminder of the frantic activity leading up to and including the night's revelries. I began to suspect that the overtime assignments that Somebody—for that is his name when it is just the two of us at home—pulled at the last minute, leaving me to host solo, reflected his own depths of discomfort with the idea of having a few friends over for an evening of good food and fun. Thus arrived the end of our actual DPTE.

· I have never had a bad time or an uncomfortable moment when my parties were confined to the page. Editors and readers envied my ability to regularly round up a convivial crowd. My imaginary guests were impeccably well behaved, admiring, attentive, and sweet. We had a shared history as cozy as a down comforter and a future as bright as the spring dawn. And while I never named names, I did enjoy the company of the occasional bona fide, albeit minor, celebrity and/or otherwise social notable. Doctors and lawyers, as well as artists and best-selling authors (who, save for *moi*, isn't these days?), were sprinkled about my fetes like croutons on a Caesar salad—the really good kind, the ones I make from cubed organic ciabbata bread tossed with shredded parmigiano-reggiano cheese (aged for at least thirty-six months) and slow-baked in a low oven, 250 degrees, on a cookie sheet, until the cheese filaments jacket the bread in a tender, golden regard. But no one ever had a better time than I, the greatest time-saving hostess trick being to make it all up. One need never break a sweat throwing an imaginary party.

Then Richard Cronenberg came along.

⫼† Red Onion and Roasted Garlic Marmalade †⫼

• •

6 medium red onions (about 2 lbs.)

1 head of roasted garlic

⅓ cup olive oil

½ cup organic chicken or vegetable broth

¼ tsp. salt, or to taste

5 tbsp. balsamic or red wine vinegar

¼ cup brown sugar

Thinly slice onions crosswise into rings, then sauté in a noncorrosive medium saucepan with the oil until soft. The large pile of onions you began with will soon cook down to a more manageable mass. Add broth, vinegar, salt, and brown sugar. Cook over medium heat, stirring occasionally, until thickened and most of liquid is evaporated, about 1 hour. After you get the onions cooking on the stove begin squeezing the garlic cloves from the roasted head. Add these to the onions about half an hour or 15 minutes before the cooking hour is up. Store covered in refrigerator for up to 1 week. Serve on anything that makes sense.

Chapter 3

BONUS TIME

*I*t started innocently enough. I bumped into Le Cronenburg at a food writers' awards evening early last October. The real point of the event was stuffing the stomachs and inflating the egos of food writers, which isn't all that difficult to do. There's nothing more thrilling to us than getting to eat for free. It's a congenital desire, lulling us into a delusion of security. When our mouths are full we can convince ourselves that the world is taking care of us. All the excessive amounts of glorious (for we don't eat just anything) gratis grub that are shoved our way will make up for the abuse we regularly suffer at the hands of editors and publishers. We may be poorly paid, underappreciated, and overedited, but at least we will not starve.

The evening's meal was prepared by a galaxy of Los Angeles's star chefs, with the main draw being several dozen pounds of white truffles flown in that morning from Alba, in the Piedmont region of Italy. The entire dining room was infused with the fungis' earthy odor, their secret attraction being a naturally occurring chemical that closely mimicked the human sexual pheromone. I was having a physiological reaction to the lumpy, ashen-looking rocks, my body tingling all over, and feeling dangerously close to the edge of an orgasm. Not wanting to appear such an obvious food whore, I was frantically fanning myself with a cocktail napkin when a voice behind me asked, "Are you all right?"

I recognized the deep voice, hints of mahogany and cherry wood, from phone conversations. He was better-looking than I'd imagined, and I'd imagined an attractive man. Tall, graying at the temples, dressed in tan slacks and a navy blazer, a crisp white shirt striped in sage, open at the neck, with a few curlicues of salt-and-pepper hair peeking heroically from below. His pale skin sported a clarity gained from eating high on the food chain and getting monthly facials. I noticed how he held his glass of red wine by the bowl instead of the stem, the warmth of his hands developing the wine's fullest flavors. I held my glass of Veuve Clicquot by the stem to preserve its crisp chill.

"Richard?" I asked. "Richard Cronenburg?"

"Yes," he answered warily.

Bingo and huzzah! This was the rarest treat I could have hoped for that evening: Richard Cronenburg of *Savoir Eats!* magazine. I'd written for him while he was at *America Cooks!* magazine in New York. Now he was at a new job based in L.A. I hoped having him in my city might lead to better assignments. Instead of eight hundred words on the secret life of capers, I'd be sent to France for four thousand words on the caper harvest and festival. We made pleasant, giddy, "good to meet you" chitchat. His wariness slipped away, and I sensed he was actually glad for my company—if for no other reason than my serving as a human shield against the throngs of other writers who were hoping to corner him in the same fashion and for all the same reasons.

He leaned close to speak, and I smelled sandalwood and verbena with a hint of moss. His eyes were the mineral green of an exotic mussel's lipped shell. I wondered if they were real or colored contact lenses.

"Those truffles aren't from Alba," he whispered. "The market's been flooded this year with Lithuanian ringers."

I knew truffles. I'd run with the yelping dogs through the oak forests of Alba in the fall, watched as their handlers sold their filthy lucre from baskets in the town's open market. That same trip I'd tucked into a plate of *pasta al tartufo* so vibrant with eau de truffle I nearly passed out, and these were the real deal. But he was the editor, so I kept my mouth shut and my passions private.

"Now that I'm in Los Angeles," he said, " you have to invite me to one of those wonderful dinner parties you're always writing about."

Was he kidding?

"I'd love to," I lied.

"Well," he said, "when?"

"Soon," I said, smiling my morning-news-anchor smile. "I'll look at my book and give you a call."

"Marvelous," he said. "You can fill me in on the secrets about this burg."

I offered a brief, back-of-the-throat guffaw, my professional-pals laugh, rather than the full-blast hyena hoot I wanted to let fly with.

Me, the secrets of this burg? I was the only secret in this burg I knew about. That I wrote about dinner parties as if I actually gave them. And the other secret was that nobody cared. In New York I would have been drummed out of the journalist corps. In San Francisco everyone would have been vying for invites to my nonexistent events. In Los Angeles no one cared. My not actually giving the dinner parties about which I wrote was not a Three-Picture Deal.

"I'll see if I can dig some up before the big day," I said.

That night I drove home drunk from the effort required to make a decision: host The Big Man in my home or concoct a mille-feuille (layered, Napoleonic thing) of excuses to avoid such an appallingly intimate social encounter, while extracting the desired string of assignments from him—like trying to make an omelet without breaking any eggs.

No one had ever asked me for an invitation, and certainly not an editor for whom I hoped to work. If I didn't give a dinner party to which he was invited while we were living in the same town, I couldn't keep writing about dinner parties as if I were actually giving them. It would be professional suicide, not to mention rude.

By the time I pulled into my garage, I decided I had no choice but to do it.

We played phone tag through the holidays until we settled on a date when he would be available. In January he agreed to a Saturday evening in mid-June. Three months to find a suitable calendar opening six months off, for a total of nine months from the initial conception. It wasn't an untypical gestation period for an L.A. party.

The next hurdle was gathering a crowd by Extending Invitations. My palms sweat and my stomach churns at the mere thought.

On this front, I envy the gall of Lady Sibyl Colefax, an early-twentieth-century English hostess, a woman Leonard Woolf referred to as an "unabashed hunter of lions," both literary and political. "She was a ruthless Lady Bountiful . . . an insensitive professional hostess" who he considered failed at "her art."

Still, he accepted her invitations. She knew how to gather a crowd. Prime ministers graced her parlor, as did the Woolfs, Leonard and Virginia. Colefax spent all her spare waking hours writing invitations to the A list of English society. The only problem was that her invitations were mostly illegible. While everyone knew from whom the invitations came ("Oh, her!"), it took them days of studying the document to decipher the where, what, and when of the event and whether to attend. Acceptance, of course, only encouraged the woman to continue sending more invitations.

In the past, I always preferred to offer my invitations by phone. I spoke clearly and, while giving all pertinent information, fully expecting the recipient to hit me with a list of excuses: their vacation schedules, work-related emergencies, imminent operations, and suddenly pending divorces ("Forget the kids, couldn't you just stay together for the next two weeks for the sake of my dinner party?"). One acquaintance begged off because of my garden. She was allergic to flowers. She said. I stopped short of offering to strip the yard. I was prepared for any and all excuses, and kept a book handy to read while they shoveled them on.

I never tried to talk them out of their flu or the trip to Uzbekistan they'd been planning for years. I might consider changing the date of the dinner to a weekend when they were available, if it was in an appropriate century, or I just assumed they were lying through their teeth and started cultivating resentments. Why didn't they invite me to Uzbekistan? How come I never got the flu? (Hostesses never get the flu—only guests, usually at the last minute. Hosting a dinner party is great for the autoimmune system.)

Whatever they said would not make me stop trying—at least in the short term. I'd ask them again. And again. And then I'd take the hint. But at that moment I had little patience with their problems. I had to get to the next name on the list.

What really freaked me out, though, was when people accepted. Didn't they have anything better to do? Why did they want to come to my house for dinner? Yes, I was a terrific cook. Innovative, unflappable, capable of conjuring miracles from the oddest of ends and farthest reaches of the refrigerator. I could build an empire on leftover rice and expired vegetables. I can solve centuries-old conflicts with my salmon in sorrel sauce. I can revive the platitudes of dead languages with my pan-roasted sea bass with fig anchoyade. And it's been years since guests had to wait until eleven o'clock and too many bottles of wine for me to rustle Alice Waters's lamb ragout to the table.

Yes my house was cozy, with great views and an enchanting garden, but we lived in the wrong part of town (downscale neighborhood, next to a cemetery. Okay, a world-famous cemetery. Spencer Tracy's ghost might be watching while they sipped my soup).

And about that garden—did I mention that it was on an incredibly steep hillside, an elevation gain of several hundred feet from the street? They'd need a topographical map to find the paths, which were roughly laid and poorly lit. Someone was certain to fall coming down after a few cocktails.

I'd serve stuff they wouldn't like, or conveniently forget what they couldn't eat (I made notes to do so as soon as I hung up).

And I should have warned anyone with a food sensitivity, I served nothing but tomatoes, wheat, strawberries, shellfish, peanuts, and dairy products with added lactose to ensure their indigestibility. The American Heart Association had posted a warning on our front door regarding our house's cholesterol and saturated fat content.

If my guests didn't swell up from a bad reaction to the food or keel over from clogged arteries, what would we talk about? The story about the new washer and dryer was good for five minutes— I'd timed it. And they didn't really want to hear about our travels. They'd think we should have spent more money and time at home, fixing up the place.

Sure, I thought of our interiors as cozy, but others might think my cozy was merely cluttered, funky, and frayed. I knew I should have subscribed to all those shelter magazines. I could never remember which way it was supposed to be—everything matched or nothing did. I'd vacuum, but still, there would be cat hair in odd places. Weren't they allergic to cats? Wouldn't they like to be?

Didn't they know that at some point in the evening I'd insult them? It was always innocent and unintentional—a fatal flaw in my *joie de vivre*. I still remember the guest to whom my parting shot was "And be sure and clean your beard when you get home!" I was young, lacking in social graces. The look on his face haunts me still.

No—they insisted. They'd love to come. What kind of friends *were* they? Did they really want me to spend the next weeks obsessing over menus and decor and the three days up to and including the event shopping, chopping, cleaning, and fretting?

They *did?*

Couldn't they afford to go to a nice restaurant instead? I'd get directions, join them there; we'd talk, have a few laughs, bridle at the busboys who wanted to whip away the plates as soon as we put our forks down. Okay, all right, I understood. My house was a busboy-free zone, and that, no doubt, was the actual reason they wanted to come over.

At this point in the process it invariably dawned on me that the real hunger in all of this was not merely for food, but for the company of others. When none of us seemed to have time for anything, including a sit-down, well-prepared meal, and everyone appeared trapped in a solo chase after things we were not even sure existed, companionship and community could be the first things cut from the to-do list. The thought of a dinner amongst friends took on the backlit glow of a Platonic ideal.

Sharing a meal with others was one way to regain a sense of society. According to a medieval Arab saying, "when you sit at the table with your brothers, sit long, for it is a time that is not counted against you as part of (the ordained span of) your lives." In other words, no matter how much time it took to organize, invite, shop, clean, fret, and prepare, life at the table in the company of others was bonus time on Earth.

Even if everyone seemed to coordinate their clocks for a half hour after dessert was served to yawn, check their watches, and announce, "We really must be going."

January for mid-June was too early to Extend Invitations. That couldn't be done until May without seeming desperate or dorky.

It would take me five months to come up with a list of potential guests. First I had to decide whom *not* to invite.

Not my therapist, even though I consider her my closest, albeit paid, friend. She'd probably talk about me to my other guests. She loved to offer anecdotal examples from other patients' histories when our sessions were lagging, even name names and occupations so there was no mistaking whom she was talking about ("Oh, yes, David the lawyer/compulsive liar, not David the city councilman/pedophile"). She'd stop short of giving addresses, though I'm sure she was only waiting to be asked.

Not other food writers. They were friendly at public events, where they knew it was required, like dinners, tastings, lunches, and product launches, unless the best goody bags and giveaways ran out—then watch your back and hope you don't get trampled in the riot. Only a fool such as I once was would expect them to answer a colleague's phone call. And if they did show up, I wouldn't have been able to stand the tension as they spent the evening, between complaints about the miseries of their vocation (stolen ideas, unreturned phone calls, rude editors, rewrite demands, kill fees, et cetera, et cetera), testing connections, poking around to see whom I might help put them in touch with, how they could turn the dinner into a paying proposition. They could run that tape at somebody else's bash. When I launched into a spiel about some obscure foodstuff, I didn't want to be one-upped by a writer who'd done a cover story on it for the competition.

So, after five months of deep breathing, rigorous exercise of my imagination, and multiple trips through my address book, I pulled a group together.

I was shocked at how easy it was. I had the editor's name to drop as a celebrated honoree, and suddenly everyone wanted to come. Why hadn't I done that before? I'm sure Lady Colefax had learned that early on.

Those on the yes list had two things in common, starting with the fact that they were available. I've decided the greatest gift anyone in our sprawling world can give is to make themselves available. It is the most generous act, to be cherished above the usual hostess payola of wine or flowers. Most people are too busy making something of themselves so that other people will want to make themselves available to them, thus making themselves unavailable to those ignoble others who might alleviate the loneliness motivating their frenzied race to success. If you live in Los Angeles, you know what I mean.

That wouldn't be a problem with Richard Cronenburg as professional bait. This was a meal in which career advancement was a definite possibility.

My second criterion for my guests was that I vaguely recalled having actually enjoyed their company somewhere along the line. There was Boyan, the artist, and his fiancée, Emily. Artists are great at dinner parties—they love to be cooked for, welcome company after the solitude of their studios, and energize any gathering with their free-range minds as long as you don't talk about the art world, a subject that can unleash a vast outpouring of grumpiness.

Kathleen and her husband, Allan, were coming. She was the editor who had been my shoulder to cry on when I felt I was dying in the Living section during my last stint as a staff writer at a daily newspaper. She'd recently moved back to the area after a number of years working for a magazine in San Francisco, and I was truly looking forward to seeing her. She had accepted eagerly, even before I promised her "no more crying."

Then there was Walter, a graphic designer, who I knew would be problematic. He blossomed in a crowd but tended to collapse in more intimate settings. I'd invited him for totally selfish reasons: His girlfriend, Marisa, was a hotshot photographer who might help connect me to the elite and glossy world of coffee table-book publishing. I wanted to know her better. I felt certain she would like to know Richard Cronenburg better.

I wasn't trying to make this a business evening, but I wasn't an idiot, either, and when you went to this much effort in Los Angeles, it had better, like the freeways, lead somewhere. That's why they called it the City of Angles. Most of the population was running on a biofuel based on fear-borne angst, and it took too much of the stuff to not turn every event into a golden on-ramp. Marisa would be mine that night.

Next I had to plan the menu. When I was doing dinner parties in the past, I always overdid it on the food front. I feared guests would be bored by a reasonable number of offerings, or go home hungry in the absence of a groaning board. So I prepared a Las Vegas buffet's worth of victuals and fancies, killed myself in the process, and numbed my own appetite for weeks afterward dining on leftovers.

Well, I'd gotten over that. This was a new age dawning. Simplicity would be my savior. I would put out two cheeses, a pâté, and good bread for starters. Then it was *carciofi alla Romana*, a composed salad, grilled squab, oven-roasted new potatoes, and homemade ice cream for dessert. I could do that.

My new excess was to write about everything that happened to me. Much of it got published. What didn't could be used down the line. So thrilled was I at having bagged a group for the week's upcoming event, I had, after far too little thought and no hesitation, called the literary agent Patrick Langtree, whom I'd met at the same food writers' awards evening where I'd encountered Richard Cronenburg.

Patrick didn't remember me at first. "It's been a few months," he said, "an eternity, really." You could take nine months to pull a dinner party together, but not to follow up on an encounter with an agent. Glorious, flaming writing careers had been launched to the heavens and fallen smoldering back to earth in less time.

"I did see one of your articles over the holidays," he said. "Something about fruitcakes, how you made them every year and gave them to your family whether they wanted one or not. A joke that may grow tired but never gets stale."

"Yes, that was mine," I said. I waited a vast expanse for something that sounded like a laugh, or possibly the cracking of a smile.

"It was very cute," he said.

Finally. Cute. Very. I took it. I pitched him on a food memoir.

"Write up an outline," he said.

I titled it *Entertaining Disasters: How to Have Company Without a Coronary*. The five-page outline just flowed. He was thrilled. Last Friday, three o'clock my time, six o'clock New York time, Patrick called to say several publishers were nibbling at the edges.

"You're on to something," he said.

I was ecstatic. I considered not making it up. Anymore. Ever again. Using the memoir to come clean with the reading public. To try to explain why I'd gone fictional and why I was now returning to the facts. It gave me an extra helping of courage to face the crowd that was piling into my house at the end of the week. I would have the strength to tell the truth once and for all.

Pan-Roasted Sea Bass with Fig Anchoyade

....

5 anchovy fillets

1 lb. fresh figs

1 small clove garlic

Cinnamon and nutmeg to taste

4 (4 oz.) pieces of sea bass fillet

Butter for pan-roasting

Salt and pepper to taste

Fig Anchoyade:

Soak the anchovy fillets in cold water for a few minutes to remove the salt; wipe dry. In food processor mince garlic clove, add figs and anchovies, and purée. Add dash of cinnamon and nutmeg, or to taste. Anchoyade can be made a day in advance and refrigerated. Also good as an hors d'oeuvre on bread, spread with goat cheese or moistened with olive oil, and topped with chopped onions.

To prepare sea bass, melt butter in large enough sauté pan to hold all 4 pieces, or do in two stages, keeping the first batch warm on a platter in a low oven. Over medium heat, brown the fish fillet pieces on each side for 4–6 minutes. After a few minutes on the second side, spoon a layer of fig anchoyade onto each fish fillet. If the fish is still pink or translucent on the inside, put a lid on the pan, turn down the heat, and cook until opaque all the way through, 5–10 minutes, depending on the thickness of the fish. Converts 4.

Chapter 4

OPERA CAKE

*I*t's Monday afternoon, six days before Saturday night's said crowd will be knocking at my door for a sit-down, kick-out-the-jams dinner in the garden. I have lined up my balsamic vinegar and Grains of Paradise routine on the kitchen counter and am considering adding another table to our already crowded arrangement to invite Patrick plus one, when the phone rings.

"Richard here!" It's the boisterous greeting of Le Cronenburg. We are on a first-name basis now.

"Richard," I say, bright as the afternoon breeze. "How are you?"

I stop short of adding a "darling." We're not on a "darling" basis. I'm not on a "darling" basis with anyone.

"Good news," he says, "for me, but bad, I'm afraid, for you."

"How so?" I say.

"I'm on my way to the airport," he says. "I'm sure you'll understand. One of our writers took ill last-minute, and I couldn't let a week of comped rooms in Paris's finest boutique hotels slip by. I'm racing off to the City of Lights to sleep around! Haha!"

"Haha!" I volley back.

"I thought of giving the assignment to you," he says. "But I didn't want to ruin the plans for your dinner party."

That was so thoughtful of him. He could cancel but I could not.

"A rain check, then?" he says.

"Yes, of course," I say. What else could I do? I wouldn't tell anyone that he wasn't coming after all, lest they decide to back out as well. I'd put too much effort into the evening already, and now there was the book proposal to consider.

"I'll think of you while I'm dining at Taillevent."

"Please do," I say.

"Have you ever been?" he asks.

"Paris, yes; Taillevent, no," I say.

"You really must try it sometime," he says. "It deserves its three Michelin stars." And then the connection breaks up and the line goes dead and I wait a few minutes to see if he'll call back for a proper goodbye, to offer a consolation assignment or make another promise he won't keep—anything, some kind of closure—and then, finally, I am alone with the reality of the situation and the thought that he may have never intended to come in the first place. That this might all have been a ruse to stir up some buzz around the possibility of hosting him in my home. And if it hadn't been a Paris assignment last-minute, it could have been something else.

That omelet-burning, *pot de crème*–sucking, petit four–licking lout—the French deserved to have him sullying the sheets at a chain of Russian Mafia–front boutique hotels he'd rave about for his scurrilous rag, as if his opinion were objective, free of the fetters of commerce or favoritism.

I go back to the kitchen. I see my pathetic effort at drumming up conversation a week in advance. Balsamic vinegar and Grains of Paradise and he will be dining at Taillevent. May he gag on foie gras before decapitation by a demon-possessed serving cart. My mind is seized by an unbidden vision of jelly squares as I grab my purse and car keys and lunge out the door.

It is 5:37 PM and I am driving between eighty-five and ninety miles an hour, going north on the 2 freeway, cutting off slower vehicles that don't share my pressing concern: whether or not to cancel the Saturday night soiree. My immediate destination is Glendale's Schautthausen Bakery. It closes at 6:00 PM and I have exactly twenty-three minutes in which to secure a comforting cup of their Viennese roast coffee and a slab of their opera cake. I have just left a highly unsatisfying emergency session with my therapist, the one who holds forth in the sitting room of her Pasadena house, my little-old-lady-from-Pasadena therapist. This is the same therapist whom I wouldn't invite, but I was hoping she would help me decide whether to have the dinner party despite Richard Cronenburg's bailing call.

"I was only giving the party because he agreed to come," I said, tears welling up in my eyes. I hated this. I always cried in her presence and hardly anywhere else. She always asked me what prompted the emotion. I never knew. She was supposed to tell me. I paid her for answers, not questions. I considered it her parlor trick. She handed me a tissue. "Now I don't know what to do. I haven't given a dinner in ten years. It will take me months to recover."

I was about to reach for the tea she offered at the start of each session when a chunk of plaster fell from her ceiling into my mug. She is highly resistant to household repairs, and her rambling, ancient Craftsman bungalow in the Arroyo Seco area of the city is crumbling, a study in deferred maintenance. While she encourages me to examine my life and "do the work" necessary to attain personal happiness, I compile "do the work" lists for the contractors and handymen she needs to call. It wasn't the first time for falling plaster during one of our sessions, but never before had a fragment looked exactly like the triangular section of the map of Glendale where we live between the 134, 2, and 5 freeways. I tried not to read too much into this. I set the tea back down.

"What do you want to do?" she asked after I'd finished describing my dilemma. This question was her answer to everything.

"Give a dinner party," I said. I realized the discomfort I felt was all in my head—she'd pounded this idea into it. Rewards were to be had. I was tired of cooking for imaginary guests. I needed something real to write about.

"Good—then do it," she said, patting me on the knee in a motherly fashion. "And have a good time."

We were a perfect pair. Each week she encouraged me to make a decision, and I did. By the following week I'd have talked myself out of it and we'd start over again. She was a disciple of the Sisyphean School of Therapy. This time I changed my mind mid-session.

"I can't do it. I can't afford the months of downtime while I recover."

"What do you want to do?" she asked without a blink.

"Not give a dinner party," I said. Richard Cronenburg had blown me off. What would prevent everyone else from doing the same? I couldn't face the effort required to survive pulling off the night. I would continue to make it all up.

"Good—then don't," she said, patting me on the knee in a motherly fashion. "And have a good time."

That was it, her answer to everything: Do whatever it was you wanted to, and have a good time. Our session was up. She gave me a hug; I gave her a check and then raced north on the freeway toward something more satisfying and less expensive than my hours spent with her.

So here I stand, desperate for the certain comforts of my favorite cake. But first, the woman in front of me, dressed in leotard tight jeans, pointy-toed spike-heeled boots, and a form-fitting velveteen hooded sweatshirt, has to commit. I am painfully aware of exactly what I want and how many minutes I have in which to get it, and this woman wearing enough lipliner and tropical perfume to stun a jungle cat can't decide on what cake to get and, even worse, seems determined to take her time while wasting mine.

She chews a chipped enamel fingernail, scans the cases, walks slowly past chocolate icebox cakes; tiramisu cakes; orange, lemon, raspberry, and coconut cakes; carrot cakes; banana cream cakes; solid chocolate and mocha cakes; domed princess cakes enrobed in pale green marzipan; and cakes topped with fruit displays worthy of a baroque still life.

"What's the freshest cake?" she asks. Her eyes sag heavily beneath thick liner and the weight of her concerns.

"It's all fresh," the counterwoman says.

"What's the most popular?"

"It depends," the counterwoman says. "What are you getting it for?"

"My family. I prefer pie," she says, her voice nearly trembling, "but last time I took pie, they complained."

The counterwoman suggests that everyone loves chocolate, that the health-conscious enjoy carrot cake, that the fruit-topped cake was as beautiful as it was delicious, that the princess cake made any occasion special.

Still no decision.

Cake, I realize, is a mere vehicle for this woman's misery. Who are these people she is trying to placate? What doubt-filled swamp have they tethered her to? I sigh audibly, roll my eyes, and tap my fingernails on the glass countertop. Nothing moves her closer to a commitment.

I watch her torment and realize it doesn't matter what cake she gets. No one will remember the cake—they will remember her anxiety over it, her apologies, the nervous flick of her eyes as slices are distributed.

People will love whatever you get, I want to shout. *Crowds love cakes. No one wants to be alone with a whole cake. Get the cake you want—and let them eat it, too!*

This sounds like my therapist. Make a choice. Be in the world and have a good time, or don't be in the world and have a good time. In the words of the Buddha, or someone else equally brilliant and several millennia dead: Pain is inevitable, suffering is optional. I decide I hate people who can't make decisions. I will have my dinner party despite Richard Cronenburg's backing out. Besides, I can't cancel on this crowd; they are the last of my prior catch-and-release victims who still return my phone calls. And if I don't have a good time, at least I will be a few steps closer to a book project, and there is Marisa, another promise of the chance to expand my professional universe—why, we could do a beautiful coffee-table book of a food memoir, featuring her gorgeous photos—and possibly, hopefully, I might feel less alone for a few hours.

Finally, after asking the counterwoman to pull out the coconut, then telling her to put it back, querying about the filling on the princess cake and about the ingredients ("You're not using margarine, are you? I'm allergic to margarine; the trans fatty acids give me a rash"), the lip-lined, leotard-jeaned, velveteen-hoodied woman chooses the triple-layer chocolate with whipped cream and cherries Black Forest cake.

While the counterwoman slips the cake into a box and I wait heroically, patiently, for her to ask for my order, my cell phone rings. It never does. I don't remember having brought it, let alone turning it on. I dig it out of the depths of my purse.

"Helloooaaahhh!" It is the raucous delivery of a stage comic who never took her act beyond a private audience. It is my sister, Hunter.

"Hunter?" I speak in a whisper, try not to sound as shocked and on guard as the sound of her voice makes me. Everything comes out too loud when you're talking on a cell phone; it feels like street theater. I enjoy eavesdropping on conversations, watching others perform their scenes on the public stage, but I don't care to be the entertainment for strangers.

"Is Mother all right?" I ask. It's the only reason I can think of that Hunter would call. Mother must have fallen, or has had another heart attack.

"What would you like?" The woman behind the counter asks as she looks at the clock and then at me. It is five fifty-seven.

"A small coffee and a piece of your opera cake," I say.

"Where *are* you?" Hunter asks. "Some *bakery*? Eating *cake*? Every time I call you're in a *bakery*, eating *cake*."

Hunter took a fervent interest in what I ate. She monitored my sugar and fat content closely, lest I become the size of Mother, which was, in retrospect, lithe compared with the supersized citizens of today's standard.

"That's two pieces in ten years."

"This phone's cutting out."

"Is that better?" I ask, moving near the glass storefront. On the street outside, a rush-hour flood of cars races by. The last time she called and got me on the phone, I had been at the Kasselwurtz Bakery in Santa Monica, interviewing Franz Kasselwurtz for a cover story for *Los Angeles* magazine's annual food issue. Just as the Austrian-born chef left me alone with a piece of his lavender syrup-infused genoise, iced in vanilla buttercream, Hunter called.

"Mother has had a heart attack," she said. I put my fork down. "She's in the hospital. I'd go up to see her, but I have a business deal in the works." It was Mother's first heart attack. Of course I went. If I didn't, who would? Numerous hospitalizations and minor concerns followed, and there was the angioplasty operation and a pacemaker and many other things, and always Hunter had a business deal in the works and I raced north because if I didn't, who would? I was well trained. All subsequent messages were left on the phone that she knew I hardly ever used.

I didn't finish the lavender-infused genoise that day. The news killed my appetite, though the cake was too sweet, anyway, and the lavender was more appropriate for a bath product than a pastry. I finished the interview and flew to the Bay Area that evening to be at my mother's hospital bedside.

I was the baby of the family, such as it was and in whatever form it still existed, and the kid they called when Mother needed a physical presence by her side. My freelance writing schedule was infinitely flexible, and my inability to ignore Mother's needs—or kill the hope that something I might do or say would someday bring her back to this planet, to a state of mind in which she might be more present, might someday be a mother or at least more fully human—made me unable to ever say no.

Hailey was always up in the air, literally, flying his pilot's route, unable to be the first responder, and Howard was stuck on the ground, seemingly incapable, emotionally, physically, or financially, of making it down the freeway, in his truck or tractor or whatever he drove, to deal with Mother's emergencies.

And Hunter had her pressing business concerns.

She never said what her business was. I didn't know where she was living. My father said he thought she said Las Vegas. The uterine-cancer message had been left a few years ago. At least this call confirmed that she was still alive.

"Mother's fine," she says. "I'm calling because I'm coming to Los Angeles Saturday. I have something I have to give you."

I hadn't physically seen her for ten years. Now she wants to drop by the day of my dinner party.

"Not Saturday," I say.

"I can't hear you," she says.

"*Not* Saturday," I say, raising my voice and stepping outside the bakery for a clearer signal. I hear, then see, the lunging, growling, demented Doberman pinscher being walked on a leash, just in time to avoid getting bit.

"I've got your address," she says. "I'll see you then."

The phone goes dead. I punch the buttons for call history, incoming, to see her return number, but it's identified as "restricted."

I turn back toward the shop just as the counterwoman flips the door's OPEN sign to CLOSED. She lets me in long enough to gather my cake and coffee to go.

I sit in my car, contemplating the opera cake's alternating layers of silken cream and gentle ground almond crunch, grateful for the pacing sips of hot coffee, buffeted by the *swoosh* of evening traffic. I try to imagine what Hunter will be like now. She is a decade older than when last seen. She has been through a life-threatening bout of cancer. Has it ravaged her always carefully composed appearance? Will I be horrified or saddened by the spectacle? Will she be as overbearing, insulting, and high-handed as the last time we met in the courthouse lobby? We were battling over her control of Mother's conservatorship. According to the court, Hunter won. It was a battle Mother and I lost, as far as I was concerned.

How will I explain Hunter to my guests if she arrives that evening? What if she comes during the day, while I'm in the midst of a last-minute panic pulling the party together? She'll have the encounter she wants and I'll be thrown off track before the guests arrive.

At least with others around it might be safer. Alone with Hunter I feel the psychotic pull of our family, dragged back into her orbit. It has taken me a hundred years, or so it seems, to withdraw a safe distance from her gravitational pull. The company of others might be a saving grace.

Then my fear is of her embarrassing me. What color will her hair be this time? How much jewelry will be jangling from her body parts? Is she still in her gypsy-carnival phase, or has she moved on to something a tad less garish? What humiliation of my past will she find amusing to mention to my guests? What dime-store, plastic, battery-operated tricks will she whip out of her purse to extend the fun—a water-spewing space gun, voice-changing microphone, or hard hat topped by a flashing red emergency light? Will I be the only one offended or concerned by her appearance, her unpredictable behavior that passes for personality? Will others be horrified or consider her a colorful, quirky character? Will I be judged by association? Would I want friends who judged me by the family I was born into and had, through no fault of my own, barely any connection to anymore yet was still emotionally enslaved to?

I was just grateful Richard Cronenburg was out of the picture. I did not want to expose my professional connections to the truth about my family. Still, could I remain standing in the ring after a few rounds with Hunter after all these years? I'd never really learned to deal with her. It wasn't a lesson she'd stuck around for. Maybe that was the lesson: Question and confront my family, and the answer is the sight of them fading into the distance.

And I can't imagine what she feels compelled to deliver in person. All I'd ever wanted was room to breathe. I'd gained it at the price of abandonment. I don't know if I really want whatever she has to give me.

I finish my cake, start up the car, and head down the road toward home.

Opera Cake

....

Almond Sponge Cake:

3 cups cake flour, sifted after measuring

2 large eggs, at room temperature for at least 30 minutes

1 cup almond flour (3½ oz.) or ⅔ cup blanched whole almonds (see note below)

½ cup confectioners' sugar, sifted after measuring

2 large egg whites, at room temperature for 30 minutes

⅛ tsp. cream of tartar

⅛ tsp. salt

1 tbsp. granulated sugar

2 tbsp. unsalted butter, melted, skimmed of foam, and cooled

Coffee Syrup:

1 tsp. instant-espresso powder

½ cup plus 1 tbsp. water

½ cup granulated sugar

¼ cup cognac or other brandy

Coffee Buttercream:

2 tsp. instant-espresso powder

¼ cup plus 1 tbsp. water

6 tbsp. granulated sugar

2 large egg yolks

1 stick (½ cup) unsalted butter, cut into ½-inch
cubes and softened

Chocolate Glaze:

6 tbsp. unsalted butter

7 oz. fine-quality bittersweet chocolate
(preferably 70–71% cacao), coarsely chopped

Special equipment: a 15 x 10–inch shallow baking pan; an offset
metal spatula; a candy thermometer; a small, sealable plastic bag
Note: If you can't find almond flour, you can pulse whole almonds
with the confectioners' sugar in a food processor until powdery. Do
not grind to a paste.

I considered giving directions for making this cake, but the
idea of anyone constructing it in their home kitchen for other
than professional reasons brought tears to my eyes. It is as time-

consuming and potentially unsatisfying as attempting to stage *Tosca* in your living room. Don't do it. Instead, find a bakery with a good version, then treasure the discovery on the rare occasion on which you should indulge in this inspiring creation.

Chapter 5

ZERO POPULATION COLESLAW

*B*ack home, the gathering twilight paints my garden in a blue-gray light that never fails to capture my heart. I climb the narrow, ramshackle stairs and see the artichoke plant has collapsed, its extravagant plume of gray-green foliage spilling across the damp black earth. It lies on its side before any buds have poked from its interior folds, knocked flat by an unknown force in what appears to be one deft and powerful gesture. I don't know what caused it: an animal or the wind, or maybe a desire of my own.

Artichokes are too tender for the heat of a Southern California inland valley. They need the coast's cool fog and breezes. I set mine toward the top of our steeply sloped garden, protected from the afternoon sun in the shade cast by a high ridge of trees and the cemetery wall. I have fretted over this plant, inspect it frequently, add more drippers if it seems dry, spritz it with the hose if I find it swarming with aphids and ants. Some years I have gotten a globe or two. I clip them to give away, a ribbon tied to the stem with a white rose and a sprig of lavender, a charming trifle to celebrate a birthday or wedding anniversary. The recipients are oblivious to the constant and heroic effort required for this modest gesture.

I wanted the plant standing for my dinner party. Can I blame Richard Cronenburg for this? Did Hunter cause this with her call? I considered the artichoke's showy plumes a signal of my generosity, hospitality, the essence of my own effervescence. Only now it looks something less than bubbly, lying there on its side, closer to the spread-eagle, clenched-fist, lockjawed panic that I'm feeling at the prospect of Hunter's arrival.

Until now I'd managed to keep my family to myself, had quarantined it from the life I'd created in Los Angeles. As far as anyone in Southern California knew, if anyone in Southern California cared, my family was standard-issue perfect. Once I'd tasted journalistic success with my invented dinner parties, I branched out into food-centric accounts of other parts of my life, making them sound transcendent and ideal.

Like my childhood. I wrote a column in which my mother, with the appropriate measure of conventional maternal warmth, passed along her hand-printed recipe card for her great-grandmother's sugar cookies. I told readers the recipe came to California via wagon train, claiming my ancestors took the daunting route through Emigrant Gap in the Sierras, hitching their wagons to a stand of trees, then hoisting them with ropes and pulleys over the high mountain ridge. They survived this ordeal, my mother claimed, with the aid of this simple, comforting recipe. These were cookies as sturdy as my ancestors, cookies that would hold their shape and keep their end of the bargain. Cookies that would see you through.

The truth was, as a child I'd dug the recipe out of the gaily painted, lidded card box, its surface dotted with batter drips, its seams grouted with ancient dough, which Mother hid on a high cupboard shelf. I have always wondered if she did this to shelter me from the burdens of knowing how to cook, or if she didn't want me to hound her for instruction. The handwriting on the original card, the ink faint with age, was a refined, well-ordered script. I never knew whether it was my grandmother or my great-grandmother who wrote it—Mother would never say. She was in her room, the door closed, refusing to answer my knocks, the day I asked her to show me how to make the cookies, so I followed the instructions and produced multiple batches myself, a supply that was my exclusive, sustaining diet for at least a month. Finally sickened by the sight of them, I tucked the card away between the pages of my childhood diary until I rediscovered it early in the throes of my fictional food-writing career.

At first I thought the story too hokey to submit, but my editor loved the pitch and gave me the assignment. She then shared her own gushing memories of a great-grandfather who might have starved, she said, long before he reached Ellis Island if a doting aunt hadn't sewn a batch of rugelach into the cuffs of his lone pair of pants.

This is the effect my food writing has on people: They want to share their own emotion-tinged, personal stories with me. I don't have the heart to tell them I'm a fake. I do wonder where they were with their touching vulnerabilities when I was giving dinner parties.

For the record: My ancestors arrived in California by train and automobile; I have no idea what they ate along the way, though coleslaw, an American roadhouse staple and a legacy of early Dutch colonialists—*cole* being a variation of *kool*, a Dutch word for cabbage—is one possibility. The recipe that follows is along the lines of what they may have enjoyed, what they might have passed on to me and I might have passed on to my children—if I'd had the courage (or is it lack of consciousness?) to have any children. I found it in *Practical Cookery and the Etiquette and Service of the Table*, from the Department of Food, Economics and Nutrition, Kansas State Agricultural College, copyright 1920. I think of this as the perfect dish for a farewell bite with the neighbors before loading the kids and household goods in the Model T for the long journey west.

Reading this recipe makes me think of my ancestors, the minions who battled their way through the millennia, those dour, unnamed faces staring out from the sepia-tinged photos buried in the dusty bottoms of decaying trunks, how they struggled to keep their chins above the muck so that I might stand in my kitchen, hacking away at a cabbage head, reducing it to a haystack's worth of shredded bits to toss with dressing, only for it to sit, rotting in the refrigerator, for weeks until I threw the bulk of it out.

The reason: Coleslaw is a dish for the many, and my husband and I are the few.

We could have made a family, a crowd to pass favorite recipes down to, as our coleslaw-slurping great-cousins did, but we chose not to. First of all, my genes are defective and not to be passed along. I would not want to gift anyone with a DNA package producing the mental distress I've enjoyed throughout my days on the planet, nor would I want to live with anyone experiencing the same. Second of all, I am terrible parenting material. I am a journalist. I observe from a distance, take notes, analyze, surgically dissect, and sew a subject back together as a written piece. Child rearing is a contact sport. Kids need more than a parent who observes them from the far end of the runway for some twenty years in hopes of getting material for a book, and that was the only reason I could think of to have a child.

One thing I've learned from my years of observation, both growing up and in our Glendale neighborhood: Children are a hazard best avoided. And if they can't be avoided, they are to be endured and survived. Small children in our current surroundings have always been a clear and present problem, teenagers are troubling, and the young adults produced by our hill tribe are teetering on the brink of doom. No one appears happy to have had kids. And since that feels like an extension of my childhood, I have decided to pass on it in this lifetime.

I did flirt briefly with the idea of motherhood a few years back. Friends who put off having children until their careers were established started reproducing. They seemed to be enjoying their offspring, even took pride in overcoming the challenges they posed. I had never witnessed this before. And as my own parents started to weaken with age, I caught a glimpse of an actual purpose for having children. Who wouldn't want an adult child to keep an eye on you in the hospital while you were in a coma? Who wanted strangers cleaning out the closets and garage when you passed away? I couldn't imagine not being an advocate for my mother, or what would happen if I weren't there to oversee her care. Neither could I imagine who would be there for me when the time came.

My therapist assured me that "kids aren't that complicated." She had four of them herself and was still talking to at least three of them at any one time. I decided what the heck. I stopped using birth control. Somebody claimed to be a willing participant. Six months passed. At my age, by that time, six months meant infertility. I went for fertility treatments. The hormone cocktail, which cost a small fortune—fully covered by insurance, thank god and Blue Cross—plunged me into a fog of despair. I wandered in pointless circles as I tried to pick up the thread of each day. I lost track of writing assignments; story pitches were issued and promptly forgotten. If my job had been to cry at the slightest hint of beauty or tenderness, I would have earned several promotions. But the only reward was the punishing length of each day as I waited for a sign that one of my rapidly aging eggs had made it past the fallopian gates, attached itself to the wall of my womb, and was actively multiplying into another human being. Or human beings. Fertility drugs made it quite likely that I would be birthing two to eight children at once, rather than just the one trial balloon I felt ready to take on. With each day I considered this possibility, and why pursuing reproduction wasn't for me.

I feared not only for the crowd I might produce, but also losing my sanity in the process. If the fertility treatments knocked me for a loop, what would pregnancy do? And what about the postpartum party? And if I couldn't handle an extra serving of hormones, what would happen when I was faced with a hormone-crazed teenager of my own making? My therapist soft-pedaled the issues, as if anticipating my long-term subscription to her weekly aid. My mother wasn't available for questioning; she claimed we'd each been born of a pterodactyl encounter high in the Andes. She'd had to sit hard and long on her eggs while exposed to howling winds and high-mountain weather. Neither was Hunter available to discuss my concerns. The lines of communication appeared to be solidly dead. But knowing what little patience she had with the needs of others, whether hormonally induced or not, I wondered if the chemical surge of pregnancy, if she had ever experienced it, would have sent her seeking a surgical solution.

After two months I abandoned the project. Somebody seemed relieved. We never discussed it again.

I put the last of the fertility-hormone prescription into one of the collection of decorative boxes on the shelves in my home office. I christened it the nursery, and that was the end of that. Having literally closed the lid on the baby issue, I was free to return to the active pursuit of solitude, cooking, and writing.

My friends and fellow journalists talk of having a baby hunger. I don't share it sufficiently to inflict myself on a child. And what was this baby hunger, anyway? Sometimes, as I watch women dragging their kids around by chains forged of guilt, exploiting their privileged position in this hallowed, till-death-do-us-part relationship, I believe some children are born of a woman's need to own something, to dominate someone, to justify their existence in the world—women who try to absorb their children for their entire lives back into the womb.

It was a vision that both repelled and attracted me. What, I wondered, would it have been like to have a mother who took a speck of interest—even if it was only enough for the occasional beating? At least you knew with every pound of her fist that you existed. Hunter talked about how our mother used to beat her as a child, before I was born, and I wondered if that had made Hunter stronger, more certain of her existence in the world, than I was. I tried to imagine a mother who cared enough to complain about me, who fought back and held tight if I tried to make a place in the world beyond her abyss, who acknowledged my existence on the other side of her bedroom door.

As for Somebody, he came from a huge family on the East Coast—his was one of the midrange births among eight kids. Even his mother, who'd been raised in a household of ten, could not keep their order straight. His father was a six-pack-a-day roofer, and his mother worked at a dry cleaner. He was left to scuffle with his siblings for food and clothes and a place to sleep and the peace of mind in which to get an education. He went to college and graduate school on scholarships, then fled for the West Coast the first professional chance he got. And while he'd seemed uncomfortable with the effort required to make friends beyond his own tribe, he seemed pleased by the physical distance he'd gained from them.

In lieu of having a child, I got a dog, thus creating a modest, fur-lined family circle.

And if I couldn't have a stab at the perfect child, I wanted the perfect dog. Other people with children could get the rescue mutts. I wanted to know exactly what I was getting, a creature beautiful enough to fill my heart with joy and cute enough to set my spirit dancing whenever I laid eyes on it. Thus arrived our Tibetan terrier, Dalai, as in Dalai Lama. I suspect mutt and rescue-dog owners think purebred dogs, especially beautiful, cute, exceptionally fluffy and barky purebred dogs, make up for the owner's sense of inadequacy in both appearance and pedigree, and in my case, at least, they'd be right. The fact that Tibetan terriers are a rare breed from an exotic, highly romanticized, essentially lost kingdom just adds to their powers of personal overcompensation.

I can't pass my recipes on to Dalai, or even delight her with a favorite dish. She has a sensitive stomach and dines on a strict, bland diet of kibble and canned food. She turned her nose up at the dollop of coleslaw I offered her. When it comes to treats she prefers the unusual—torn leaves of radicchio or elegant ribs of endive.

Would my sepia-toned ancestors in their decaying trunks find cowardly our reluctance to make a family, pathetic our hesitation to pull a crowd together for a plate of soggy cabbage salad? Would they fear for the future of the human race, or the continuation of the family line? Resent our isolationist ways, our paltry appetites, after all they did to deliver us to this place? Or would they understand, wish they'd had the luxury of social isolation, the unconditional comfort of a dog, the grounding clarity of a few more solo meals?

I didn't know these people who died before I was born. When my parents spoke of them, it was only about the mystery of their origins, as if dodging direct inquiries into our own living relations, yet I do know them as well, in certain respects, as I know myself. They are part of me on a cellular level, yet remain a mystery of specificity. I made this slaw once—it was, after all, something commonly eaten by people such as they in the time and place in which they lived—in an effort to know them, and therefore myself, better.

It wasn't interesting. There were so many other more wonderful things to eat, like a tangy Thai beef salad and an orange-cashew pilaf. There was homemade aioli with crisp crudités, a last serving of Bavarian cream with berries, a smidgen of smoked trout, a small chunk of artisanal cheese called Humboldt fog. The giant bowl of coleslaw got mushier by the day as it skulked in the middle of the refrigerator. It took up too much room on the shelf. We never ate more than a single plate each. While I ate it, I saw the faces of my ancestors speaking to me from each cabbage splinter, urging me to eat, to share, to invite a few folks in. Finally, I threw it out. I offer it to you here as a warning.

Zero Population Coleslaw

....

½ head cabbage, finely chopped

½ cup cream or evaporated milk, undiluted

2 tbsp. sugar (if too sweet, use 1½ tbsp.)

Juice of 2 lemons

1 tbsp. celery seed

2 tsp. cider vinegar

½ cup mayonnaise

Put chopped cabbage in a bowl. Add sugar to the cream and mix thoroughly, then add lemon juice. Combine with cabbage. Add celery seed, vinegar, and mayonnaise. Chill thoroughly while striking out in search of a crowd to foist it on.

Chapter 6

COMMANDER AND CHEF

Mrs. Isabella Beeton was the voice of middle-class Victorian domestic authority, guiding women in all aspects of household concern, from what to look for in a housekeeper to the number of teeth to expect in a hog's mouth. She was one of the first professional careerwomen of the Industrial Age, striving heroically to combine career and motherhood, finding time between researching and writing books and countless articles to give birth to no less than four sons.

Tragically, she was also among the first to ignore her own advice. She warned against leaving infants in a draft, lest they catch a life-threatening cold, then, according to some accounts, lost her firstborn, Samuel Orchart Beeton (named after her husband), to a killer air current before he was five months old. She advised against traveling too far from home with young children, yet took her three-year-old second child, also named Samuel Orchart Beeton, as if she were determined to get it right, on holiday to Brighton, where poor Orchy, as he was also known, contracted scarlet fever and died.

Along with producing two other sons, Isabella wrote a prodigious number of articles for her publisher husband's popular domestic magazines, and at least two advice and cookery books, before she herself died, sadly, at the age of twenty-eight in 1865. While giving birth to her fourth baby, the leading proponent of household hygiene contracted puerperal fever, an agonizing infection of the vaginal tear caused by the delivering physician's unclean hands. She died after enduring a week's torment.

Despite her youth, Beeton had a surprisingly mature, authoritative writer's voice, as well as a vast store of knowledge regarding household operations. Born Isabella Mary Mayson in 1836, she began her domestic education in a middle-class home in Cheapside, England. Her father died when she was young, and her mother remarried the clerk of Epsom Downs racecourse. Isabella was the eldest among a teeming brood that eventually grew to twenty-one children. The family's rooms were under the racecourse grandstand, and the track was the children's playground.

No wonder she likened the female head of a household's duties to those of the "commander of an army, or the leader of an enterprise." Isabella was sent away to be educated in Heidelberg, Germany, where she became fluent in German and French, as well as an accomplished pianist. She met and married Samuel Orchart Beeton, a successful London publisher, who believed an intelligent wife was "one of the greatest boons heaven has bestowed on man."

She certainly was for him. Isabella became a regular monthly contributor to Samuel's *Englishwoman's Domestic Magazine.*

"It ought, therefore, enter into the domestic policy of every parent," she wrote, "to make her children feel that home is the happiest place in the world; that to imbue them with this delicious home-feeling is one of the choicest gifts a parent can bestow."

Isabella died before she could so gift her children, and Samuel never recovered from the sorrow of her death. He died twelve years later, orphaning their two surviving sons.

I consider the possibility that Mrs. Beeton's less than scrupulous attention to her children's welfare stemmed from her greater interest in her work; that the position of mother and housewife that society pressed on her was not her first job choice, though it was the job that she was so successfully training other women to execute down to the smallest, most confining details. I wonder who the educated Mrs. Beeton would have been if birth control had existed in the nineteenth century. I wonder, as well, what the outcome of the natural tension between giving life and living it would have been, or what her writing topics might have been had she time to venture beyond the domestic. I wonder if she would have been a Mrs., or a mother, at all.

I wonder, if my mother's mind had held up and carried her through, if she'd been able to service her maternal contract, and our family had survived in some viable form, if I might be able to write about something other than food, family, and the pursuit of domestic bliss, whether real or imagined. I wonder as well, if her mind had not given way to the darkness, if she would have stopped having children at a manageable number—maybe just one, two, or even three. I consider that if it weren't for the darkness, I might never have been born.

*W*hen inventing my blissful childhood scenarios involving my mother's recipes, I didn't mention her need for ingredient lists and instructions to help organize the chaos of her mind. How her mental disarray kept her from getting even the simplest recipes right. That she berated herself every time she made anything, because she left out a key ingredient or got the measurements wrong. A cake flat for lack of baking powder, or a casserole seasoned with a cup of salt. Cooking became her highest form of abuse. After her last trip to the sanitarium and her divorce from my father, and before she gave up cooking completely, there was a time when she refused to throw out anything gone bad. Milk curdled and rancid with age still deserved a place in her chocolate layer cake, pancake batter, or cream sauce.

As a result, I developed a heightened sensitivity to the taste of food. The first inkling of an off flavor meant Mother had made one of her terrible mistakes. Not swallowing was the only recourse. No matter how hungry I was, I could never take for granted the contents of my plate. A glass of milk was tentatively sipped until the taste buds gave the "all clear." The plate heaped with chicken and homemade noodles was carefully forked through in search of foreign matter. My survival required that I pay closer attention to food than any of my peers did.

*M*y mother had once been a passionate, enthusiastic, confident all-American cook holding forth in the kitchen of our Castro Valley home. She made scratch biscuits, bubbling casseroles of macaroni and cheese, spaghetti with meatballs swimming in long-simmered sauce, raisin-studded rice pudding, and eggy custards, their taut, enameled skins freckled with nutmeg. For special occasions there was rare roast beef redolent of garlic, or broiled steak piled high with a velvety heap of sautéed mushrooms. A devil's food cake was always on the sideboard, or a pie, possibly lemon meringue (her specialty), or my favorite: apricot pie made just once a year from the fruit of our backyard Blenheim apricot tree. Its season was short, and its offerings all the more delicious for it.

I also never mentioned in print how the stove turned on Mother once my father left. Up to that point it had been a dependable, supportive companion. Mother spent a large part of her waking life tending pots and fry pans over its gassy blue flames. Its heated belly never failed to give forth a billowing warmth when its door opened. The stove and Mother were co-conspirators, creating the daily bounty that sustained our family.

After the divorce, it became as temperamental and difficult as she did, often refusing to light. Mother developed a daredevil dance with a flaming length of twisted newspaper set to the pilot light. Timed right, the oven lit. Timed wrong, it exploded in her face, the gas escaping too fast for her flaming paper jig, ravishing the air like an overeager lover, rattling her nerves and singeing her eyebrows for a permanent surprised look.

I suppose it was as simple as the switch mechanism breaking, but nothing was simple or possible after Father left. It was all part of a punitive decay process Mother seemed determined to submit to. We children countered her crushing beliefs by being as clever and resourceful as orphans in a medieval forest, or the kids who overcame adversity and got their stories told on TV. Like the boy on *The Wonderful World of Disney* who was crippled in a horseback-riding accident, only to go on to become the youngest person to fly an airplane around the world. I knew if I could just get my hands on a horse, I could eventually learn to fly as well.

Repairmen, let alone getting on a horse or riding the jet stream around the world, weren't an option in our house. Husbands fixed things until the day they packed their bags and pulled out of the driveway. Eternally deferred repairs were the price a woman paid for a failed marriage and a man's desertion.

Bridges to the outside world were burned; oil was spread on the water and torched with a dying cigarette butt.

Cooking was the only thing Mother continued to care about. Fingerprints and dust built up around the house. Darning went undone. Laundry languished in the garage and we wore the same outfits for days on end, until our clothing started to smell—or that's what my classmates said, prompting me to learn how to use the washing machine myself.

When the oven stopped lighting altogether, Mother retreated to stovetop cooking. Her favorite recipe was fried frozen ground beef à la smoking skillet. She'd slap the block down to sizzle until its Styrofoam topcoat slid away, then turn the cauterized flesh to sear on its still-raw side. The meat was done when its surface looked like dried earthworms all squiggly on the sidewalk days after a rain. Mother cut this into four square servings, dished up with a bottle of ketchup on the side. Scarlet juices ran from the wounded center; the outer crust was carbon black. Mrs. Beeton would have been horrified. We refused to eat it.

Mother's cooking became suspect and foreign. She was crazy, and crazy women couldn't be trusted to cook food. The vegetables in her soup weren't uniformly cut, like they were in the can of Campbell's. They were uneven, unpredictable, and imperfect, a

mirror of her defective mental state—Mother's crazy soup. As soon
as she left the TV Room where I'd been served another loony bowl
for lunch, I'd climb up onto the couch, open the high clerestory
window, and throw the soup out into the bamboo patch by the side
of the house. My siblings were similarly on edge. Everything was
eaten carefully and with a large measure of concern, or not at all.
We all practiced the art of excusing ourselves from the table and
tossing dinner down the toilet.

And while I never considered it at the time, I'm sure our refusal
to eat her offerings helped kill off what small measure of Mother
was left after the doctors and the divorce were done with her. Back
then, however, there was no question in our minds that the only way
to retrieve our sane mother was to totally reject the crazy one. But
considering the fact that we soon came to see everything she did as
crazy, I don't know how we imagined that plan could ever succeed.

One evening Mother forgot her meat-frying project and
took to her bed to smoke a few cigarettes. The smell of vaporized
Styrofoam came wafting into the TV Room. I raced to the kitchen
to discover a marbled puddle of plastic and incinerated beef.

"Damn stove" was all she said. After that, she stopped cook-
ing anything that didn't include an alarm or automatic shutoff.
Her culinary repertoire was reduced to instant coffee from the
whistling kettle and toast. Goodbye—and even—for good Mrs.
Paul's frozen fish sticks and Chun King chow mein. The toaster was
abandoned the day a mouse scrambled from it as Mother inserted
a piece of bread.

Hunter adopted a hamburger stand, Chuckle's, a name that
always made me think people who ate there were laughing at the
rest of the world, something Hunter loved to do. Chuckle's was one

of a vast array of hamburger stands to choose from on our town's main boulevard. Hunter dined there nightly on burgers wrapped in waxed paper and dripping with a slurry of juices and mustard, ketchup, and relish, always accompanied by a side of fries as tender and melting in the mouth as rice paper. Despite this steady diet of grease, fat, and sugar, she managed to retain an enviable figure and the clearest skin of any girl at Canyon High School. Howard, my brother, got an after-school job at a Chinese restaurant, where he lived on batter-fried shrimp dipped in an incendiary sauce of ketchup and hot mustard, and egg rolls, their crisp skins translucent with stale grease. He'd come home with flakes of egg roll skin, like evidence of some transgressive act, still clinging to the slickened corners of his mouth. Hailey, my oldest brother, turned eighteen the year my parents separated and, after a short spell sharing an apartment with my father, got a job as a mechanic and moved into a place with roommates his own age. He got to eat whenever and whatever he wanted, a sustaining dream for us all.

Too young to drive, get a job, or move out, I claimed the kitchen as my territory. No longer was it just a room in which to play house or conduct baking soda–and–vinegar science experiments; now it held the promise of my survival and the possibility of conjuring that "delicious home-feeling" Mother no longer chose to provide.

But first I had to light the stove. "Good luck," Mother said, offering me a couple of wooden matches and a rolled-up swath of newspaper. "I don't know why it should light for you."

I lit the twisted ribbon of the day's *San Francisco Chronicle*, Herb Caen's bald head and smiling face crumbling in the blaze, his convivial, man-about-town persona lending bonhomie to the act. I held the torch as far away as possible while opening the oven door and turning on the gas. The line hissed open as I swung the swooning lick of flame down to the broiler ceiling. A familiar fringe of blue fire poofed from parallel rows as the oven's temperature soared. Within an hour I had a tender potato waiting for butter, salt, and sour cream. I climbed up on a chair and plucked cookbooks off the kitchen shelf. I read recipes. I followed directions. I made things happen.

*M*other stood next to the stove, her nylon robe aluminum-colored in the twilight, burnt cigarette scars dusting the front like shrapnel wounds.

"What's that?" she asked, as if some foul mistake were brewing.

"Moroccan lamb tagine with prunes," I said, lifting the pan lid. The sweet-savory steam rose from meat simmered with prunes, cinnamon stick, turmeric, honey, and ginger, a recipe from the "Foreign Intrigue" chapter of a red gingham–covered cookbook Father gave Hunter for her birthday but Hunter never touched. I made it because it was Moroccan, and Morocco was in North Africa, according to the globe in the TV Room, and very far away. I made it in hopes of finding escape.

That moment in the kitchen was a standoff of sorts, a score registered, impossible to settle. Mother hated us for rejecting her cooking, the only possibility she had left for acceptance by others in the world outside her head. We hated her for being crazy, for not acting like all the other mothers, because it stole her from us.

She looked at the savory, simmering lamb, a simple combination yet more exotic than anything she'd ever tried, and said nothing more. I was going places and her traveling days were done. She sucked the glow brighter into her cigarette, turned toward the trail of smoke, and shuffled back to her room.

Lamb Tagine with Prunes

· ·

1 large onion

3½ lbs. lamb shoulder (with bone)

1 stick cinnamon

½ tsp. turmeric

2 pinches ground ginger

3 tbsp. olive oil

Salt and pepper

1 lb. prunes

3 tbsp. honey

1 tsp. ground cinnamon

1 tbsp. sesame seeds

Chop peeled onion, and in a large tagine, earthenware, or cast iron casserole dish combine the onion with the meat, cinnamon stick, turmeric, ground ginger, olive oil, salt, and pepper. Put the dish over a medium high flame, throw in enough water to just cover the meat, then bring it all to a boil. Just as soon as it's boiling, reduce the heat down to a low simmer and cook for 1½ hours, with the casserole lid partially on. Toss in the prunes and drizzle with honey and sprinkle on the cinnamon. Simmer this for another 15 minutes or more, until the meat is thoroughly tender. Heat a small fry pan and brown the sesame seeds in it. Sprinkle these over the lamb dish. Serve hot with couscous. Enjoy while watching travelogues on PBS.

Chapter 7

WHERE THE THISTLE GROWS

I became a hostess. I gave parties. The families I watched on our seventeen-inch black-and-white Zenith television while I traveled the world, eating my Moroccan lamb tagine, my quiche Lorraine, my Hawaiian chicken, and my fiesta tamale pie on a dented TV tray, inspired me. Television families had people over. It seemed natural, unless the guest was their boss; then it was nerve-racking, which meant funny in a sitcom, but we didn't have a boss, so I didn't worry about that. The important thing was that an invitation meant people other than one's family would come to a house, anyone's house, maybe even our house, and eat the food served. It was like a temporary family, with actual rules to follow called etiquette, rules Emily Post put in a book Mother kept in her room, another gift Hunter refused to touch.

My first party was for my tenth birthday. I did a spaghetti dinner (the recipe for the sauce came from the back of the spaghetti's cellophane wrapper: It was a red sauce with an added fillip of warmth coming from a surprising touch of cinnamon), games (culled from library books with instructions on how to play, score, and make props), and store-bought cake and ice cream. I made a centerpiece for the dining room table, a table we no longer used, of a cardboard Snoopy sleeping atop his doghouse. I copied it from the newspaper cartoon page. I admired Snoopy for his rich fantasy life, his ability to relax and to dream.

I set the table with plates of carrot sticks and pitted black olives, which I was now too old to eat off my fingertips, and onion dip that I'd made from an envelope—my first time-saving hostess trick. I filled our beach ball-size yellow mixing bowl with two bags of ruffled potato chips—more festive than the flat kind—and set out giant bottles of Coke to be poured into fire engine-red paper cups. We played relay games in the TV Room, the room added on to the original house, a room we at first called the New Room, but never the Family Room, which I guess now, when I think about it, it was meant to be.

Still dressed in her bathrobe and threadbare socks, Mother came out of her bedroom just as I was about to cut the cake. Unfortunately, it hadn't completely defrosted in its supermarket freezer package. I finessed the moment, as the best hostesses must sometimes do, by suggesting to my guests that it was an ice-cream cake.

"There's no ice cream in it," Naomi Albrecht accused after taking her first bite. "Yes there is," I said. "There's cream in the cake batter and now it's turned to ice." She gave a surprised wobble of her head and finished the cake without saying another word.

*L*avender is growing next to the rosemary, which is next to the strawberry tree, and beyond that is the artichoke bush. This is my piece of Italy in L.A.—the perfect world I planted and that has flourished in this Mediterranean climate. The rosemary is generous; it releases its oils, gives up its scent willingly as I brush by. I will clip some to put into the roasted potatoes with orange zest, which I will scrape from the blood orange taken from my own tree. The roasted potatoes will be for my guests.

Hunter has never been here. She has never walked through my garden and shared a moment in the fading light, taken in the scents, the sights, the views. No one in my family has. My mother doesn't travel. My father no longer says he hopes to visit someday. My brothers never call.

I wonder what Hunter will think when she comes through the garden gate and sees the hill covered in cascades of yellow Lady Banks rose and climbing iceberg roses, mounds of lavender, Mexican bush sage, and towering succulents that force her gaze to the sky. Some people gasp. They are amazed that we have achieved so much beauty in such a difficult space. Will she hurry to shift the attention back to her own patch of personal concerns, as if frightened by the garden's presence, like my dog who looked away from the coyote she once met on our evening walk, as if refusing to see it rendered it nonexistent? Will Hunter deny that I have a garden that thrives beyond the grasp of my childhood home, beyond her small circle of desires—that I thrive and exist beyond the same?

In my childhood garden there was a robust artichoke bush, always a large number of chokes pushing forth in the spring, swelling into full, handsome globes. But they never made it to the kitchen. My mother said they had infantile paralysis, or sometimes she said it was elephantiasis—that our limbs would swell up like an elephant's and stiffen and stop working if we ate them. They were always left to go to thistles, spiked domes of waxy purple needles, a beautiful waste. They stayed on the bush until they faded to mauve and fell apart in the winter rains.

My mother liked artichokes, enjoyed the ritual of cooking them (when she still cooked), the slow, meditative act of eating them, but insisted on buying them from the supermarket. She would set them smartly on their trimmed flat bottoms in an inch of water in the steel saucepan and cook them, covered, over a low flame, until a fork easily pierced the biggest choke's flank. We dipped the end of each leaf in lemon-flavored mayonnaise, then tugged it across our bottom teeth for its small measure of tender flesh. The heart of the artichoke is where the thistle grows. We scooped out the compact, inedible quills, and holding hearts the size of tumbler bottoms in our hands, we slathered them with dressing and ate them one sweet, starchy bite at a time. This was the best part, our reward, and we ate the hearts silently, without looking up, becoming lost in our own artichoke universe, as if each of us were sitting at the table alone.

It was the first school year without my father living in our house. I was nine. On the last Saturday in August, a week before I started fourth grade, Hunter drove my mother and me across the Bay Bridge to San Francisco, where she went to modeling classes at the Chateau du Charm to learn to paint her eyes like Cleopatra, suck in her cheeks for a gaunt look, and walk with a slicing, toes-pointed stride. Our father would never have allowed

Hunter to go to charm school. He constantly fought with her about her wearing makeup, and he would have resented the expense.

On the drive over Hunter smoked cigarettes and listened to KSAN, an FM radio station that was known to play an entire album by the Jefferson Airplane or the Beatles without a break. Its disc jockeys talked slow and low, like the conversation was just between you and them. I suspected they were smoking something mellower than Hunter's Kents.

Hunter spent the drive making fun of the other girls in her class, like the one who had "the personality of a dead squirrel," or the girl whose face was so bumpy with pimples that "blind people were always trying to read her." I always laughed at Hunter's put-downs. She didn't stop her attacks until the only people left standing were those who shared her humor. That was her real charm.

While she went to class, Mother and I went shopping. Our first stop was a flower cart, where she bought two gardenia boutonnieres, marking us as a special pair. With our flowers pinned to our fronts, encasing us in a cloud of exotic perfume, we walked beneath the formal pagoda curls of the Grant Street gate into Chinatown, where everything was different, weird, and riveting. Eyes narrowed there and turned upward, like black guppies caught by their tails. Women wore silk pajamas with stand-up collars and black slippers, the fronts of their blouses closed with intricately knotted cords my mother said were called frogs instead of buttons. Mother walked with a light confidence on the city's streets, not the reluctant or weary walk of home, as if she enjoyed the bumping of strange bodies on crowded sidewalks. I held her hand tight as we darted like koi amid the throng.

The late-summer light was amber and jade and filled with the smells of tea and wooden crates from across oceans, of salted dried fish, preserved plums, and ginger. Everywhere there were dragons and chrysanthemums splitting into a thousand perfect petals, a black enamel certainty wrapped in edible rice paper. Windows held live chickens, fish moving like sequins in wind, mahogany ducks, preserved snakes and roots shaped like humans, steel bins of luminous pink noodles, ceramic women with salt-and-pepper-shaker breasts.

In Chinatown we ate pork-filled buns baked a high chestnut brown and sipped green tea from porcelain cups without handles. Sharp and flippant words punctured our ears. It didn't matter to me whether they were shouts of greeting or warning. Even anger sounded safe in this foreign place.

We walked back toward Union Square to see Macy's windows, crossing the park beneath wheeling pigeons and palm trees that looked like Fourth of July explosions. That fall the mannequins wore short burgundy wool dresses and camel-hair coats. The coats were the soft dun of lions, the color of August grass covering the hills surrounding our town. Inside the store, I ran my fingers over the creamy wool sleeve of the A-line coat I'd admired most in the window, smelled its faint oil of lamb and grass. I was surprised when Mother encouraged me to try it on, as I believed we couldn't afford anything since Father left. When he lived with us I believed we couldn't afford anything, either, but Mother still spent money on clothes and household linens for us, ignoring his complaints. Now she made the fuss and we believed her when she said we were broke. When I slipped my arms into its sleeves, the coat's copper-colored satin lining went cool to a reassuring warmth against my bare skin.

"The buttons are real tortoiseshell," the saleslady said.

"It's lovely," Mother said. The store smelled of distilled roses and baby powder, mixed with our own gardenia scent. The light was blue-white and brighter than day. In the mirror I saw myself on the cover of *American Girl* magazine. Hunter called it *American Clod*.

Mother fingered the price tag.

"It fits her perfectly," said the saleslady.

"My artichokes," said Mother.

The saleslady offered a concerned tilt of her head.

"I left a pot of artichokes on the stove," Mother said. "The pan will melt."

"Oh, my," the saleslady said. "Maybe you could call a neighbor."

"The house will catch fire."

"We don't have any artichokes," I said, shoving my hands into the coat's pockets, hunching my shoulders as if to laminate the fabric to my skin, permanently encasing the *American Girl* me.

"I bought them Monday at East Hills Market," Mother hissed.

"Not in the refrigerator."

"They're in my bedroom, where the neighbors can't find them."

Mother's bedroom closet looked like the annual food drive at Marshall Elementary School, with Cream of Wheat boxes, Del Monte fruit cocktail cans, and bags of dried pinto beans—things no one wanted to eat, but she swore the neighbors would break into the house to steal the minute she left.

"Let me know if I can be of any further help," the saleslady said, shifting her attention to a woman with twins tangled in a blouse carousel.

I slipped out of the coat and watched Mother's face stiffen as she stabbed the hanger into its sleeve, still warm from my body, and put it back on the rack. She squeezed my hand as we marched up the hill to the Chateau du Charm, where Hunter was in the midst of a runway turn, demonstrating the smooth-gaited walk she'd been practicing in the TV Room all week when we slammed through the classroom door.

"Artichokes," Mother said.

"Not again." Hunter rolled her eyes.

"Hun-*tur*!"

Hunter seized her pearl-buttoned teal cardigan from the back of a chair, grabbed her handbag by its fashionably skinny straps, and left without a word. She smoked Citrus Kiss–tattooed Kents and gunned the Tempest's engine all the way home.

"That's the last time you're coming to San Francisco with me on a Saturday," Hunter said. My entire fall wardrobe—a skirt, a white cotton blouse, a pair of oxfords, and a quilted nylon jacket both for good and for play—would come from Daughtery's Department Store, a drab emporium whose only attraction was that it was about a mile from our house—what Hunter considered within walking distance, even though nobody walked in our town.

Hunter launched the Tempest into the air as she sped across the drainage ditch fronting our housing court, knocking the ashes from her cigarette and making me bite the inside of my lip.

"Slow down, young lady," Mother said.

"I'm just trying to get home before the house burns down."

"Don't get smart with me, Miss High Hattie."

No signs of smoke or burnt vegetables waited inside—just the damp, soap-scented air from drying laundry. The dryer had broken the week before and the wash was draped over dining room chairs, lamps, and the entrance to the bedrooms' hall, where it slapped and slid across our faces like an insouciant chanteuse.

Hunter's bedroom door slammed shut.

Mother snatched the lid off the empty stockpot on the unlit stove. Its cold copper bottom reminded me of the camel-hair coat lining.

"Damn neighbors," she said.

*F*or my dinner party I will make *carciofi alla Romana* with young artichokes from the Hollywood Farmers' Market. I will trim them down to the tender remains, stuff them with a mix of diced parsley and garlic, and cook them through in a pot of water, wine, and a healthy dose of olive oil, the way I learned to in a hilltop villa in Umbria, an area of Italy north of Rome filled with green rolling hills topped by medieval towns—a fairy-tale place much like Tuscany. The instructor said that if you were concerned about the amount of olive oil that went into the pot, "don't even bother making the dish." So when I make it, I just pour.

My artichokes will be completely edible.

Carciofi alla Romana

. . . .

8–10 medium-size artichokes with stems

¼ cup minced garlic

¼ cup chopped parsley

¼ cup chopped basil

Olive oil

1 bunch green onions, trimmed and cleaned,
  with a few inches of green remaining

Remove all the coarser, outer petals of the artichokes and trim off the rough tips of the remaining petals with kitchen shears or a sharp knife; trim stems down to white inner core, keeping them 5–6 inches long. Scoop out inside of artichoke, the fuzzy "choke" part, with a knife and/or a melon baller or sharp spoon. Keep the trimmed chokes in acidulated water until ready for cooking. Mix garlic, parsley, and basil together. Stuff mixture into the center of each artichoke, distributing evenly among them all. In a stockpot large enough to hold all the artichokes, place them facedown, stem up. (Side of pot needs to come up around the stems.) Add enough water to come about an inch and a half up the sides of the artichokes, then add an equal amount of olive oil. Toss in the green onions. Cover the tops of the artichoke stems with parchment paper, domed as much as possible. Cover this with a lid, if possible; if not, cover with aluminum foil. Simmer until artichokes are tender all the way through, about 45 minutes to 1 hour and 15 minutes.

Chapter 8

HORSE AND CARRIAGE

I brush the dead bronze leaves and toyon berries from the top of the willow table we'll be using for Saturday night's dinner. It's not long enough to seat our evening's total (now eight, possibly nine, people), so we'll add to its length with a second table we keep folded in the basement. A large cloth will help hide the fact that one is actually two. The overall effect of linen, china, silver, and candles outdoors amid the blousy overgrowth will be that of civilization staking its claim in the wilds.

The dog barks as Somebody appears at the back door. He joins me at the table with a kiss hello, then lifts the cover from the barbecue.

"Honey, where are the barbecue tools?"

"Grilling tools. It's the twenty-first century."

"The fork, the tongs, where are they?" he asks.

"I'm not sure," I lie. I put them in deep storage, on a high shelf behind boxes labeled CAMPING GEAR, by the water heater in the basement. I don't want him to use them. Not with this crowd. He never finds his grilling legs until the end of August. It's still June. I'll be tending the meat for the party.

"Maybe Somebody could check the gas level," I suggest.

The Thanksgiving we invited a crowd in for grilled turkey, Somebody didn't check the gas level, which was empty, until the bird was ready to cook. Somebody had to run out to the one place in town that was open for the holiday and could refill the tank. The fact that it was open made me suspect Somebody wasn't the Only One to forget that Major Detail that Special Day.

"Maybe Somebody already did," he says.

"Are you sure?" I ask.

"I'll take it with me to work tomorrow and have it checked on the way home," he says. "If they're still open."

This last suggestion is in hopes that I'll take pity and offer to get the gas checked myself, tomorrow, during the day, when we both know the barbecue shop will be open. I offer him a quizzical look instead.

"I'll get it checked on my lunch hour," he says.

"Hunter called," I say.

"Is your mother all right?" he asks.

"She's fine. Hunter says she wants to stop by Saturday. She has something she has to give me."

"Did you tell her not Saturday?"

"The call dropped before we could discuss the alternatives."

"Well, that should make you crazy," he says, rolling his eyes.

"And Richard Cronenberg canceled," I say.

"He heard Hunter might be coming?"

"No, he called first. He's off to Paris for an assignment."

"Cancel. Let's go to a movie instead. Remember movies?"

"I can't. No one will ever talk to me again. So don't take a last-minute assignment for Saturday."

"Then find the grilling tools."

"I'll try," I say. What I mean is that I'll think about it.

"The rank which a people occupy in the grand scale may be measured by their way of taking their meals," Mrs. Isabella Beeton wrote in *The Book of Household Management* (London, 1861), "as well as by their way of treating their women. The nation which knows how to dine has learnt the leading lesson of progress. It implies both the will and the skill to reduce to order, and surround with idealisms and graces, the more material conditions of human existence; and wherever that will and that skill exist, life cannot be wholly ignoble."

I came across the above passage several days ago, when I woke in the predawn hours in a panic about the prospect of doing an actual dinner party. This was before Richard Cronenburg packed his bags for Paris and Hunter surprised me with her travel plans. I wanted to know exactly who had invented this sickening social ritual of seating a group of guests at your table to dine on food you've prepared for them. Why, I wondered as I lay staring at the bedroom ceiling, parking a fleet's worth of regrets, had our species given up on the wholly ignoble? Why couldn't we just continue to scavenge for grubs and worms and tender shoots of grass? We could live like pandas, with vast tracts of land, individual foraging territories between us, overlapping occasionally for an impromptu exchange of grunts, comparing grass or bamboo qualities, before we went our merry, very solo way. There'd be far fewer of us, since we'd rarely get together to procreate, let alone break bread, making the encounters all the more enjoyable. I would never have to experience the terror and anxiety surrounding the giving of a dinner party.

Who invented this horrifying custom? I had to find some answers. I rolled out of bed, put on my slippers, went over to my shelves of Gastronomy, Hisory of Texts, and searched the various indexes for "prehistoric man," to see if I could find anything about his communal meal habits. I discovered that dinner parties were to blame for civilization itself.

It was the Ice Age. Quick bites were becoming increasingly scarce. Woolly mammoth appeared on the menu as a necessary, but huge, source of protein. And it took a group to kill and drag one back to the cave. I imagine the first primitive hosts thinking, *Why not invite everyone to stay for dinner? A deboned mammoth yielded more than a ton of meat, there was plenty to go around, and who wanted to face all those leftovers?*

The first invitation to a dinner party was probably a simple gesture, a smile aimed at a nearby tribe, accompanied, possibly, by a wave toward a retreating mammoth. The first excuse no doubt followed. The nearby tribe waved in the opposite direction, indicating that they would love to come if only they hadn't made previous plans to migrate across the Bering Strait.

For the first few million years, these shared meals appear to have been beyond bleak. Language hadn't been invented, so even if there was something to talk about, there was no way of saying it. Cooking hadn't been invented, either, since man had yet to learn to control fire. Invitations were to unheated caves for bloody slabs of meat.

The Neanderthals learned that flames applied to flesh equals succulent flavor around 75,000 BC, when, it is believed, one beetle-browed member of this otherwise evolutionarily dead-end group dropped a piece of meat into the fire and barbecues were born.

I suspect that the size of dinner parties grew as a natural response to the tempting smell of roasting flesh. Wafting clouds of savory smoke were all the invitation some primitive neighbors probably needed. If not the first words formed in the human lexicon, "What's cooking?" no doubt must have been a close second.

Man the party animal soon took off. Communal meals became a vital thread in our social fabric. Those first casual cave affairs encouraged organizational bonds that led to tribes. Tribal banquets led to civilization. Civilization gave us royal feasts and peasant unrest. Peasant unrest led to revolution, fraternity, and equality. Equality led to democracy and the suburban backyard soiree, with its roasting flesh, savory clouds of smoke, and the piqued interest of primitive neighbors.

But I digress.

The chairs scrape loudly across the concrete pad as I push them close to the table, trying to assess the margin for movement before the pad runs out and people start falling into the flower beds below the concrete terrace on which we'll sit.

It's a snug, but manageable fit.

Barbecues are what you did in the suburbs in the '50s when you wanted to have people over, when you were the kind of family other families invited for an evening or relatives insisted come for the holidays, and whenever you could, you'd do the same.

This is the kind of family we once were, used to be, back in the beginning, before the stove broke, before Mother came permanently undone. At least I think it is. It's hard to tell. Sometimes the memories remind me of the Silly Putty I stretched and pressed over the funny pages to copy onto my drawing pad. I'd give the characters new words to say, and the story a different ending.

Maybe these moments, what I consider to be our True Family moments, the perfect state in which we were intimate, easy with each other's company—moments I have always imagined were lost in the chaos to come—maybe they are a consoling fiction that has existed only in my mind all these years. And if that's the case, couldn't something similar exist in the minds of the others, in their own peculiar version of happiness that falls under the heading "Family"? If that is true, could it also be true that these imagined, wholly fictional moments are where our True Family, if it ever existed, continues to reside?

My father, George, his solid, square hands with splayed fingernails stained proudly from the long hours spent in his garage-turned-workshop, built a brick barbecue on the patio from mail-order plans he got from some *Popular Mechanics* he had read when he wasn't mowing the lawn, pruning fruit trees, or building a boy's bedroom dresser or a girl's skirted vanity in his workshop. He built the barbecue in the evenings, when he came home after a full day at his work—twenty bricks a night, until it was done and time to start another project.

The house was a labor of love—or at least a labor. My father built out and improved on its structure. My mother, Lenore, filled it with the children she birthed, hung the closets and packed the dressers with the clothes she sewed, cooked meals planned while lying awake at night, and scrubbed the floors weekly on knees red and thickened from work. It was an industrious, thrifty, well-intentioned house. The yard held enough fruit trees for George and Lenore to feed their family through the summer, make jams for the winter, and still have bags of fruit left for neighbors and relatives. In the fall the ample spread of a walnut tree showered nuts onto the ground, busying me for hours as I cracked their mottled tan shells by the living room hearth, collecting enough of the soft meats for my mother to chop in her wide wooden bowl for adding to brownies, nut bars, and Toll House cookies.

There was enough room in the garden to plant vegetables, instead of flowers and shrubs, if it ever came to that.

The house sat at the head of a court flanked by similar homes, and had a clear, straight view of the street beyond and the traffic that whizzed by but always slowed when turning toward the houses, forced into civility and deference by the drainage ditch, like a medieval moat blocking the court's entrance.

The court families felt safe within their intimate circle of fronts, like a wagon train gathered around, and connected through their children. Everybody had kids then—raucous, unruly kids. They played games in the court, like One Foot off the Gutter, or Indian Tag, or Hide-and-Seek, all variations on the same basic threat of "Tag, you're it," which no one wanted to be. The games were really just an excuse to run and shout and slap at each other. Or the children fought over who had the best front-yard tree to sit under while eating from a brown bag filled with early summer cherries. I insisted the cluster of three aspen in the upper corner of our front yard was best. Russell and Paul, the two British boys next door, preferred their curbside magnolia. And Judy, Janet, and Harry, Jr., the two sisters and brother next door to them, lobbied for the root-rutted ground beneath their front camphor. The only thing we all agreed on was that backyard trees wouldn't do. The fruit-eating session had to be in front of the house, where everyone could be seen.

Our mothers watched us from their kitchen, dining room, or living room windows, as all the houses looked out onto the court's center. And because all the houses had the same floor plan, everyone felt closer knowing each family occupied the same exact set of rooms. It was as if no one had any secrets.

At cookouts on the patio where my father built the brick barbecue, everyone drew close to the smell of hamburgers and hot dogs frying, fat dripping and sizzling onto the charcoal fire. My father always started a pile of logs burning in the fireplace he'd built next to the barbecue, to keep the kids occupied poking sticks and staring into the flames until the food was ready. So excited by the blend of charcoal smoke and hamburger smells and summer night air, I had to calm myself with a hand pressed flat against the bricks' radiant heat.

My mother set out generous bowls of potato and macaroni salad, flecked with velvet bits of bottled red pimiento and the crunchy green of finely diced celery, and we children got to drink Hawaiian Punch, competing with each other to see who got the bestest, reddest mustache. All the families fit into the narrow pen of a patio behind the house, like the box canyons rustlers herded stolen cattle into. There was a wooden gate at one end of this imagined canyon, its walls formed by the house looming high on one side and a woven-wood-slat fence on the other. The house's foundation was edged in brick planters with trellis-climbing vines, a fine-veined veil of tendrils and leaves, stretching up and outward, struggling to find purchase on the sheer vertical face of the clapboard siding. We children sat in what my father called the pygmy chairs at an equally diminutive table. When I looked up from my plate heaped with food, I saw a square of sky that looked to me like a pool of water stretched between the roofline and the fence, with stars floating across its surface, the last traces of the day's light marking its shore.

After dinner, when everyone was full and the kids were quiet and mostly still, when the Eskimo pies were unwrapped and contentedly gnawed, the waxy chocolate coating crackly against the softening vanilla ice cream, my father set up the movie screen, with a screech of metal scraping metal, and the projector and showed our family's vacation movies, just like we were at a drive-in. It was as if the 8-millimeter reels were proof to others that this family could exist, just as it was, somewhere else.

When the movies were done, my father snapped the screen back into its metal tube, collapsed its tripod stand, and returned the projector to its portable box that looked like a suitcase, with its handle and nickel-plated latches, as if he were going to turn it into a traveling show. For sitting still, we children were rewarded with marshmallows to roast over the last of the glowing briquettes, which reminded me of the lava flows in *National Geographic*.

One year, a good year, my father took a photo of his four children with a Brownie camera, the kind you now find at flea markets, for sale alongside the bins of Peggy Lee albums and stacks of ancient *Life* and *Look* magazines. We lined up in front of the fireplace in the New Room. We were arranged by height and age, boy, girl, boy, girl. It was a neat equation, a mathematical output: seven years between the boys' births, seven years between the girls', two years between the oldest boy and girl, and two years between the youngest boy and girl. My sister and I dressed in matching starched party dresses, white with inky sashes tied in bows at our waists, and my brothers wore dark slacks and ties with white shirts. The print had a scalloped white border like a doily's. Each of us held up a black chalkboard with a section of the message MERRY CHRISTMAS AND HAPPY NEW YEAR. We looked like two perfect child couples issued from one, as if it were all planned, fated yet scientific, meant to be, desired and flawless.

I navigate the broken concrete path up through the garden, scouting for flowering possibilities to cut, interesting branches I might pull together the day of the party, for a few elegantly disheveled arrangements. The bush sage is an easy decision; if it doesn't get trimmed, my guests may founder for lack of a clearly marked path. Lawsuits could result. I will nip the branches close to the base for long stems; the purple velvet blooms dangle on their stalks, like rows of elbow-length gloves waiting to applaud at the opera's end.

The other flowering candidates are harder to choose. The scarlet penstemon catches my eye, but there is not enough to spare. The hummingbird sage, its fuchsia blooms like oversize cups resting against felted saucer leaves, is too perfect to relieve of its post.

Everywhere I look I see tragedy in the act of trimming. Plucked and put into a vase, the blooms will be for the temporary enjoyment of a few. Left uncut, they will continue playing out their natural roles: bird perches, seed providers, islands of tranquility.

Gardens are supposed to submit to the will of the gardener. That's their purpose: to give us the false comfort that nature can be ordered, organized, ordained by our shaping desires. My garden, however, controls and organizes me. I walk through and see the need to fertilize. Then the growth I have encouraged demands to be cut back. Weeds beckon to be pulled. I can't help but stop to watch a beetle crawl along a petal's ridge, diving headfirst into a soup of pollen and dew. A distant chattering steals my attention. A squirrel hangs upside down from a branch, testing gravity while gnawing on a clawful of red berries.

I do the trimming myself because when I ask Manuel, the gardener, to trim things back, tell him it's because I'm having a party, the garden ends up looking like a plague has swept through. As if Manuel believed the garden was an unwanted guest at its own celebration. Or possibly he thinks there's something fundamentally wrong with my garden's appearance. He's just waiting for an excuse to make it sit upright, comb its hair, and straighten its tie. I wonder, too, if Manuel's other clients prefer prim, close-cropped gardens, and mine strikes him as excessive, exultant, threatening, and out of control, something other than the acceptable norm.

My garden is tame compared to Mother's garden after Father left. Or maybe it's best to call it a yard, for that's what it became. A plot of land is called a yard when the inhabitants are left to their own devices. It takes on the appearance of the unintentional and opportunistic, like some families do when parents get overwhelmed with the upkeep, move on to other things, or just retreat into their own world, let the grass go to seed, let the kids fend for themselves.

"*N*othing grows," Mother said, fishing a cigarette from a pack of Winstons, igniting it from the smoldering stump of a filter in her hand. Just the opposite was true. Everything grew, and all too well. No one trimmed anything back anymore. That was the problem. The pyracantha bush that was once a low, box-shaped border edging the patio's cement outline became a towering canopy, its branches bent overhead from the weight of their scarlet burden. My mother fed the plants on kitchen dross and beef tea, even the gardenias. A basket of white blooms hung from the back porch's eaves. Their virgin cream petals were like upturned petticoats, set in leaves the color of cave water as they steeped in their own musk.

"Whatever I plant, the neighbors come and take," Mother insisted. Her hand rose to shade her eyes from the whittled sunlight sifting through the branches. Mother's suspicions grew like a high barrier hedge around our house, enclosing our yard and us in it. The world beyond our property was suspect.

"Let's open a teahouse, Mother," Hunter said, slipping a cigarette from Mother's pack. Hunter brought up the teahouse whenever Mother started complaining about the neighbors.

"Oh, I don't think so," Mother said, brushing pyracantha bugs from her blouse front. It was printed all over with clocks, and Hunter called it her eternity shirt because it made Mother look like she had all the time in the world.

"No, Mother, it would be perfect," Hunter insisted. She flipped through a copy of *Ladies' Home Journal* with an unsinkable Debbie Reynolds on the cover. Eddie Fisher left her for Elizabeth Taylor, and Debbie went out and found another man. She didn't sit around and chain-smoke and rant about the neighbors. My mother would never find another man. She had too many other things to find first. Like the can of Bon Ami she swore she'd bought to clean the windows with on her last trip to East Hills Market.

"We'll serve cheesecake, finger sandwiches," Hunter said. "We'll put more tables out here."

My sister drew the ribbon of smoke rising from her mouth through her nostrils in what she called a French inhale. Hunter cultivated the exotic, like the entrance to her bedroom hung with a curtain of Moroccan glass beads that sounded like a hail shower when she closed the door. Her room smelled of the pine and patchouli sticks she used to cover the burnt-rope smell of the marijuana she smoked while listening to Bob Dylan and Barbra Streisand albums. An easel in the corner displayed her painting of a dark blue sky and a gray planet with people melting as they reached toward a fiery orange ball of sun. She called it *Ennui, #9*.

Mother pulled the enameled Oriental cigarette holder from the bun in her hair and stared into the middle distance, as if imagining the public seated at tables on her patio. This look remained from a time when suggestions still held the promise of possibility. It passed in an instant, and Mother's eyelids descended like parchment shades as she twisted the fresh cigarette into her holder's tip.

"I don't want strangers tromping through my house," she said.

"I've got a great cheesecake recipe," Hunter said.

Hunter learned to make cheesecake in her high school home economics class. Cheesecake was the essence of worldly sophistication—New York, artistic, bohemian. Barbra Streisand and Bob Dylan ate cheesecake. Hunter didn't eat cheesecake. She feared being fat as much as she feared being trapped in a suburban marriage ("I think that's what drove Mother insane," she said to me once, while we drove down Castro Valley Boulevard in the Tempest).

Making cheesecake was a domestic gesture and, as such, a daring act for Hunter. She offered it to Mother as a crucible, a self-sacrificing path to save our family finances and bring the world back within our borders. It was fattening, but it was also moral.

I saw this cheesecake hovering above us like the heavenly visions shown in the Episcopal Sunday school class our neighbor Mrs. Conrad took me to once. It was a leaden disc like a collapsed planet, like the fiery orange ball in Hunter's painting, only this cheesecake was red. Its raspberry glaze was the color of the blood of Jesus and was spilling across the cheesecake's top and down its sides. A decorative sprinkling of candied violets marked the edges where the Sunday school illustrations would have placed a crown of thorns. I imagined that each slice we cut from it would be miraculously replaced by a transcendent spirit greater than the sum of our own, greater than the power of all three television networks and Mr. Wallstrup, the school principal, combined. Its dark, crushed-graham cracker and butter crust would feel gritty, like sand, in our customers' mouths before the cream cheese spread inside them like an oil-slick blessing.

"You can hold cheesecake for weeks," Hunter said. "It stays good until your customers come."

"And what if they don't ever?" I asked.

"Then you can eat it all," Hunter sneered.

"We're not opening a teahouse," Mother said. "We have enough problems."

She pulled the gathered hairs from her comb and set a match to them in the ashtray. They sizzled like the fuse to a bomb; an acrid human incense seared the air. I thought of the smell children made when the wicked witch put them in the oven, or the drifting scent of the fires when they burned, the flames settling into coals shaped like bones, the smell of their burning bodies drifting over the countryside miles beyond the witch's walls—a form of escape. Mother's molecules were in this smoke signal, an act of self-incineration, our incandescent mother.

Could the neighbors smell this? And if so, did they ignore it, for fear they would have to take some action?

Hunter and I couldn't stand the smell. We left. We thought offending us was why Mother did it.

She lit a fresh cigarette from the glowing butt before tossing it at the base of the feral pyracantha hedge. She hummed and tapped her toe in an absentminded rhythm, then began to sing softly, as if to a small creature huddled at her feet. "Love and marriage, love and marriage, go together like a horse and carriage." Her high, lilting soprano followed the smoke vapors up and over the rooftop. "You can't have one, you can't have one, no you can't have one without the oooooothhhhher."

I can't decide on anything in the garden. I want it all to stay, a form of visual sustenance. Besides, none of my garden blooms care to cooperate with my need to drag them indoors. The last rose I clipped dropped its petals, as if signaling horror at its fate, immediately upon landing in a bud vase above the kitchen sink. I will buy flowers for my dinner table. The neighborhood shops always have lilies and roses for their customers visiting Forest Lawn. I won't buy lilies, lest they draw further attention to my no-longer-living neighbors. I don't want to make my guests any more uncomfortable with their mortal thoughts than they may already be.

Death thoughts have not always been banned from the dinner table, mind you. They were once encouraged. In ancient times, hosts regularly passed a preprandial skeleton around to remind their guests that life was short—enjoy it while they could. Then Christians were invented, and with them the belief in delayed satisfactions, that foregone pleasure in this life brought eternal reward in the next. The skeletons were tucked away.

I'm sure this constant reminder of death—life's end product— is one reason I find comfort in our proximity to Forest Lawn. It's a perpetual cattle prod to happily soldier on. I know some people are superstitious about living next to a cemetery. I'm not afraid of anyone there. I consider the dead to be at peace.

It's the living who haunt me.

I'd prefer to find a tortured soul from the cemetery next door floating in the hallway in the middle of the night to the tricks my living, immediate family members play.

Standing at the top of the garden, I am struck by how welcome a sight our house is, like a companion waiting at the foot of the stairs. I imagine that the glow reflected off its stucco sides is born of gratitude for all the things we have done to it since we bought it fourteen years ago. My husband and I have an intimate understanding of its needs. It provides shelter while we provide repairs.

Constant repairs.

It's an old house, built in 1924, with a number of previous owners, the last being a cocaine-snorting video editor whose wife left him, taking off with their infant child shortly after they moved in. It had been on the market for over a year and was in terrible shape when we bought it: broken windows, stained rugs, and ceilings damaged from a leaky roof and a poorly patched-together drainage system. We have been on alert and in a panic ever since the first day we moved into this, our rescue house. In our first month of occupancy, we had a team of five plumbers excavating our front yard to keep the toilets from backing up and onto floors. No one knew how long it would take, what it would cost.

They never do.

One of the plumbers trimmed the front-yard bushes before proudly informing me they were roses. Another day this same plumber, arriving winded and struggling for breath at the top of the stairs, laughed and said, "In this house you don't have to pray to God; you just get up in the morning and shake hands with him!"

The first rainy season after we moved in, we discovered that water ran through the basement of our hillside house, across the first floor's carpeted entry, and out the door. Or sometimes it chose instead to fill our kitchen cabinets and then seek exit out the kitchen door. Sometimes it did both things at once.

We replaced the cracked, crumbling stucco coating the entire house and, section by section, every wood deck, all eaten down to the nails by ravenous termites and a particularly cancerous dry rot. Bee experts responded to our pleas for help when a mystery buzz in the dining room wall turned into a plague of insects crawling out of the electrical outlets; they were determined, I suppose, to pollinate the chandelier before moving on to the floor and table lamps. Rat experts have had to plug up holes to keep large rodents from traversing our living room, escorted by our useless cats. Clouds of termites have risen from the wooden floors and expired on our window screens in an effort to escape. This happened once while we were in the midst of entertaining. My husband diverted the guests while I swept a living carpet of termites out the kitchen door. The termites were smart. They were seeking an exit. We stayed.

And anything that we do launches a chain reaction of other things that need to be done. The house's exterior is perpetually in need of painting, the blistering Southern California sun eating away all efforts, it seems, before a coat fully dries. We have had the foundation bolted to the ground to prevent full and total loss during earthquakes. During the course of the annual fire season, brought on by the hot, dry Santa Ana winds of fall, I entertain fantasies about the place burning down. I often wonder if the Santa Ana winds are generated by the wishful thinking of tortured homeowners such as us.

It is only in the calm between storms of house repair that I can contemplate dinner parties. Like now. We have just replaced a dishwasher, what I call our $3,000 dishwasher because it took $2,500 worth of virgin wiring before the installer would plug in the fresh, comparatively inexpensive, dishwasher. We had initially been relieved that the new dishwasher wouldn't require us to remodel the entire kitchen, because the opening left by the old one was, we were certain, going to be either too small or too large for current models to fit.

And while we have been caught up in all of this damage control, I have not, in fourteen years, changed the shelf paper in the cabinets—something I'm sure most people would consider top of their to-do list on taking up residence. I simply haven't had the time or the interest. And if it isn't broken . . . well, you know the rest.

*T*he thought occurs to me, as I stand at the top of the garden and look down on this house that has taken so much concern and cash and constant vigilance, that it is the opposite of the house in which I grew up. That house was unsullied when my family moved into it. Additional construction increased its size as our clan grew. That house was well maintained and in showcase condition until the day my father left. In the absence of his vigilance, neglect and decay came to roost.

Piece by piece, the house began to fall apart, and there was little cash or willingness to take responsibility for maintenance or repairs. Curtains shredded with age. Paint peeled and was never replaced. The roof leaked and buckets were put out to catch water, for lack of a proper remedy. Mattresses sagged and backs bowed. Hot water heaters broke and we boiled water on the stove for baths, holding the pans and stockpots with bunched-up towels as we carried them, trying our best to keep the scalding contents from sloshing over the sides and burning hands or feet as we minced past the dining room table and down the carpeted hall. While I was doing this I imagined I was carrying a pot of nitroglycerine, and that if I spilled just one drop it might blow us all up, the house included, like in some movie thriller. My life and that of my family's and our future happiness all depended desperately on my success. Or sometimes I imagined that I was a ballet dancer crossing the stage on tiptoe in search of an impossible perfection, my hallway performance propelled by an imaginary symphony and a demanding, sophisticated audience. If I managed to reach the bathtub without losing a drop of water, the applause was deafening, the critics' praise fortifying, the rewards of the hard-won bath all the more pleasurable.

Hunter had moved into Hailey's room, with its own shower and hot-water heater, so she didn't have to participate in this ritual. Our struggle against our house's decrepitude and Mother's decline set us apart from the other, more conventional homes: We were bohemians, nonconformists in a conforming world. Our membership in the middle class had expired, and we were better off for it, as Hunter constantly reminded us. Hunter hated normal, so I kept my desire for normalcy to myself. Normalcy meant connection to the larger world; normalcy meant escape from the boundaries of our exceptional family.

Clothes dryers broke, and the damp wash was hung inside the house. In the summer we could escape outdoors from the wet fabric, which slid across our faces as we passed through the hall and doorways where it was draped. In winter it was unavoidable as we moved through the house, and indoor drying added a pervasive, moist chill to the interior air. London was said to be cold and damp in the winter, and I fancied it was similar to being inside our house. I built a fire in the TV Room's fireplace and roasted whatever I could find in the refrigerator that could be stuck on the end of a fork and shoved into the flames, like people did on busy urban street corners to sell to the passing throng. In lieu of chestnuts I did bacon strips which sputtered happily and fragrant on the hearth and never did get crisp, and tried making toast, but the bread got more black from smoke than firm and tan like it did in a proper toaster. There was no passing throng to sell my goods to, so I ate them myself, cheered by this primitive act.

Sometimes, like when I'm walking up the stairs with four bags of groceries tugging at my arms, I wonder if we bought this house as a punishment. Or as penance, as my lapsed Catholic husband might venture. Survivor's guilt, possibly, having survived my family, the family my mother did not. I would saddle myself with a house full of disasters, in a decaying neighborhood filled with stubborn, flinty people who seemed to me, when I was in a dark state of mind, haunted not by ghosts from the nearby cemetery but by their life's regrets. If we stayed long enough, I feared we would feel the same.

Overcoming these burdens will prove me stronger and better than my mother, and possibly rescue her in some way.

How, though, I don't know.

Extreme Unction
Raspberry-Glazed Cheesecake

1½ cups graham cracker crumbs

3 tbsp. sugar

⅓ cup butter, melted

4 (8 oz.) pkgs. cream cheese, softened

1 cup sugar

1 tsp. vanilla

1 tsp. lemon zest

4 eggs

⅓ cup raspberry preserves

Candied violets and/or crown of thorns for
decoration

Preheat oven to 325 degrees F. Pulse graham cracker crumbs in a food processor with 3 tbsp. of sugar, and butter; press this mixture firmly onto bottom of springform pan. Beat the softened cream cheese, 1 cup sugar, vanilla, and ½ tsp. lemon zest with an electric mixer on medium speed until well blended. Add eggs, 1 at a time, mixing on low speed after each addition, just until blended. Pour over crust.

Bake 55 minutes or until center is almost set and top is golden. Loosen cake from side of pan; cool before removing side of pan. Gently warm raspberry preserves with the other ½ tsp. lemon zest in small saucepan, or microwave in microwave-safe dish just until melted. Using spatula, spread over top of cake, letting raspberry drip decoratively over sides of cake. Sprinkle a ring of candied violets and/or crown of thorns around edge of cake. Refrigerate 4 hours or overnight. Store leftover cheesecake in refrigerator.

The calorie count on this entire cake lands just south of 6,000, including 400 grams of saturated fat, and 256 grams of cholesterol. Do not eat it in one sitting, even if you are feeling extreme. Better yet, open a teashop and use the cake as a major menu item and customer draw.

Chapter 9

THE SICK ROOM

My mother always said she worked in a place she called the Clause. I imagined it was dark there, and cold, like the hollow carved by fire in an ancient tree, the heartwood eaten away by recalcitrant flame. It smelled of sweet decay from decomposing leaves, copper, scarlet, and amphibian green scales fading to a pliant black. Wind sliced through, fingers rushing into hollows, stripping etched grain. It was a lonely place. My mother was the only one there. She worked in it day and night. The exact tasks remained as mysterious as the rewards. It couldn't have paid much, as she still relied on support checks from my father. I suspected it was a frightening place, as her hazel eyes often held a haunted look when she came back from the Clause.

Black-and-white snapshots showed a beautiful woman at ease with youth's glow. Startling eyes beneath a brow as smooth and tan as the sandstone cliffs on which she watched the razored horizon. Ocean breezes lifted molasses-dark hair. Her fleeting smile daring beneath a tilted straw brim. A trim waist meant for confident hands; an apple-filled mouth waiting to be kissed. A twist of high spirits moving gracefully toward the edge.

The Clause was the place my mother went when others went to offices or shopping. She disappeared there, moved freely, worked while she was asleep. When she was smoking cigarettes and watching television or burying the wet kitchen trimmings in the garden, I knew she was really in the Clause. When she was brushing her extravagantly long hair, shot through with shock-treatment gray, its waves tapering to a waist thick as a silted riverbank, I imagined she was spinning straw in this dim and distant place.

The one benefit of working in the Clause was that Mother had information available only to her. She received advanced warning about dormant volcanoes beneath our house that might someday blow, and she was sensitive to impending earthquakes.

Possibly in exchange for this information, Mother made a pact with nature: It could take over the house while she worked in the Clause. Trees and shrubs were allowed to grow over its windows, filtering and blocking the light, replacing the pinch-pleat curtains rotted to a crude lace.

Mother lost things in her Clause, silly things: broken Haviland china plates, stray sterling silver forks and spoons in a sweetheart pattern, veiled velvet hats, pearl-handled opera glasses, a garnet good-luck ring, a high school graduation watch rendered delicately in gold gone dull with age. The thing she lost most often was the Chinese enameled cigarette holder she stabbed into her bun like some Oriental concubine, always patting the top of her head in search of it, always swearing she'd lost it in the Clause.

This girl, this Hunter, wasn't Lenore's fluttery-eyed, easy-peasy firstborn, her son, her Hailey. "Oh, your life will change forever," people warned her when she was pregnant with Hailey, as if a child's birth might bring something less than joy. Joy and its accompanying bundles were the only things ever mentioned before she first got pregnant. Once she began to show, the terrible warnings began: "Oh, your life will change forever," they said. "Your life will never be the same."

She loved her life—married, grown-up, out of her parents' house, cooking and cleaning in her own house, graduated from college. She didn't want this life to change. Then her Hailey came and he was perfection, a cooing ball of bliss, named after a comet that made only rare appearances. He was a once-in-a-lifetime occurrence. She'd never been happier, so of course she wanted a second, when the time was right. And it soon was. She named her daughter Hunter because she wanted her to be a strong woman, a courageous woman, a woman with the instinct to survive.

But how would she survive Hunter, who cried constantly, insistent cries that sounded like animal howls, cries that Lenore wasn't able to stop, no matter what she did? When she first called her mother, Ellie, for help, Ellie came and walked the floor, patting the baby's back, murmuring, "Now, now" and, "There, there" until the tiny infant, the helpless, innocent baby Hunter, fell asleep.

"You have more patience than I do, Mother," Lenore said. "I can't bear the sound of her wailing. I don't know what I'll do if she doesn't stop." Ellie assured her it would get better with time.

Ellie lived only a few miles away but had her own house to take care of, and soon Lenore's father refused to drive his wife to his daughter's "every damn time the baby cried."

"It's not every time," Ellie said.

"It's enough. It's her baby; she needs to learn to care for it proper."

*L*enore took up smoking to calm her nerves, just as the advertisements promised. Each tangy, sulfurous puff loosened the knots, mildly disengaged her mind, just enough to blot the sleeping child's cries from her consciousness. A couple of cigarettes a day, a walk or two, her babies in a double stroller, the park and back—she could handle that. The other mothers talked only about their babies, the best pabulum formulas, the discomforts and indignities of breastfeeding, sleeping schedules, and precocities.

She had gone to college, studied history and politics, and earned a teaching credential for this? To entertain pabulum opinions? Did anyone read the newspaper? Had they heard the one about the toddler in Hiroshima who stood in his doorway and saw the sun explode before it burned his skin away? What would happen to all of them, all their private, self-propagating concerns, if there were a flash in the sky and their flesh began melting from their charred limbs? Wasn't anyone concerned about that?

When these thoughts came, as they began to more frequently after the birth of her second child, Lenore couldn't look at Hunter and Hailey without seeing the photographs of dead babies killed in the war. A phrase repeated itself in a voice reminiscent of her late grandfather's, as if he were speaking from the beyond, knew what was ahead: *They are not safe, you are not safe, in this world*, the voice said.

The voice didn't stop until the children began to fuss. Loudly. Forcing their imperious demands on her. Breaking the spell.

Bringing her back to the moment. A moment in which the world seemed wobblier than before.

I climb into bed alongside Somebody, who is sitting propped up against the pillows, reading the latest *New Yorker* magazine.

"I called my mother today," he says.

"How is she?" I ask perfunctorily. She's always fine when he calls her. Still, I ask. It's the dutiful thing to do. He calls her as part of his role as the obedient son. She rarely calls us and does so only if she isn't fine and all her other children up and down the list (a chart, really), which she's maintained according to the chronology of their births and their current geographical distance from her, aren't otherwise available. Somebody is a midrange child but lives the farthest away, so when his mother does call it's a virtual certainty that she isn't fine. And if one of his siblings calls, an even rarer occurrence, it's only because she definitely isn't fine and they're seeking Somebody to deal with whatever her problem is.

"She's fine," he says. "She's coming west for a visit to see Sam and Susan and Seeley and their kids, but not this far west."

Sam was Somebody's older brother, who lived in Idaho with his wife and two teenagers; Susan was a divorced younger sister in Phoenix, raising three kids under age twelve from two separate fathers and one marriage; and Seeley was the youngest of the lot, who'd married the year before and had had her first child a month ago. Somebody's mother's allergies prevented her from coming to California, or so she claimed, though I suspected our failure to reproduce was as much a concern to her as the local pollen count.

Her refusal was our punishment (in that if we wanted to see her, we had to make the trip), or, as I saw it, our reward (in that I never had to host her in our house).

"That's too bad," I say.

"You don't mean that," he says.

"Anything good in the *New Yorker*?" I ask.

"My mother is a good person," he says.

"She is. But not when she refuses to visit her children who haven't gifted her with grandchildren."

"That's not true," he says.

"She's never been here, not once," I say.

"Her allergies."

"Allergies? You're the only child not to go forth and multiply, and her response is a cool distance."

"We get a card and a check at Christmas."

"With so many children, her check-writing arm must get exhausted. No wonder she has no energy to ever place a call." I felt bad for Somebody that she seemed so disinterested in us. I'd hoped when we married that an extended family might be included in the deal. But the only deal was a list of family obligations in which our participation was expected, even if our pleasure was not. Like attending the General's (for that is what I called Somebody's mother, though not in his presence) Big Birthday extravaganzas, staged by the inner circle of Major Breeders who'd stayed close to home and created a village's worth of clan members.

He flips through the magazine, stops to chuckle at a cartoon he won't share with me unless I ask him what's so funny, something I refuse at the moment to do out of sheer exhaustion with a side of annoyance, then puts the magazine down, reaches over to pull me close, and kisses me on the lips.

"How about a date?" he asks.

"Are you kidding?" I am exhausted by the thought of Hunter's imminent arrival and Richard Cronenburg's departure.

"No," he says.

"I'm really not in the mood."

"I want to make love to my wife."

"I'm not in the mood. And neither is your wife."

I hated when he referred to me as his wife. What happened to me, the woman he married? Had our marriage reduced me to a wife? I never referred to him as my husband, unless it was to a stranger or I was making a consumer complaint. It was my trump card. "My husband hates the color," I'd say, or, "My husband couldn't follow the assembly instructions to make it work," and it was understood, no more questions asked, return accepted, refund granted.

It was cowardly and lazy, sure, but it got the job done. So what if it was me who hated the color or me who couldn't make the damn thing work? When it was just me facing down the world, there were certain sorts who wanted to turn it into a production, rustle up an argument, pull an attitude, make a power play. If I blamed the discontent on my husband, it wasn't just between them and me—it belonged to an absent third party, and I was just an agent in the game. So, yes, you could say I used Somebody's role as a husband to get a job done. But what was he doing when he wanted to make love to his wife, instead of me?

I indulged his need to order in a restaurant, prefacing his remarks with "My wife would like," and there I would sit, playing that part for the evening, an actor joining the cast of a domestic situation, whether comedy or drama. But at some point he'd started making reference to me as his wife in most all situations, private and public. As if that was what he wanted from the union most—not me, but "a wife," or, more specifically, "my wife." A generic possession, easily replaced or repaired if broken. I wasn't sure when I'd left the room, or who this wife was and if we had anything in common besides clothing and shoe sizes, but it was a topic he and I might need to discuss.

Did he have a problem with me, but not with his wife, the one whom he wanted to have sex with that night? Was he a polygamist in that sense, married to two women, his wife and me? Or was the wife designation just made in the interest of getting a job done, and was sex a wife's job? Was that my job if I were to agree to be his wife? I had, way back, agreed to be his wife. I was in love. I'd failed to look closely at the job description. I thought we'd work it out. I'd have to reexamine the contract. But not tonight. Tonight I was tired. Too tired for anything.

"I want to make love to you," he says, turning back toward me, looking directly into my eyes. He kisses me. I don't pull away, even though his wife might.

"How about a rain check?" I ask.

"Are you sure you want to do Saturday night?"

"Yes, I do," I say. "I need to spend an evening with friends. I need to feel like more than just your wife."

He turns away, pulls up the covers, and shuts off the light. I turn my back to him, move away so our bodies are not touching, and turn out the lamp on the table on my side of the bed. "Good night," I say. "Right," he says.

"*Etiquette* is the name given to the rules of society, and society is a game which all men play." I read this in the introduction to *Practical Cookery*. It's the book in which I found my coleslaw recipe. "If you play it well," it went on, "you win. If you play it ill, you lose. The prize is a certain sort of happiness, without which no human being is ever quite satisfied."

I'd always thought of dinner parties as trials, at the end of which my worth as a human being would be judged for ill or good; or a test I'd pass or fail; or an audition for a place in the world. I'd never thought of them as games, like tennis or basketball or chess. Your life didn't depend on games. If I looked at it as a game, a dinner party became something to practice and get better at. Something that could be enjoyed while playing. I could watch my guests in the midst of the match and see how they played their positions.

Somebody practiced his social game at the office and on business travel to Europe, Asia, and the major megalopolises of the world. Except for quick trips to Napa for an olive oil conference, or a day run to Santa Barbara for a tour of an organic farm, I stayed home, perfecting my game of Solitaire. I was rusty at the social game, and my familiarity with the rules was fading. I was hungry for that "certain sort of happiness" provided by a well-played game.

"What if Hunter shows up?" my husband asks.

"I can handle it."

"You couldn't before and it's been ten years."

"I've had ten years of therapy."

Somebody seemed determined to retreat into the private world of our marriage. I knew couples that did this, but I needed more.

"Well, I'll help you with the dinner, but you're on your own with Hunter."

"I know," I said.

She was the wild card in this game. All my culinary efforts, my house, my laborious efforts at cultivating friendships, even my pathetic gastronomic musings, would be trampled by her feather boa–topped, mirrored-caftan, snide but always amusing, one-woman brass band. I would be lost to the role of younger sister and forgotten as Hunter took the trophy for the evening's most memorable personality, even if it was for being crass.

When we were still talking, Hunter never accepted my dinner invitations. Instead, she would call as we were sitting down to our dinner, a meal I'd spent hours cooking. This was considered the family hour and she always wanted to talk about "the family," but only the one I'd been born into. She hadn't bothered to start one of her own, and without having birthed any babies, my marriage was too dull for discussion. These calls seemed to be all the family she needed or could stand.

Then we had our falling-out. There were lawyers and a court appearance. I sought her removal as my mother's conservator. Her behavior seemed increasingly erratic and unstable. I was concerned for her mental health, her ability to conserve our mentally ill mother's estate. The calls stopped. Never having known how to survive in a world shared with Hunter, I treasured the silence.

Then the calls began again. Mother had her first major heart attack. Conversation was restricted to the topic of her care and condition. These calls no longer came during the family hour—that was now Hunter's time for the gym: running on the treadmill and lifting free weights, rapid breathing, toning muscles, maintaining strength, energy, and a youthful appearance. These calls came at the onset of morning business hours, just a few minutes after nine, as if she were waiting for me to settle in at my desk before she snagged me with her latest dire concerns.

"Mother's systems are shutting down," she would say, and I'd race north to visit her in the hospital after a minor heart attack, take her to the emergency room for a dog bite, convince her to let me dispose of a beloved but four-days-dead cat. So afraid for her welfare, so concerned that no one else would or could take the necessary actions, I devoted myself to her care, enslaved as if by a spell.

When I exhausted myself from the constant travel and began to realize how much of my life I was no longer living, I began to gather a network of caretakers who stepped in when I couldn't. There was Eva, the visiting nurse; Marla, a paid companion who sat with Mother for chats in front of the TV and did her grocery shopping; and Christos, the Greek immigrant gardener, who mowed what was left of her lawn, tried to keep the trees from collapsing onto the roof of the house, and beat the bamboo back from the border fences, something Mother used to consider her job but no longer had the energy or physical strength to do anymore.

"When did your father pass away?" Christos asked me one day.

"He's still alive," I said. "They divorced when I was a child."

"He divorced her?" he asked, incredulous. "How could he do such a thing?"

He said what we, Mother's children, never allowed ourselves to think: Apparently, the Greeks operated under a different code.

One day, while Lenore stood at the stove heating formula, Hunter slung over her shoulder, the baby began crying, a rusty knife stabbing in Lenore's ear. As Lenore held the hot bottle to her wrist to test the temperature, the girl squirmed and kicked the bottle out of her mother's hand. Shards of hot glass covered the freshly washed linoleum floor in a milky tide. The baby cried even louder. Lenore knew the only way to stop her was to heat another bottle. There wasn't time. She wouldn't survive the stabbing in her ear. Lenore slapped Hunter hard across her face.

Hunter stopped crying. Then, after a blessed moment of silence, she felt the impact's full sting and began screaming hysterically between frantic gulps of air.

Lenore couldn't think straight for the child's howls. Now the floor had to be washed again. And another bottle prepared. She set the baby in her high chair, where she continued to howl. Lenore plucked at the glass and sliced a finger, the dripping blood blending with formula. A ribbon of red flowing into a faded pink—such a pretty parfait of fluids, she thought.

It occurred to her to put the baby's face in the bucket of water she'd used to clean the floor. Not long enough to drown, just long enough to shut Hunter's flower-bud mouth. To show her what was what. Lenore wiped the dripping formula from the bottom of the high chair. She wrapped her hand in a kitchen towel, poured Spic and Span in the bucket, grabbed the mop, and attacked the floor instead of the baby. She wrung the mop and the soap inflamed her cut. She feared disappearing into the baby's cries.

Drown out the baby's sound instead of drowning the baby. Good. She said this aloud as a reminder she still existed. Who was shouting at the baby, and why didn't the baby shut up? Dammit, right now! That baby should listen; that person was as loud and angry as Lenore was. Was it her father? He got mad. Was it her? How could that be? She tried so hard to control her temper. All that effort lost in a moment with this child.

This had to stop.

Lenore shoved the tub handles on full force, water flooded the white enamel basin. She ripped her clothes off her body—buttons shooting across the room, zippers snagged, blood and formula stains; pressed herself into the tub's coffin shape, her bone marrow turned to lead. So heavy, she'd need a crane to get out. Her bleeding fingers tinted the water the color of Mexican primrose.

A primitive voice welled up from inside; a volcanic charge escaped her lungs as she held her head under the water's torrent. "Love and marriage," she began to sing, "love and marriage go together like a horse and carriage."

The water flowed over the tub's edge onto the hallway's wooden floors, the wooden floors she'd waxed on her hands and knees. Every month, when she wasn't pregnant, when she could get down on her hands and knees and buff the wax with a cloth the way you were supposed to; when she could still keep up with the household chores. Not like now, when she was always behind, always exhausted, too exhausted to think or even sleep. How she missed sleep.

*I*t is Tuesday morning, and I call my father to see if I can tease a contact number out of him to reach Hunter. I can't stand another minute of not knowing when she thinks she's coming by. Either she'll make it early morning, so I'll have time to recover before my guests arrive, or she'll have to reschedule.

My father's phone rings. He only picks up after I start to leave a message on the machine.

"I thought you were a telephone solicitor," he says. This is his excuse for screening all his calls.

"I was calling because Hunter called me and . . ."

"What? I can't hear you," he says.

"I was calling because Hunter called me and . . ."

"I can't hear you," he says. "Just a minute while I get to the other phone."

He lays the handset down by the phone in his kitchenette, and I can hear his footsteps as he slowly shuffles into the back room, where he keeps his computer and a phone on which he can hear a caller. It is a long journey for him in his shuffling stage.

"Are you there?" he says finally.

"I'm here, Dad."

This is our ritual.

"Dad, why don't you get a phone in your kitchen you can hear calls on?" I ask.

"Why would I want to hear a solicitor?" he says. "They never say anything I want to hear. You're not a solicitor, are you?"

"No, I'm not, Dad," I say.

"Good. What's up?" he asks, in a jovial way that means, *Get to the point*.

"Hunter called," I say. "She says she's coming by my house Saturday to give me something."

"That's nice. It's about time you two learned to get along."

"No, it's not, Dad. I'm having a dinner party Saturday."

"I thought you made those up."

"Not this one."

"Set a place for Hunter."

"She didn't tell me when she was coming before the call dropped."

I don't say that I can't think of anything more horrifying than having Hunter at my table with the few people I've managed to gather together after all these years in Los Angeles whom I consider friends—the few people who would show up if I gave a dinner party.

"How can I help?" he says.

"Can you give me her number? I seem to have lost it."

"Let me see if I can find it for you." He lays down the phone, and I can hear his footsteps as he shuffles into the next room, where he keeps his address book. I hear him sigh and shuffle back.

"Here's the number: (818) 555-1212."

"Dad, that's Information for my area."

"Now, why would I have that written down here by Hunter's name? Let me look here . . ." I write down the number he gives me in the 818 area code. We exchange comments about the weather. Whatever is happening where he is will soon be at my location. It's raining up there. It's sunny down here. "Good luck," he says.

What was Hunter doing in my area code? Selling real estate in the Valley? Producing porn movies in one of the beautiful, empty houses owned by one of her absent friends, of which she boasted a collection? I dial the number. I get myself. "I'm sorry, I'm not available. Please leave a . . ." My father gave me my own cell phone number. I never call it, rarely give it out, so I didn't recognize it.

I call my father again. He shuffles back to the office to talk on the louder phone, then shuffles to his room for the phone book, then shuffles back to the office, and finally gives me a 702 number. A Las Vegas area code. That makes sense.

"I thought she was still in Las Vegas," he says. "I was wondering what she was doing in the 818 code when I gave you that last number. Sorry about that. I must be getting old."

It's still raining where he is. It's still sunny where I am. We bid adieu. I call the number. A recording says the number has been disconnected. It's late morning. I don't have time to call my dad back and try a third time. I have errands to run and shopping to do. I'll wait for now; maybe Hunter will call back on her own. I put my cell phone in my purse and make sure that it's on.

I move "wine store" to the top of my destination list. I need to get a few bottles for the party, and after the go-round with my father and failed phone calls to Hunter, the errand takes on new urgency and appeal.

*G*eorge found the girl in her chair, spittle on her chin, her eyes and cheeks flushed from crying, quiet now. Her diaper was wet against his suit as he walked down to the nursery, where he found Lenore lying on the rug, her bathrobe open, her blood-streaked body exposed. The chenille marks from the nursery rug carved a flamelike imprint on the side of her face.

"I was just so tired," she said. She laughed at this because her voice reminded her of Rosalind Russell's: methodical, sharp, intelligent, trying to get herself out from the midst of a screwball muddle. She'd been feeding the girl, came to the nursery to check on the boy, and then lay down for just a minute.

"I must have fallen asleep," she said. Bette Davis. It was more Bette Davis than Rosalind Russell. The shimmy in the shoulders was definitely Bette Davis. "I must have fallen *a*-sleep!" she said with a comic emphasis on the "a" and a fillip on the "sleep," and ending in a batty-eyed smirk. George didn't know what else to do but slap her hard across the face.

Neither of them said anything for a good long spell.

She didn't know how to explain the blood. She didn't remember anything about the blood. It wasn't her period, or had she lost track of that, too? A gash in her finger continued to ooze. She was Lady Macbeth stifling a laugh. Certainly, Shakespeare had a more layered tragedy with deeper meanings in mind? She'd explore that at greater length, use this as an anecdote when they came to that place in the curriculum. When she got back to her students, when she was up off the floor.

"I think I was opening a can. That must have been it. Damn can opener."

Her father bristled at the expense of the private sanitarium they agreed to pay for. "You coddled her," he accused his wife. He grew up on a Kansas wheat farm. No one ever coddled him. "From the age of four I spent my summers working the fields dawn to dusk, planting, weeding. School didn't start until after harvest. They put a pancake in my back pocket and that was lunch. It made me strong."

"Lenore's not you and she wasn't raised that way."

Lenore's mother hadn't told her father all the details George shared with her of the condition he'd found Lenore in that morning. It upset her to discuss it with anyone, even her husband. It was too much like her brother Leo's daughter Helene, Lenore's cousin, all those nightmares they'd suffered with her. Fine-boned Helene, a Lalique vase of sorrows, an internationally touring dancer, never married, twice admitted for treatment—a nervous condition, they called it (all that travel, no doubt)—and there was a man to blame as well; she had spoken of a man. She'd collapsed into herself like the frond of a prayer plant.

Certainly, Lenore's mothering instinct would save her; she'd stay in this world for her babies. If not, what would become of Ellie's grandchildren, her daughter and the family she'd begun?

Private treatment was the only respectable solution. No one else was to know. The indignity of a public hospital was not for *her* daughter. If the neighbors asked, Lenore was recovering from a ruptured appendix from which she'd nearly died.

The women understood. With two babies, a woman might forget to take proper care of herself.

The diagnosis was postpartum depression. Many women suffered from it, the doctors told Lenore's family, to varying degrees. There was no reason to believe Lenore's wouldn't fade with time. It was just part of the after-healing, like the vaginal tear, from making babies—a rip in a woman's solid sense of things that, with a return to the rhythms of daily life, a reattachment to one's inherent domestic duties, would gradually and inevitably repair itself.

"*W*hoever the invalid may be, whether the mother, father, or sweet youngling of the flock," wrote Marion Harland in the "Sick-Room" section of her 1882 volume *Common Sense in the Household: A Manual of Practical Housewifery*. "the foundations of the household seem thrown out of course while the sickness lasts. . . . All other thoughts are swallowed up in the all-absorbing, ever-present alarm." It was in this manual that I found the following recipe I consider appealing for the potentially therapeutic benefits of pounding the raw chicken. Beyond that, I make no claims.

Chicken Jelly. (Very nourishing.)

....

Half a raw chicken, pounded with a mallet,
    bones and meat together

Plenty of cold water to cover it well—about a
    quart

Heat slowly in a covered vessel, and let it simmer until the meat is in white rags and the liquid reduced by one-half. Strain and press, first through a colander, then through a coarse cloth. Salt to taste, and pepper, if you think best; return to the fire, and simmer 5 minutes longer. Skim when cool. Give to the patient cold—just from the ice—with unleavened wafers. Keep on the ice. You can make into sandwiches by putting the jelly between thin slices of bread spread lightly with butter.

Chapter 10

YELLOW WALLPAPER

$\mathscr{I}$ drive to the Glendale wine store everyone says is the best, but I've never stopped at before because it looks like a real estate office. Instead of photos advertising houses no one can afford, the window signs promote the latest deals on cabernets, chiantis, and fumé blancs. Suddenly the world seems possible again.

No one drinks in Los Angeles. This despite civilization's booze-soaked roots. Agriculture began when hunter-gatherers discovered a pleasant buzz from beverages made with fermented grain. A steady supply of raw ingredients required staying in one place to tend crops. Former nomads needed a drink at the end of a day in the fields to soothe their wanderlust.

The ancient Greeks valued drinking over dinner. The after-dinner drinking party known as the symposium was the main point of their evening. Great literature resulted, including Plato's *Symposium*, and *Apology*, featuring the classic icebreaker "The life which is unexamined is not worth living."

In Los Angeles I've found it best not to examine life too closely. In Los Angeles there's a slippery slope in every sip. This is due largely to Los Angeles's being a driving town, a distances-between place. This is good for preserving lives, but bad for society. Society needs to get pickled every once in a while.

New York and San Francisco are walking towns, and when I lived in those cities I got pickled on a regular basis, along with the rest of the residents. In New York drinking is a necessary form of stress reduction. High achievers drink in New York. Of course, you have to be a high achiever to drink in New York, because booze costs so much.

In San Francisco drinking is affordable entertainment. San Franciscans love their drinkers like they love their crooked streets and gear-grinding hills and perpetual fog. San Francisco employed its favorite drinkers as newspaper columnists: Herb Caen and Stanton Delaplane and Charles McCabe, who used to walk down the hill from his North Beach apartment to start his mornings with a stiff one at the local Italian social club. People read them over cocktails, a Ramos Fizz with the morning edition, a martini with the afternoon final. Drinking was always part of San Francisco's character, its morose charm.

Los Angeles packages character, produces character, markets character, and that's a sober undertaking. Movers and shakers in Los Angeles bend themselves into yoga pretzels or jog past the urge to have a pop. Angelenos believe that an hour lost to an alcoholic buzz is self-abuse, an opportunity missed to put you a step closer to that Three-Picture Deal, starring role, or prime piece of real estate. Then you can have a drink. Or two. Or three. You're even allowed a few stabs at rehab, as long as it's in the right places: Betty Ford's in Rancho Mirage, or Promises Malibu.

In Los Angeles drinking is tainted with pathos. It's considered noir. Drinkers are those people who sit in their short-sleeved Hawaiian shirts[2] in the dark on blindingly bright days in the bars lining Western Avenue, talking about what might have been. And their sagging guts and flabby arms, their flaccid thighs flopping out of their shorts, are another reason not to drink: Consider the high caloric content of a single glass of merlot or shot of tequila. Mention carbohydrates, and I can hear the last drinkers in Los Angeles dumping a luscious sauvignon blanc as they permanently switch to water. We're all smiley faced and dutifully driving the freeways here, scared straight and on edge.

Not that I want any more drinkers in Los Angeles. It's hard enough to stay between the lines on an eight-lane freeway at ninety miles an hour when you're sober. I'm grateful to everyone who abstains. Still, I'd like some relief from what passes for life here. I welcome earthquakes for taking us outside the quotidian, something a daily drink or two could do. I wonder if these geologic upheavals aren't tied to our pent-up tension.

The wine store clerk welcomes me with a smile and direct gaze. Dressed in a red sport jacket boasting a white plastic nametag announcing Bob, he looks like a real estate agent.

"We'll be grilling squab," I say.

Bob acts truly interested, and for that I am grateful. It's hard to find anyone in L.A. who is even willing to fake interest. He nods

....

2 Think Harvey Keitel or Mickey Rourke.

his head and sucks in cheeks still soft from their morning shave, as if he's mentally picturing a row of petite poultry carcasses sizzling in the night air.

"Red-wine lovers," I say.

He ducks his chin, braces his mouth, and leads me to a Napa Valley pinot noir.

"Light enough for poultry," he says. "Full bodied enough for red-wine lovers. Spice and blackberries, with a round finish." It sounds irresistible, like some summer fruit dessert I would want served with a side pitcher of crème anglaise.

I take three bottles. There will be eight of us for dinner for sure. I'll be surprised if we open the second. Unless Hunter comes. Then I'll have the third for myself after everyone has gone.

I began my drinking life as a teenager—blackout binges on weekends, a shared gallon of dago red tipped back after school. I preferred alcohol to marijuana, which only made me hungry—which might make me fat, which scared me—and I never did like the wobbly mental state it put me in, not with my concerns about crazy. Even worse were the hallucinogens, the acid-induced loony cartoon landscape from which there was no escape. Mescaline was mellower; the kids all claimed it came from mushrooms or desert cacti, some magical plants—organic material, an argument in its favor—but still, it never agreed with me. Alcohol was a controlled substance providing the short-haul trips I preferred. A couple of hours, or a night lost to its woozy embrace, was fine.

In college I enjoyed a daily bourbon habit that continued into my late twenties. I was just being polite, since all my friends, most of them many years older than I, hard-driving professionals in San Francisco media, drank far more than I did; several eventually confessed to and recovered from alcoholism. Then there were those who never confessed, and thus never had to recover, getting to tipple along until their liver or some other part of their life gave out.

Not me. I curbed the habit, became a productive, sober adult. Now I only drink to stupefaction on rare occasions, usually when I'm alone and most comfortable with the company I keep. I'm more vigilant in social situations, monitor my intake, know my body chemistry to the point that I imagine I can feel the alcohol molecules flooding the fat cells, and alternately take glasses of water with glasses of wine. I rarely ever have more than two glasses of wine in public, and with age have come to feel the aftereffects the next morning more strongly, even from just a few sips the night before. It's as if I've lost an old friend, a reliable habit that greeted me unconditionally at the end of the day. Like most folks I know, I see it far less than I did before, and when we do get together I question the value of continuing the relationship. I weigh the health concerns with the sanctifying legends and lore of viniculture—anything this complex must be good! The effects invariably are the same, despite the effort squeezed into the bottle's artful content. My mind is still turned to jelly, my time stolen. The older I get, the more I regret such losses. It's become a productivity issue, rather than a chance for social intimacy. Social intimacy lost out long ago.

I miss the rip-roaring days of brown liquid on the rocks, cigarettes, and the easy flow of talk. Waking up the next day and taking two cups of coffee to remember what it was I'd done the night before. Now I can't forget. Work is the answer. Work is all anyone ever does anymore, no matter where they are or what they're doing. We work at our jobs, however defined, and work at social relationships.

To this end, alcohol just gets in the way. No longer can we drink to the bottom line; we must instead soberly and wholeheartedly devote ourselves to it. It is the only thing, after all, that matters anymore.

*I*n the sanitarium, Lenore feared that if she didn't respond to the hot baths, quiet surroundings, and talk therapy, didn't enjoy visiting with other patients in the sunroom or delight in the exchange of small, token gifts—like a pump dispenser of hand balm that looked to her like semen, or a small bud vase with an artificial rose, gifts for a patient's birthday or wedding anniversary—they'd have to take her treatment to another level of concern. The doctors and nurses never said what that other level was.

"Shock treatments," the attendants said when she asked.

"You don't want that," the attendant said. "Your hair will go gray and you won't remember a thing. They say that's why they do it: so you forget why you're sad."

*L*enore resolved to act happy instead, despite her fear that she couldn't care for her children, and her anger that her husband and her parents had put her there.

When Lenore came home after two months, everyone said how well she looked. She smiled, made self-deprecating comments, and dismissed remarks about her appearance.

Why were they so concerned with her appearance? What did her appearance have to do with it? Did they think her appearance reflected her ability to function? Did they think that someone who looked happy and competent was? Were they really that stupid?

She insisted she was fine, even if she didn't feel completely all there, even if her limbs felt hollow, her mind unsteady, and she didn't know what to do with her hands. She hoped she would soon feel herself again, for she didn't ever want to have to go back to that place.

"Louise," she shouted again.

Lenore knew that Louise saw her. She knew why she turned away. She might have done the same thing. Who could tell? It didn't matter. Louise turned away, disappeared around the corner. Louise didn't return her phone calls. Neither did Genie Morton. Not since she'd come back from the hospital. She'd been the captain of their high school soccer team. No one in the East Bay knew about the mental hospital. Just a bridge span away, that's what George said.

There was nothing to be ashamed of; how could he think that? As if it were her fault that they had to move away from the town they'd grown up in. Why couldn't he make enough money to buy a house here, with their friends, in their hometown? Maybe he should get a second job instead of spending every spare minute at his father's, building bookshelves and barbecue carts, every silly thing he saw in those woodworking magazines. They didn't need more things, they needed more money. Maybe she should have married a man who'd gone to college. Alice and Genie had, and they didn't have to move to the East Bay.

Lenore had pushed the stroller to the park, where the chestnut trees bloomed with flaming white candle flowers. They'd have five-gallon saplings in the East Bay. No shade, nothing big enough for the birds to even bother with. She would have liked to talk to Louise, to catch up. They hadn't talked since the hospital. She wouldn't run into old friends in the East Bay. The East Bay was filled with hayseeds from out of state. Anyone who'd grown up here knew that, knew better than to move to a new place, a place that was beneath them.

"And we're just a train ride from the City here," she'd told him the night before.

"When do you have time for the City?"

"We'll go when the children are older."

"The country atmosphere will do your nerves good."

"The boredom will kill me."

Maybe a private yard would be better than a park, she thought now, as she watched the silhouetted figure of her girlhood friend disappear. George said there'd be room for fruit trees—plum, apricot, and walnut for baking. She pushed the stroller harder, walked with a fast clip toward home.

I sit at a stoplight in Glendale, waiting for it to change to green. I am heading in the direction of Mario's Delicatessen on Broadway to pick up a few more items for Saturday night. All the things that must be done before my guests arrive are scratching at my brain, tugging on my sleeves, and mussing with my hair, like obstreperous, demanding children. I've yet to finish taking care of my shopping list and, good domestic soldier that I be, I'm already whipping up a sweat racing through the lengthy to-do list in my head: iron linens, change candles, polish candleholders, sweep, dust, straighten, hide, switch, and freshen basically everything. Mrs. Beeton would approve of my rising flood of concerns.

I think of Charlotte Perkins Gilman, a leading feminist theorist of the late nineteenth and early twentieth centuries. She railed against everything Mrs. Beeton encouraged. She believed in kitchenless homes, professionalized housekeeping, and child daycare centers. As the great-niece of Harriet Beecher Stowe, author of *Uncle Tom's Cabin* (which, by the way, Samuel Orchart Beeton made a fortune publishing the first English edition of before he wed Isabella), she rallied for women's emancipation and was considered a radical in her day, writing such revolutionary feminist tomes as *Women and Economics*, *Concerning Children*, and *The Man-Made World*. I don't think she would have indulged for one liberated minute my need to give a dinner party.

She gained her greatest writing fame with the 1892 short story "The Yellow Wallpaper." It's about a woman whose physician husband drives her mad by administering the "rest cure." It was based on Gilman's own experience with suffering a "dark fog" of depression after the birth of her daughter, which prompted her husband to send her to a leading "rest cure" practitioner.

Women diagnosed with "hysteria," what today is most often called depression (so much depends upon the naming), were sent to their rooms to rest. They lay quietly in bed, body still, hands limp, and mind allegedly inactive for hours, days, and months on end. All stimulation was avoided: No reading was allowed; even needlework was considered too exciting. If the woman suffered from postpartum hysteria, as Gilman did, the newborn might be put in the room with her. Male doctors ordered the treatment and husbands enforced it.

After two years of participation, Gilman decided it was driving her insane. In 1888 she fled the East Coast for Pasadena, California, taking her daughter and abandoning her husband. She eventually divorced her husband, then sent her daughter back east to live with him and her best female friend, who soon married Charlotte's ex and raised Charlotte's child. "The Yellow Wallpaper" proved a hit and gave Gilman an independent source of income through her career as a lecturer, editor, and writer. She was ever a pragmatic woman: When breast cancer rendered her unable to work, at age seventy-five, she committed suicide.

⁄ The light changes to green. I accelerate toward Mario's. My to-do list will have to wait for now; I've got to get some olive oil, among other things. I need a good oil for the *salsa verde* I'll be making to serve with the grilled squab at dinner. The recipe is from a Mediterranean food conference I attended in Napa. Like all great Italian recipes, it's simple, but dependent on the best ingredients. This has parsley chopped finely and a whole lemon, juiced. Salt ground. I will whisk these together with extra virgin olive oil. I will do this while standing at my sink; I will look up and notice the light on the boxwood hedge, the sparrows. I will take a grounding pleasure in this modest moment.

"You are so simple," Hunter said. She takes pride in her complexity, a buffer against what she considers the emptiness of Mother's life. I see summer light, window sparrows, and emulsified oil, my mind free to roam, standing at the sink, alive with the prospect of becoming. I see a rich complexity in simplicity. This is my refuge and salvation.

Albina, a native of Italy's Piedmont region and Mario's wife, recommends Sasso oil, a brand she uses every day. "Eggs fried in it are delicious," she says, her freckled face lit with pleasure at the thought. I take a large bottle for the common good, and a smaller, more precious oil for the salsa. I picture a jade-colored thread of it swirling into the whisk's cage.

*J*t was November in Assisi, a tour of an olive oil–pressing operation, the plump, fresh-picked mix of green, speckled, and burnished purple fruit—olives are fruit and must be pressed before their juices spoil—crushed and then spread across sieves stacked like pancakes, where the watery juice and oil mixture dripped down like honey through a comb. Our guide, a well-bred and charming young man from the American South, talked the press's owner out of a five-gallon jug of the luscious green gold. We fried fresh anchovies in it that night back at the villa.

Returning home, I launch into the task of carrying the provisions up the stairs. Halfway to the house, I hear a buzzing overhead and set my packages down to study what might be the problem and where's it coming from. I scan the upper front of the house until I see a swarm of bees dripping from a main branch of the deodar cedar, and another cluster at the corner of our upper deck. It's been years since we've enjoyed a bee infestation. Word must have gotten out in the insect world that I was having people over this weekend. I will now have to call the bee man for an extermination visit. Meanwhile, I'll keep the cats and dog inside, so they don't get stung, and hope the bees don't get into the house, as they have in the past.

I pick up my packages and continue up the stairs. The weight of the bottles of wine and oil makes me think of all that I have ever carried up these many stairs, and I feel like a beast of burden, a common laborer. It's a shameful feeling, as if someone else should be doing this for me.

But who, and why? What is wrong with common labor? Would it be more dignified if I did it while dressed in a monk's robe or a nun's habit? Why must housework seem such a burden and never a joy?

Why does my blood chill at the combination of two words: "female" and "domestic"? I live in fear of the two being applied simultaneously and directly to me. Female domestic. Domestic female. Either way, a failure in the world's eyes. What this means is that I can't run the vacuum unless I can become an expert on the subject, with a string of published how-to titles and a cable network show. That accomplished, I won't have time to do my own housework, even if I have discovered that it's the only thing capable of keeping me sane.

Run a vacuum, become a female domestic worker. Dressed in this straitjacket of contemporary, middle-class American–induced fear, I hire someone to run the vacuum for me, even though the mindless hum of the vacuum is soothing, the results satisfying. My modest standing on the socioeconomic scale renders me incapable of acting in my own interest. Instead, I worry about how others see me. As if the neighbors watch as I carry my packages up the stairs and pity me. As if anyone sees me when I am home behind a closed door, running the vacuum.

Because others in my social class, in this classless society, do so, I must hire a woman from a lower social class to do my vacuuming. In Los Angeles this means an immigrant, probably Latin American, possibly illegal. I don't know if this is what Charlotte Perkins Gilman had in mind. I know Carlotta is the first two; I haven't asked about the third. I am supposed to do my acceptable work, writing, while she bangs around the house, doing as much damage, I imagine with every *thud* and *plunk* and *crash*, as possible. I further imagine that all this banging of cabinets and bashing of doors is because she's unhappy that this is the only work available to her.

Together we are two miserable women stuck playing our parts. I'm surprised the house doesn't explode from the misery held inside.

When Carlotta is gone—and I can't wait for her to leave—I get out the vacuum cleaner, before Somebody is home, because I don't want him to know, as he'll feel guilty because he's not contributing to the household chores and because he hasn't the time and energy to do so (another reason he'd prefer an independent third party to be paid to do the work). I go over the house with the vacuum again, so it will be done the way I want it done, the way Carlotta refuses to do it because—I guess—she's so unhappy. When I'm done, I'm thrilled with the results and the certainty that my secret is safe. I assume Carlotta is happy as well, for not having done what I asked her to, because it is important that none of her employers, a different homeowner for each day of the week, can lay claim to owning her.

Maybe that's what keeps the house from exploding: In the end, we are both happy slaves with our stolen, secret freedoms.

Of course, Carlotta has an advantage over a housewife, which is what I am embarrassed to think I am when I find myself doing these things. She is paid for the work she does, work she is doing outside her own home. She has an identity in the world, money of her own. Even if it is only janitorial work she does. Without that foot in the world beyond a woman's front door, she is dependent property, the chattel of the man who has the job outside, the man in whose name the mortgage or the lease is held, the man whose name is on the children as well.

I know what happens to women who can't do their job.

I find a bee struggling slowly across the living room floor, as if it is on its last legs. I wonder if I should be honored that this symbol of industry has come here to expire. Several other bees lie dead below the front window, through which I can clearly see a hive forming in the main branch of the deodar cedar. The buzzing is faint and unnerving. I call the bee man and leave an urgent message. I sweep up the dead bees, then seek some measure of solace in the three-ring binder from the Napa food conference that I pull down from my kitchen shelf. I flip through the pages, as if it is a hymnal, until I find the recipe for this simplest sauce.

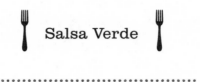

Salsa Verde

¼ cup lemon juice, freshly squeezed

½ cup extra virgin olive oil, the best you can afford

1¼ cups chopped parsley, preferably the flat-leaf Italian variety

Ground coarse salt to taste

Whisk salt into lemon juice, then begin whisking in olive oil in a thin stream until fully emulsified. Add parsley; whisk thoroughly. Add more salt if desired.

Chapter 11

GARLIC MAKES US INTERESTING

*R*ecipes. I once followed them exactly, blindly, putting my faith in the author, known or not. I collected them freely, like rubber bands or those little cards with extra buttons and yarn that come with every piece of clothing you buy, believing fully that I would someday get around to using them. Like the newspaper clipping for tortilla soup that's anchored to the refrigerator door beneath an Edvard Munch *The Scream* magnet. It symbolizes the thousands of recipes that beg me to save them each day. If I dare to rescue one, the clipping screams, every recipe will be there for years. Years! And for years I will feel guilty for not making them.

It's dangerous burying oneself too deep in recipes. It can take years to climb back out. And no matter how many you make, you can never satisfy certain hungers. Sometimes you end up consuming yourself instead.

I finally realized I couldn't save every recipe. I had to admit the braised lamb shoulder with olives wouldn't provide the perfect welcoming note to the table some winter night, because we don't have winter nights in Los Angeles. Stewed meat dishes make no sense in this desert climate. When it's cool enough to stand at the stove, Somebody is working late or is out of town, and spur-of-the-moment dinners aren't done in my L.A. So I think and write about cooking more than I actually do it.

Still, there are recipes that haunt me and that I can't help but make in my mind, like my mother's garlic-cream cheese dip. She served it in a fluted and etched crystal dish, a fixture on the white damask tablecloth when we were still a family that entertained. I have never made this recipe, I have never even physically tasted it since I left my mother's house, but the thought of its lingering pungency floods my senses as I roll a plump clove in the rubber peeling tube, remove its crisp, translucent outer sheath, and drop the ivory crescent like a talisman into my palm. It was a tongue-searing unguent that both excited and calmed me when, as a child, I licked it off a finger furtively dipped into the mixing bowl.

I see my mother forcing this garlic through a square metal press, the mordant juices dripping onto the white knobs of cream cheese. She scrapes the mashed garlic remains from the press's bowl, its stench blooming as thick as a swarm of summer gnats, and mixes it into a cup of mayonnaise and a stick of room-temperature butter, stirring by hand, pressing hard until it is lump-free, the wooden spoon leaving ridged traces in the thick yet pliant blend. She wipes the spoon clean with the firm pad of her finger, flicks the last bit of dip back into the bowl, and hands me the spoon to finish with my tongue. The lush paste looks as bland as our suburb, but overwhelms me with a fiery and seductive foreign zest.

"Enough?" she asks.

"More" I say.

Fresh garlic was a foundation of my mother's kitchen before she abandoned it, an inheritance of her French ancestors. She sprinkled French words throughout those days, as spirits needed lifting, and she used garlic to the same effect. She made garlic bread with thinly sliced cloves tucked into the buttered cuts in a long loaf of San Francisco sourdough, real sourdough, the stuff that got its tang from the sweat of North Beach's Italian bakers. Other mothers slapped slabs of spongy, tasteless white bread they called "French" on the table, slathered with jaundice-colored supermarket spread, or pretty but tasteless prepared loaves painted in a too-bright yellow wash and dusted red with paprika that looked like clowns' rouge.

A clove of garlic went into her salad dressing (only inferior families bought bottled), and minced garlic topped buttered steaks before they were slipped into the broiler. A side dressing of raw mushrooms cooked down into a sop of garlic-infused meat flavors. Mother would never have agreed with Mrs. Beeton's warning against garlic. Mrs. Beeton blamed it for inducing too sound a sleep, "so sound that you do not wake till an hour after your usual time in the morning, and then you feel half stupid, your head aches, and the taste in your mouth is abominable. Should wholesome food produce such symptoms? Certainly not. . . ."

We savored the abominable, reveled in our mother's garlic dishes, and for all the garlic in our house, no one ever complained or teased anyone about a smell, even though we teased each other about everything else—the clothes we wore, things we said, friends we made, as if nothing else mattered; the only true good was garlic. Neither did anyone run for the mouthwash, which we didn't have, or mints, which we never kept, lest they wipe garlic's comforting afterglow from our mouths. Garlic was a secret, shared pleasure we never discussed, because we treasured it so.

Garlic made us interesting, if only to ourselves, set us apart from our neighbors whose houses held no special odors, were nothing more than common shelter for their benign, boring, blank breath. And when this mother became another mother and stopped making her garlic dip and her garlic bread, stopped putting out the damask tablecloth and using the good crystal and china, we remembered her garlic recipes, made them and tasted them in our minds.

*W*ednesday morning, 7:00 AM, I wake to the sound of the phone ringing. I jump out of bed to answer, in hopes that it's the bee man. It's Kathleen.

"My dad went into the hospital last night," she says, emotion tearing at her voice. "He's got pneumonia."

"I'm sorry," I say. And I am—but not just for her father.

"I've got to drive up to Santa Rosa," she says.

"Of course," I say. I mentally reset the table for the loss of two more guests if Kathleen and her husband do not come, and one unwelcome relative if Hunter does.

"But only for a few nights," she says. "The doctors believe he'll be fine. I just have to see for myself."

"I understand," I say.

"I hope to be back by Saturday."

"Of course, I understand," I repeat, even though I don't. Why does anyone's father have to go into the hospital with pneumonia the week before I've scheduled a dinner party? Pneumonia and hospital stays and business trips are forbidden the week before all my dinner parties. As are bee infestations. That is my deal with the universe. Now the universe is backing out.

"I hope he's all right," I say.

"Me too," she says.

"Take care and drive carefully," I say. I add this for extra karmic coverage. If nothing else, any events adding to Kathleen's misery will not be attributable to my lack of well wishes. That is clearly stated in the small print of my contract with the universe. Elsewhere in this contract it is noted that if I manage to do a dinner party right, no one gets hurt and everyone gets to go home alive.

I call the bee man. He says he can be here by mid-afternoon. I have only a few hours to get to the Santa Monica Farmers Market and back before that. I throw on some clothes, run a comb through my hair, and head west on the 10 freeway.

After Kathleen's call I need the spirit-lifting sights, sounds, and smells of the market to stoke my crumbling enthusiasm for the dinner party, to keep me from canceling it after all, to wipe the thought of Hunter's presence at the table from my mind, and all the horrors that conjures.

"Try our Fuji apples, sweet-as-a-kiss Fuji apples," the produce monger shouts. "'Tis the season for heirloom tomatoes; don't miss 'em," another urges. Dinner parties used to be my excuse to go to these markets. When I stopped doing those, I still went because the markets felt like medieval village fairs, with chockablock crowds, bumping bodies, noise, authentic air, and surprising possibilities. It is always a welcome break for a few hours from the house's solitude.

I slowly parade past the bounty of canopied booths lining the streets. Shouts and murmurs, cooking tips and sales pitches, mix in a thick stew of sound sauced with the smells of onion, garlic, fennel, and peach, smells that grow more pungent as the day's heat rises. There are the cheese people from Northern California, with their hundreds of goats, all individually named; and the Asian couple from Riverside, with their backyard-raised bins of eggplants white, purple, and black that shine like Chinese lacquerware. Roses glory in the imperfections of the homegrown with their subtle, eccentric colors and ebullient perfume. I think of my uncle Garland, who bred roses and once told me of the rose he tried to develop but that had so many petals, "it never opened properly."

Farmers markets are the opposite of the supermarkets I grew up with—East Hills was our regular, closest-to-home haunt, while Safeway was the deluxe palace downtown, the anchor at the main intersection along the boulevard. Both shared a sense of containment and order, prescribed abundance promised in perpetuity, pink lights to make the meat look blood-flushed, and fruits waxed to a patent-leather shine. Muzak infused the shimmering, sterile air of aisles packed with canned vegetables, bottled juices, instant meals, cake mixes, and frozen treats. People roamed there in a concentrated daze, guided by lists and coupons. At the end of the trip, when all the items on the list and everything called for by a coupon had been checked out, paid for, and crisply bagged, the reward was Blue Chip or Green Stamps to buy more things. Small, easily broken things.

When I lived in New York, supermarkets held an anxious air, with their bins of withered vegetables, bruised fruits, and meager supplies, as if the world would soon end. Some shops even sold fruit by the piece, which struck me as a form of rationing that one might experience in wartime. I now realize that buying by the piece wasn't necessarily such a bad thing, that having to think about how many apples or bananas you might need until your next shopping trip could help you plan for, anticipate, deal with the future in an organized way. But buying fruit by the pound was my suburban heritage. If the peaches started to go bad before all had been eaten, then the competent kitchen commander should drop everything and bake a pie. And brown bananas required a batch of banana-nut bread, even if I hated banana-nut bread. Buying fruit by the pound and never knowing what it might lead to was one of the reasons I returned to California. I hadn't been schooled in the eastern ways of looking ahead, making do, and dealing with. I felt unprepared to compete for what I saw then as the limited resources of New York's premeasured, shrink-wrapped, doomed world.

At farmers markets, the goods reach out to grab me, instead of the neat Safeway shelves' contents begging for hands to grab them. I go not just for the produce, but to check the blooms in the pavement green-room plant stalls, and to sample the food vendors' wares: the *pupusas* stuffed with zucchini flowers, the fresh spinach omelets, or maybe the strawberry crêpes. I go for the bread people, the wild-mushroom people, the seafood trailer smelling of fried-fish people, and the beautiful blond Spanish woman who speaks authentic, tongue-tip–touching–teeth Spanish while dishing up plates of saffron-tinted paella. The market was the closest I'd found to a free-flowing community in Los Angeles, yet even that had its limits. I considered how food and its intake had replaced social intimacy, how lively conversations about something other than food were as scarce as a decent tomato in winter. And just as the best of chefs chose canned tomatoes when the fresh winter ones became cardboard-hard and tasteless, I resorted to canned conversation, stock social pleasantries, just to feel as if real conversation were taking place when no one seemed interested in anything beyond the predictable and ordinary.

/Standing in line for a duck–and–goat cheese tamale at the Corn Maiden booth, I look down at the pavement and notice the bare toes of the man in front of me. They look like cocoa beans poking out of his leather sandals. His loose-fitting, softly draped exercise pants cling to muscular thighs and a trim waist. I scan the length of his body, arrive at his face, and realize he is a model from a recent painting class. I have seen him naked and remember his perfect, tawny features, miniature and irresistible as the baby vegetables in my shopping bags. I imagine how his buttocks, which look as perfect as a pair of French breakfast melons, must feel ripe to the touch. These are not Safeway thoughts. I stifle the urge to act, focus on my tamale order.

Neither do I say hello or remind him where we have met. Accidental encounters with a recognizable face are so rare in Los Angeles that they typically never rise above awkward. I decided long ago to avoid them if possible. I have learned if I want to contact someone, I email them or call their answering machine and wait for a reply. Otherwise, I have come to believe, people would rather pretend they are still in their cars than deal with an unexpected personal connection. Especially with someone who has seen them naked, or so I imagined, along with all else I was imagining about him as we stood silently together in line.

At Coastal Organics I find organic artichokes, a large globe variety with a good length of stem remaining attached. I buy eight, one for each of my guests. I would prefer baby artichokes, but those must be ordered special through a local brick-and-mortar market. Otherwise, they are virtually impossible to find; the reason, I was told when I stopped one day in Castroville, where much of the country's artichoke crop comes from, is sinister: The babies are sent off to processing as marinated artichoke hearts. A crime when they are so tender and succulent eaten fresh. A fresh baby artichoke can be sliced paper thin and served raw as a salad, with arugula and shaved parmesan dressed lightly with lemon, salt, and the best olive oil. The fully mature chokes can never be enjoyed this way.

As usual, I buy more at the market than I can ever use, unable to resist such things as the Arkansas black apples I discovered last fall—I had never seen them before, and I thought if they were sufficiently terrific I would turn them into a story. So I got enough to bake, slice, and sauce with, cooking up multiple articles in the process. That is the pleasure of food writing: I get to enthuse about things. I have had it with investigative exposés that fail to save the world, heartstring-thrumming human-interest pathos, and celebrity puffery. Now all I crave is an honest apple to crow about. And a fetching clutch of red peppers, a glowing few celadon globes of sweet fennel, some plump bunches of French carrots.

Only when my arms can't carry any more do I head for the car. That's when I pass a bin heaped with apricots labeled BLENHEIM. I sample a slice; a familiar sharp tang with a softening sweetness lingers on my tongue.

Blenheims are different from other apricot varieties in that they ripen from the inside out, requiring pickers to develop a special visual sense of when their moment is due. If they wait until the fruit looks ripe, with a full orange flush, it's too ripe to ship to market. Buyers need to buy before the apricots are fully golden. This makes them a poor commercial crop, even though their flavor is superior to that of any other varieties. I thank the man for the sample but pass on the opportunity to buy. These are overripe and will be bad by the next day. I'd have to eat them all tonight or drop everything I was doing, which I can't, and make a pie.

My cell phone signals loudly and insistently from my purse that I need to call voicemail. To find out why it goes straight to voicemail rather than ringing so I can answer the call, I'd have to read the manual, and to read the manual I'd have to find it first, or take an hour troubleshooting with a technical support person in Bangalore, India. I don't have the time. I call voicemail. A message has been left from a restricted private number and there's no possibility of calling back.

"Helloooooooooooooaaahhhhh!" It's Hunter. "I'm still coming by Saturday, but I'm not sure what time—either early afternoon or late. I'll let you know as soon as I know. And if nobody else has told you this, your answering message is too long and too sarcastic. Change it! Byeeeeeeeee!"

Hunter was always full of helpful suggestions. I had stopped taking them long ago. After the last physical encounter we shared, I left with a list of appearance-improving surgical procedures, several blouses she no longer wore but thought I should have (not because I might enjoy them but because they were hers), and the name of an entire new makeup regimen that would transform me with a swish of a brush and a wave of a mascara wand.

When my mother stopped being my mother, Hunter stepped in. I needed a mother, so I needed to believe she was a reasonable substitute. She both loathed and loved the part. She took her primary parenting inspiration from *Ripley's Believe It or Not!*. She loved to tell about the millionairess who was so cheap that when her daughter injured her leg, the mother let the wound fester instead of taking her to a doctor, and the leg had to be cut off. *Believe it or not!*

⸌ The most unbelievable thing about Hunter was that she, who ate nothing but Chuckle's hamburgers throughout her prime teen-parenting years and little else after that, was always telling me what to eat. I'm sure it's another reason I was drawn to food writing. I write about eating a vast range of food in good quantity. As far as I know, Hunter has never read any of these pieces.

When I was in graduate school I read how, toward the end of his life, Leo Tolstoy devoted much time to telling others what to eat. In that respect, he reminded me of Hunter. He preached about the virtue of meeting needs versus the impossibility of satisfying appetites. In the matter of diet, this meant forsaking the hedonistic feasts he'd enjoyed as a youth for simple repasts meant to provide nothing more than the energy necessary for work. Hunter's diet regimen was for the purpose of preserving a slim and youthful appearance. Pleasure was not part of either's equation. Chocolate was banned from Tolstoy's house. In his novel *Anna Karenina*, he described many elaborate meals, including ostentatious buffets laid with such rare and expensive delicacies as fresh oysters and pineapples. But the most delicious food taken was a midday scupper of creek water and peasant bread shared with a field worker. Needs satisfied goals. Appetites were desires, like a fire in an underground coal mine: Once ignited, they could be dampened but never fully extinguished.

Tolstoy wrote convincingly on the issue of needs versus desires, as if he had the one true recipe for life. Yet he was working both sides of the issue—I defy anyone to read his banquet scenes in *Anna Karenina* without craving a taste of the dishes described.

Tolstoy in private was different from Tolstoy in print. He kept and consumed chocolates, despite his declared ban. We desire to trust writers. We need to not.

Hunter's tales were never written down, but she loved to entice with stories of delicious, exotic meals she'd enjoyed on her adventures. Since she never enjoyed anything she ate in my presence, I had to imagine that sometime other than in that moment there was enjoyment to be had.

I sought to find the truth of it through my writing. I have come to realize that the entire aim of my food writing, all food writing—and of Hunter's tales, for that matter—is to ignite an audience's appetites, add to the unquenchable desires eating away at them, help spread the guilt and frustration, and share the misery, rather than alleviate it. To activate an audience with temptations and the promise of pleasures. To sell magazines or books or newspapers. I don't know what Hunter really ate or what she enjoyed most, but I have never experienced anything as delicious as what she described to me when I was young, and I never believed that her stories were anything but true.

In an effort at redemption for my food writing, I offer this recipe adapted from Tolstoy's description of what he considers one of the finest meals available to man.

Tolstoy's Field Workers' Delight

....

1 full day worked alongside others in the field, scything hay, preferably begun well before dawn

1 scupper creek water (if giardia is a concern, boil for 5 minutes or run through a purifier)

½ tsp., or to taste, finely minced mixture of hay and assorted weeds

Several thick slices of dark peasant bread, artisanal variety if available—the older, the better

When the sun is high overhead, sit in shade near creek with coworkers, add finely minced ingredients to water, stir, raise scupper to lips, and enjoy. Alternate with bites of bread. If bread is too old to bite easily, dip in water before consuming. Sense weariness of muscles and bones, energy drained from body by hard manual labor resulting in a fine sheen of sweat covering all, and feel deep within soul how water and bread provide renewal. Share self-righteous smile with grumpy, exhausted coworkers. Delicious!

*T*he San Mateo Bridge was a low span that went on for five miles, a nauseating eternity, hovering over the bay's muddy whitecaps. When it opened in 1929, Lenore's father, an engineer, crowed that it was the longest span in the world. As if that were a good thing. He took his family across within weeks of its opening, and Lenore hated it from the first. He treated it like an entertainment, this miracle, ending as it did in the farm fields and orchards at the other side. All this way for a bag of oranges for their week's juice. She couldn't drink it. The sight of its foam sloshing in the glass made her stomach sour, made her want to throw up.

She always felt as if they were driving on the water when crossing the San Mateo Bridge; the stunted railing couldn't possibly keep the waves from sweeping them over its sides. Their Plymouth sedan would become their coffin; they'd sink into the bay's bottom silt.

They would have to travel this bridge each time she wanted to return to visit her mother or childhood friends in Burlingame, each time she wanted to go home.

George piled Lenore and the children into the car and drove them across this bridge to a housing tract he wanted Lenore to consider moving to. It was bordered on one side by a field of mustard, in the middle of which stood a clutch of curious donkeys, a hundred or so yards off, staring dumbly at them as George parked the car at the end of a cul-de-sac. Across the bare dirt yard in front of them was an assemblage of upright sticks outlining their future.

The ground felt less solid here to Lenore than on the Peninsula, and the blue-white light wasn't the light she had grown up thinking of as light. There was a high haze here, this far inland, that made it harsh, a hot blue light that stole shadows, made her feel partially erased. If she said anything he'd think she was crazy.

The children remained asleep in the backseat, heads back, mouths open like baby birds waiting to be fed. She looked at the circle of future houses; the faces of strangers looked back from the yet-to-be windows. She doubted there was even a public library.

No one here would tell him how sorry they were, they'd heard about the wife, they hoped it would turn out all right for him and the kids. Or look down on him because he was Irish. The East Bay was a place on its way to becoming. The Peninsula believed it had already arrived.

"What do you think?" he asked.

"I don't know," she said.

The silence that followed reminded him of a length of rope waiting to be tied into an elaborate knot for a specific purpose.

"We should go," he said finally.

She returned to the car and he backed it up, out of the court, heading toward the bridge for the trip back home to Burlingame. She considered the possibility, as they rode along in silence, that she was being unreasonable. That they should move here because he thought it best, because she shouldn't be unreasonable. Being reasonable would mean that she had a reason for her doubts. She couldn't claim that. She didn't know what it was that made her not want to be here. All she knew was that it seemed to her like a kind of death. And that would strike any reasonable person as unreasonable. Absurd. It wasn't a death. It was a new life. A house, a garden, a family. She should be happy. They should move here because he wanted to. He was, after all, the husband and she was the wife.

Garlic–Cream Cheese Dip

....

1 (8 oz.) block cream cheese, brought to room
   temperature

½ cup mayonnaise

1 stick butter, brought to room temperature

3–4 cloves garlic, more or less

Whip cream cheese and butter together with an electric mixer; mix
in mayonnaise to a smooth consistency, but not so stiff it will break
chips. With garlic press, press cloves of garlic in, then whip further
until fully incorporated. Serve with ruffled potato chips and a crisp,
bubbly *prosecco*. My mother enjoyed serving this with a gin martini
made with aerated gin. She civilized the gin by attacking it for
several minutes with a hand-cranked eggbeater, thus taking out
all the spirit.

Chapter 12

THE BEE MAN

Hedonism was in its heyday by the time of Julius Caesar, as Romans surrendered to their highly developed appetites for both food and drink. Tolstoy would have been horrified, considered them unsalvageable souls. They considered themselves *dediti ventri*, slaves of their stomachs. They entertained lavishly in their villas to satisfy the desires sparked by the excesses of their world. One Roman, Lucius Lucinius Lucullus, a general and epicure who entertained in the first century BC, is immortalized by the adjective "Lucullan" for luxurious feasts. He invited the entire city of Rome to his military retirement party and devoted the rest of his life to hosting. "Some of this . . . is for your sakes," he allegedly told the guests of honor who protested his extravagance at one over-the-top banquet, "but more for that of Lucullus."

Seafood was among the most extravagant and expensive foods in the Roman diet. The softer the flesh, the harder it was to preserve, and thus the more it cost. Oysters and other shellfish were the highest-priced delicacies, and therefore the most impressive to guests. Private fishponds were kept in certain elevated circles in which moray eels were prized as pets, their owners adorning them with jeweled earrings and necklaces. An evening might be enlivened by throwing a slave into the pond for guests to watch as the victim was torn apart by the pampered eels.

Romans reclined on couches while dining, eating from small individual tables that slave servers continually replenished. The onset of the Christian era introduced chairs for sitting upright at communal tables, with food taken from a communal pot. During the Dark Ages, hosts entertained to distinguish themselves from the invading hordes determined to destroy civilization. They wore their etiquette like a badge, a protective shield.

Medieval lords regularly hosted huge banquets to reinforce their control over their land and people. Everyone from titleholders to field workers was invited. As populations grew, the riffraff were dropped from bloated guest lists, and smaller, more exclusive dinners became the trend. Banquet halls lost favor to private dining rooms.

By the nineteenth century, a formal dining room in a middle-class home became a mark of civilization, a sign that the middle class could have dinner parties. One gained status by being invited to a private dinner party, and even greater status when their invitation was accepted.

Then came television. Urbanites fled to the suburbs and the seclusion of their own personal planets. Social climbing took a backseat to lawn mowing. Television kept people entertained and provided companionship when household chores took the place of human interaction. TV dinners, along with TV dinner trays on which to eat them, were invented, and suddenly Americans were doing as the Romans had done, dining sprawled on the couch, taking their food from small individual tables while being entertained.

I return home from the farmers' market, and there is a message waiting on the landline phone's answering machine. Walter asks that I call him back. I do and am shocked when I don't get a machine, when he actually picks up. He is double-checking the date, time, and number of people in attendance Saturday night. He wants to know whether it is a party, as in a large group of people milling around at a low boil, or a dinner, as in a sit-down, sit-up-straight, act-grown-up kind of thing.

I sense anxiety.

I explained all of the particulars when I invited him and Marisa, his girlfriend and my night's golden opportunity. Small group, formal table settings with accompanying chairs, babysitters booked. I suspect he is experiencing a common form of early-onset social meltdown. Signs include last-minute confusion regarding the evening's details—suddenly a brunch is meant for late afternoon, a dinner marked on the calendar for another day. Or the directions get lost or you forget how to read a map. Or you wake suddenly to discover you're pacing panic circles, trying to divine what to wear, say, or bring besides your miserable self.

"Can I bring Jackson?" he asks.

"I'm afraid he'd have a terrible time," I say.

"I'll bring movies."

"He'll be the only child."

"He's used to it."

I refuse to sacrifice my dinner to his six-year-old son's tantrums and tears. The garden is a minefield of cactus and aloes and steep, stumbling stairs. If he doesn't come, all I'll have to contend with are his constant cell phone calls to his father.

"I'd really rather you didn't bring him," I say.

"All right," he says in a petulant voice.

I know it isn't all right, but I didn't know what else to say. Is it my fault all our friends are raising toddlers when they should be writing college tuition checks? Is a childless hostess required to welcome underage guests when uninterrupted, undivided adult conversation is what she is dying for? Several hours pass. I am still suffering visions of Jackson playing horsey on my giant paddle cactus, when the phone rings again.

"Are you sure I can't bring Jackson?"

"It would really be a problem."

"I've got him that night."

"I thought you were bringing Marisa."

"She's in Prague for a shoot. He'll be my date."

"Marisa's not coming—why didn't you mention that in the first call?"

"I just found out. She just found out."

"Jackson hates my dog."

"You could put her in the garage."

My dog is not a car or a lawn mower or a spare piece of furniture, and she doesn't go in the garage. Marisa was the reason I'd invited Walter. If it hadn't been for Marisa I wouldn't have asked Walter. He's a fan of the Big Mingle and hates intimate social gatherings.

If it were just him, he'd blow it off first chance or at the last minute. This time, though, he seems determined to destroy it instead.

I say nothing.

"I'll make some more calls," he says. "I'll see if I can find a sitter." I mentally rearrange the menu and seating to handle the possible loss of Walter and certain absence of Marisa, the question mark of Kathleen and her husband, Allan, the possible presence of Hunter replacing the departed Richard Cronenburg. I consider whom I might call to replace one or both or all and realize anyone worth inviting will be busy, or claim to be, or insulted by the last-minute invitation.

The bee man calls. "I'm sorry," he says. "I ran late at my last call, and the traffic heading to your place is a bear. I'll have to come first thing in the morning."

I can hear the bees buzzing beyond the front living room window.

"See you then," I say. What else can I say?

The thought does occur, after I hang up, to invite him to dinner Saturday night and tell him to bring a date.

*L*enore sinks to her shins in lawn turned to pudding as she runs toward her children's cries for help. The muck holds her back. Where are they? Is that the smell of sulfur? Are frogs and locusts next?

A shadow sweeps overhead, a woman riding a white donkey through the sky. Its hooves paw the air as if climbing a slope. The woman wears her snow-white hair in a bun like Lenore does; her skin is the charcoal of film negatives. Her incandescent eyes and mouth swell and collapse like germinal storm clouds as she yells silently. Her children dangle behind the donkey, a rope looped around their necks in the curdling air.

A scream strokes upward like a swimmer rising from the depths, punching through sleep's membrane. George lies still by Lenore's side, his hip and shoulder a mountain beneath the heaped blankets. The donkey woman visits her each night in this new house. She doesn't tell him, lest he be alarmed.

By week's end he had to go it alone if she refused to come. "Don't go," Lenore suggested to George one Sunday as he prepared to leave for his day of sailing. She would not join him, insisting the children were too young. He missed her help as crew to his captain, missed the sight of her hair blown back from her high, bisque brow, her laughter and whispered poetry known by heart. He needed the grace of a boat skimming water, heeling to the whims of the wind; his time at the helm necessary to endure another week on land, in an office, anchored to the job that supported their growing family.

"The fruit trees need pruning," she said, "the lawns need fertilizing, and the children would like to see their father for the day."

"You come along," he said, his hands around her waist as he pulled her close, smelled her freshly soaped skin. "Ask Bev if the kids can stay with her for a few hours."

"Just go," she said, then pushed him away.

She watched from the kitchen window as he loaded the boat onto the trailer from their side yard. His captain's hat set jauntily on his head, he checked lines, tightened the trailer hitch. She imagined the sound of flapping sails, the satisfying tug of the jib line, the bounce of hull against waves, a picnic seasoned with salt air. It seemed like she only left the house now for groceries.

The last time she'd seen the Bay was crossing the bridge to visit her parents in San Francisco before they moved south to Los Angeles. When she closed her eyes and stood at the sink she could still feel the soft weight of her mother's hand against her palm, the plump pads of her fingers smoothing her skin, the strength of her hug. Now there were only long-distance phone calls, clouded with concern for their expense, and a husband who spent his days sitting at a desk or skimming the water's surface.

And no one ever to talk to.

The neighbors here filled their bookshelves with bowling trophies and lined their gardens in abalone shells they'd yanked like ravenous animals from rocks along the coast. They thought San Francisco was dirty and crime-filled. Their interests ended at the edge of their lawns. Lenore once mentioned to Beverly, the bowling enthusiast, her fondness for Chekhov's play *The Cherry Orchard*, how she'd once seen a traveling production, starring Lionel Barrymore, in the City. "If you like cherries," Beverly replied, "we just planted a tree. When it fruits you'll have to come get some."

She was drowning in this court. She was sinking to their level, too tired to keep her head above the muck.

He had his sailboat. He was happy.

She began stuffing crumpled newspapers into the fireplace, surrounding the stacked logs. The scratch of a match, and leaping flames billowed out, the flue shut. Flames licked at the mantel front, seized the happy ducks and kittens congratulating a birthday girl, and threatened the framed watercolor painting hanging above. It was an anniversary gift by a California plein air painter they had discovered at the Palace of the Legion of Honor's *Sanity in Art* exhibit. Titled *Safe Harbor*, it depicted two rowboats resting at low tide. Lenore couldn't see it now for the smoke and flames.

She laughed at Hunter's screams as the girl pranced like a hotfooted chicken down the front steps to her father, coughing and flapping her arms, as if in a cartoon. Lenore stood at her kitchen-sink post, running the water and singing operatic nonsense to drown out the din.

George knocked her aside, heaved the water-filled dishpan at the flames, drenching the mantel, the hearth, the tweed patterned wall-to-wall carpeting they'd chosen solely for its ability to hide dirt. The flames expired with sizzling, hissing smoke, like some dying beast.

"Geesis H. Keerist, what's the matter with you?" he said.

"My nose was runny," she said. "The heat would clear my sinuses."

"I have to paint and repair the wall, replace the rug," he said, massaging his head with his hands as if trying to prevent some imminent explosion. "It's going to cost a fortune."

His outburst felt good to her, like a conversation. No jokes, like a boxer's feint, deflecting her approach. It was a spectacle worthy of MGM, more thrilling by far than a painting of two boats stuck in the mud. The fire's charcoal residue lent a sfumato effect to the image, granting it an emotional depth, an air of foreboding that she considered a substantial improvement.

He repaired it in his clever way, cut lengths of wood to replace the mantel's charred sections, rented one of those vacuumlike devices from the market to shampoo the rug, then repainted the living room in the most popular color of the day, eggshell white.

*T*he sun has set behind the ridge and the bees have gone to bed. I have almost forgotten about the infestation and am working on forgetting Walter's call when Somebody comes home, a convenient distraction. I pull together a light supper of salad, bread, and pâté and ask him to crack open a modest sancerre. We sit at the dining room table.

"What's this?" he says, holding a bee corpse up by the wings.

"Where did you find that?"

"It was resting on the place mat."

"I've called the exterminator."

"And?"

"He's coming tomorrow morning."

"Not again," he says.

We sip and nibble in silence, and I consider the previous invasions we've suffered over the years, none of which I care to discuss. When we're done I put things away and start out the door, wine glass in hand, to head up into the garden. I need the lift only the sight of the shimmering city lights from the pergola can provide.

"Mind if I come?" he asks.

"Not at all," I say. We work our way up through the garden. It's not easy to see in the descending dark. He curses as he stumbles. We settle into the straight-backed chairs of the bistro table. It is here that I look forward to gathering my guests, whoever they end up being, to serve sparkling wine and appetizers Saturday night. Somebody swats at something in the dark by his head. I see the silhouettes of an expedition of silver dollar–size spiders rappelling off the overhead lodgepole beams.

"I'll spray the seat cushions for bugs," he volunteers.

My eyes will burn and my nose will run from the pesticide-soaked chairs.

"Don't bother," I say. "There'll be plenty of chances to poison the atmosphere. The spiders are more afraid of us than we are of them."

"Fine. One less thing to bother with."

I remember his previous mosquito abatement program—citronella torches spewing black smoke, like the Kuwaiti oil rigs in Desert Storm. Their flames shifted, grew, and danced with the wind until I feared either the lodgepole pergola or a guest would catch fire. That night was when it first dawned on me that maybe Somebody really didn't want to entertain. As I studied his beaming countenance through the citronella fog, I wondered if his yeses all these years might have actually meant no.

"We could use more cushions if you want to be helpful."

"Try one of those Mart places," he says.

It's the onset of summer. Outdoor cushions are a seasonal item. If you haven't bought them by the week before Memorial Day in Southern California, you can set your alarm for next year. Consuming here is a competitive sport: Winners anticipate the seasons, losers are left to react. Wait until it's cold to shop for sweaters, and you'll have nothing to choose from but a rack of leftover cardigans in safety orange, size XXXL. You'll end up looking like a roadside warning. You have to plan ahead to find a proper-size pullover in a decent color, and use your imagination, because you'll have to hit the stores in July.

"Maybe you could do that Friday," I say, referring to the hopeless cushion hunt.

"If I have the time," he says.

We both know it will be futile, yet one of us won't be able to resist spending an entire day doing it, at the end of which we'll invariably drag the wrong thing back. It depends on which one of us is suffering the greatest guilt by Friday for suggesting that the other one do the shopping and feels most in need of deliverance. This is the secret of our marital success—giving each other wide enough berth to pick our respective psychic scabs. And when we get the too big, too small, too dark, too light, too ugly, or too complicated thing home, haul it out of the car, schlep it up all the stairs, and discover it is unacceptable, inappropriate, and/or deeply offensive, well, that's what the basement is for. Our need for the item will now have to wait until next year. We are always running behind a list of goods to be got.

I see mosquitoes glancing off the silhouetted curve of Somebody's head.

"I'm going in," he says, flailing at them.

"You might want to build up your resistance for Saturday."

"Why?"

"We're eating in the garden."

"We *are*?"

"Don't act so surprised."

"You never told me we were eating dinner outside. Just drinks."

"Inside smells like cat pee and there's no time to replace all the carpets."

"It's just the downstairs entry."

"It permeates all three floors of the house."

"You never told me we were eating outside."

"I did, I did, I did, I did."

I probably didn't, but I've told him enough things in the past that he's conveniently forgotten that I refuse to grant him this one.

"You can smell the cat pee," I say. "You should have known." He sighs the sigh he always sighs at such moments and drops his gaze down and away to the broken concrete floor of the pergola, a forlorn, abandoned little boy.

The truth is that he is so rarely home, he probably hadn't noticed. Then, as he always does after sighing the Big Sigh, he silently rises from his chair, kisses me on the cheek, and starts gingerly down the path to the house. His habit of gentle abdication is maddening. He never stands his ground. Maintaining all the territory I've gained through our years together has worn me out. Were we in this together or was each of us, in truth, on our own?

I try to imagine where our marriage exists. We share a bed a few hours a night. There are two names on the deed to the house; proof can be found there. And somewhere in the household files there is a marriage certificate. And snapshots of the wedding. It was a casual affair. I lacked the courage for a public event. We did city hall. If we'd done the church before hundreds, might our union feel more real?

Was my marriage as much a phantom as my ghost family? Could we drop shopping, maintenance, and schedule talk to remap the borders of our lost bond? Could we spend less time getting things and more getting each other?

Could we ever make our union as comforting and supportive as those elusive lounge cushions? Is this why people had children—the only hope of intimate human ties? Had our lack of children doomed us from the start? Or was it what kept us together? Instead of staying together for the sake of the children, we stayed together for the sake of their absence. Without children, we had only each other. With children, you could leave a spouse and still not be alone.

Had rescuing this decrepit house and creating a garden in this impossible yard distracted us from our loneliness in being together? Was I married to this house? Had I become a housewife—and wasn't that the job my mother fled for the Clause?

A siren ribbons its way through the streets at the bottom of our hill, and Forest Lawn's pack of resident coyotes howl their encouragement. I stare into the glowing portals of the houses across the hill and consider the possibility that my phantom marriage and ghost family are responsible for my uncontrollable urge to entertain, what I have diagnosed as my adult onset obsessive dinner disorder. It isn't, after all, the public schools, a horribly flawed state university education, bad brain chemistry, not enough One-A-Day Vitamins, too much television as a child, or too much faith in the media as an adult. It's my inability to breach the impossible distance between myself and the people I love. That's why I feel most at home and least at ease entertaining strangers at my table.

Sitting at the top of the garden, spiders dropping like flies, coyotes spooking the populace, mosquitoes supping on my blood, I consider the possibility that I will never recover, that my AOODD is terminal, that all these years in which I invented dinner parties for the page were just a period of remission from the disease. Fully inflamed again by the symptoms, I realize my fate is to give horrible dinner party after horrible dinner party, inviting all the wrong people, saying all the wrong things, serving all the wrong foods, until the day I die.

Maybe this simple understanding of my plight was the most I could hope for. It was the icing on Saturday night. Or maybe the gravy. Whichever. I could make both better than most.

The Gravy

....

While meat is roasting, be it a turkey, pork tenderloin, beef, or a whole chicken, make the roux for gravy: In a small skillet or saucepan, melt 3 tbsp. of butter, then whisk in 3 tbsp. of flour. Whisk and cook over a medium low flame for 2–3 minutes, until cooked but not browned. When roast is done, remove meat from pan. Put roasting pan over a medium flame and deglaze with 1½ cups of appropriate wine: red for beef or white for poultry and pork. (Deglazing is simply scraping up the delicious bits of roast from the pan with its drippings and mixing in wine, the alcohol of which is cooked out while leaving the condensed flavor.) Cook this wine mixture down until it is ½ cup of liquid. Next, whisk in the roux, continue cooking and whisking until it's well blended, then whisk in 1–2 cups of stock, either beef, chicken, or vegetable. Continue whisking and cooking until desired consistency is achieved. Season with salt and pepper to taste. If the wine proves too tangy, tame it with 3–4 tbsp. of cream whisked in and some chopped fine herbs such as parsley, sage, and maybe a touch of lemon zest. Simplify the entire matter by leaving out the wine and just do the roux and stock routine with any tasty juice and bits tossed in from the roasting or fry pan. This is not as elaborate a gravy as those found in cookbook recipes requiring chopped sautéed vegetables and onions and straining, but it's quick, simple, and easy to remember, a major gift on the rare occasion gravy is ever called for or desired.

Chapter 13

WELCOME TORTURES

"She's just looking for an escape from work," George's mother said. "She's just lazy." Fiona Kerry came from an Irish immigrant family that suffered enough prejudices it was natural she'd harbor her own. She had no tolerance for laziness of any sort, and that was what she considered Lenore's problem— what the doctors, overpriced and all too willing to indulge her daughter-in-law's excuses, insisted on calling *mental illness*. The world was going soft, and it wouldn't benefit anyone to indulge such crippling tendencies.

She, Fiona Kerry, had personally survived the 1906 San Francisco earthquake, lived for months in a tent cabin in Butcher Town with her entire family—mother, father, seven brothers and sisters—in a single room, cooking whatever they could find over an empty coffee can filled with coals. She'd lost a brother to the First World War and a son to the second, and she was still paying off the funeral parlor bill on her husband. In between she'd faced the full brunt of the Great Depression, making do on homemade noodles and bacon rind and chard grown in the backyard of their Peninsula row house when her husband's lack of work didn't stop her four children from being hungry. No one ever went to bed without a full stomach on her watch. And there was always coffee and oatmeal to send them off in the morning. She never failed them that. That was her duty.

"I'd keep an eye on her if I were you," she told her son. America was on the cusp of the greatest prosperity the world had ever seen, and this silly girl who had never known any hardship—Fiona had watched Lenore's family drive to Saturday market in a new-model roadster when everyone else lacked gas money—was crippled by the prospect.

The girl's family had come here in the new century. Midwest emigrants. Arrivistes and parvenus. Stepped off a steam train instead of tumbling out of a covered wagon. That was the problem: They still hadn't settled in. They had not earned the right to prosperity. Lenore's brother returned from the war intact, with a college degree paid for by Uncle Sam. Government largesse. A boondoggle perpetrated on the taxpayers.

The Kerrys took care of themselves. If they couldn't afford college, then they didn't need college. Look what it did to that girl. She'd graduated with a credential to teach, which she did for all of a single year. Now she was crumbling from the challenges of two beautiful, perfect babies. Just two. Fiona spoke to the Lord on the subject and he agreed: Fiona did not have to take care of those children if anything happened to this worthless girl. She'd done her time raising babies.

"As the pope is my witness . . ."

"Don't." George knew what she was about to say.

"I'm telling you. An annulment. There was something wrong with her from the start. She married in bad faith."

"She's trying hard to get better."

"You could start over. Men do."

"I'm sorry I mentioned the fire."

"It won't be the end of it."

"She's still my wife."

He couldn't explain it. The dark-haired beauty with the quirky, surprising sense of humor and a sharp wit, educated, a reader of texts beyond his understanding. Stylish. Like a movie star sometimes, in her broad-shouldered coats and slim-waisted dresses, hair swept back and pinned with a tortoiseshell comb, a brooch set perfectly on a jacket lapel, a rakishly tilted hat with a veil begging further investigation. Gloves, always. His first mate standing on the boat deck, her hands clinging to the mast, smiling into the blunt propelling forces, the generous legs of her pants flapping back, revealing the outline of her thighs. He was jealous of the wind; he wanted to be the sun and the fabric and the salt air clinging to her face, her thighs. He wanted his Lenore back desperately.

"Promise me no more children."

"Show me that light switch, Ma. I've gotta get going."

He believed Lenore's explanation, an accidental overstuffing of the fireplace, a silly mistake not to happen again as she grew more accustomed to the house, its systems, its limits and preferences. Who could truly know a fireplace's capacity until it was tested?

This new town was as good as a sanitarium. No Depression memories and immigrant desperation, like on the Peninsula. This pavement was too new for oil slicks or cracks, the homes bristling with first-owner pride, no taint of history, other people's misery. The supermarket's aisles flooded with orchestral music as you shopped, like in a dream; yardage shops filled with everything a clever and stylish woman who sewed needed to compensate for the lack of fashionable clothing stores or the funds to shop in them. You did it yourself here. You took responsibility for your own needs and desires. You drove yourself to the acres of parking. A tonic. A miracle. A place to forget where they'd been and live for all they could become.

Lenore said less than she would have liked to. When she did speak, she felt no one understood. Offbeat comments only raised quizzical looks. She'd rather be left alone, keep her thoughts private. The workings of her mind were her business. There would be no more outside probing of the only clandestine territory to which she could still lay claim.

She put her energies into conquering the household chores—this despite often finding herself, in the middle of the day, exhausted, desperately craving sleep. She refused the urge, fearing she'd be thought a sluggard, a shirk, a lazy loon, or a worthless nut. Laundry was done, shirts ironed and starched, buttons replaced, socks darned, cakes baked, and three meals a day served on time.

Thus applying the strength of will her father considered a flaw in a woman, she felt confident the outside world considered her recovered, returned to normal, no trouble to anyone but herself. For the most part she was able to ignore the melancholy pull she felt beneath the flow of daily routines. Sleep was a nightly challenge, the donkey-lady dreams stealing what little rest Lenore achieved. Without sleep she didn't have enough energy for the day.

The house made her dopey with its never-ending squall of work.

She scrubbed the stained grout on the bathroom tile with an old toothbrush. She did this with furious, tight strokes, as if brushing the house's teeth. Stains led to cavities and decay. She had lost her mother to the distance between the Bay Area and Southern California. It would be too sad, then, to lose the white of the grout as well. She wouldn't be able to bear that loss. So she used a rougher hand, a greater intensity, quick circular motions, until her arms flamed with the heat of her effort. She didn't stop until the grout began grinding away.

The special challenges of linoleum were another pressing concern. She studied the issue of waxy buildup thoroughly, and had determined the only answer was preventative: Simply do not let it happen or suffer the consequences. Every week get down on hands and knees to strip the floor free of wax with a brush held in both hands, working it in a zigzag pattern, pushing forward and pulling back, skirt raised up from the knees, hem tucked in at the waist to keep the fabric from the water, knees slick with soap. Then from the same doggy position, spread a fresh coat of wax with a soft, dry cloth.

Rub the bar of Bon Ami, as if it were a bead from mother Kerry's rosary, into a fulsome gray lather, a filmy prayer to slather across the windows, a slimy, unctuous measure of effort dripping from the brow. The price of bodily fluids. The cost of sweat. Earning one's keep.

Done fogging over every glass pane in the house—and there were plenty of panes in the house—back to where she started, to the dried, opaque mask. Now wipe it away for a crystalline view of the court's houses. They look back at her like a medieval council of burghers. What could they possibly want?

A man's temper is so unattractive in a woman. Spank the children's bottoms bruised for stealing your time, then press charges. Children are your charges. They'll be held against you. What *was* the crime?

Lenore knew the poem from a translation assignment in her college poetry class. How could she have forgotten it? "Amor Mysticus," by Sister Marcela de Carpio de San Felix, a sixteenth-century nun.

> *Let them say to my lover*
> *That here I lie!*
> *The thing of His pleasure,*
> *His slave am I.*

Slap their creamy cheeks or take a switch to their legs until they jerk from the sting. Threaten to slap them silly—as if you could ever explain that one—or announce your wish to kill them. That was always good for some quiet time.

> *Say that I seek Him*
> *Only for love,*
> *And welcome are tortures*
> *My passion to prove.*

That bride doll Hunter begged for until you scraped the money together, went without, worked all the harder—then she left it on the floor. You tore the head off, then walked through the house, the yard, the head in one hand, its satin-and lace-clothed body in the other, calling, "Hun-*turrr*!" You found her curled in the dust in the closet corner, making those mewing, kitteny sounds. You dragged her out by her wrist, swatted the dirt from her bottom, and told her if she was so tired, she could just get into her pajamas and go to bed. A gift. A treat. You wished it for yourself.

Someday she'd understand. When she was a mommy herself.

> *Love giving gifts*
> *Is suspicious and cold;*
> *I have all, my Beloved,*
> *When Thee I hold.*

George asked why Hunter wasn't at the table.

"She was feeling fluish," you explained.

He didn't ask again.

I wake Thursday morning at seven o'clock and Somebody is packing a bag.

"Where are you going?"

"A car's coming in an hour. I've got a meeting in New York Friday. I'm taking the red-eye home that night. I'll be back Saturday in the AM."

"Unbelievable," I say. The last time this happened, he dragged his carry-on up the stairs behind the first guests. It was one reason I'd stopped doing dinner parties. I'd forgotten until now.

"It's the best I can do."

When he isn't dispatched last-minute, there are weeks of warning but still no repair for dashed plans and crumpled commitments. Everything flies out the door with him—high-priced theater tickets, hard-won invitations. Now my dinner party hangs in the balance.

The dog explodes in a barking frenzy. The driver has arrived forty-five minutes early. Somebody is ready.

"I love you," he says, hoisting his bag like a sailor's duffel before heading out to sea, then kisses me hard and hugs me close and dashes down the stairs.

He loves me. He says so—*all* the time. As if one of us ever doubted it for a minute. Was this a Post-it note "I love you," a reminder, or was it a warning? "I love you"—*watch out!*

I look out the living room window at the graceful drape of the deodar cedar branches and see a hive dripping its increasingly large swarm of bees. I can hear them buzzing. They are starting to drop down the chimney and crawl across the floor when I hear a truck pull up to the curb on the street below. I see with relief that it is the bee man, and I go down to the street to meet him. Dalai comes with me on her leash so that she won't get stung following bees across the floor. The bee man is ready for battle in his bee suit, a netted helmet and a white jumpsuit. He takes his ladder into the front garden and sets it against the tree.

"Please don't crush my border plantings," I say. Alejandro and I have recently collaborated on an edging row of primrose.

"I'll try not to," he says. The garden always ends up paying a price when the house is ministered to. I point out a second infestation, at the high corner of the house, and go back inside to leave him to his task.

He comes up the stairs when he is done.

"I think I got them all," he says, "but if they come back it probably means there's honey inside the walls. You'll have to break the walls open, scrape it out, and repair the stucco."

I hand him the credit card for payment. He takes it down to his truck to process it. In a few minutes he's back.

"This isn't any good," he says. "The card company won't put the payment through."

I feel a hot flash of humiliation spreading across my cheeks and brow.

"Can I give you a check?"

"We've done business with you before?" he asks.

"Yes," I say.

"I guess so," he says. "I've got to get going here."

I race upstairs, all the way to the den on the top floor, write out the check, and race down to hand it to him, sweat now moistening my brow previously colored by humiliation. I loathe asking service people to come up the stairs for payment; I'm embarrassed by the number of flights, a condition I've arrived at after so many years of listening to workers complain about them. *Life is hard enough* is the feeling conveyed, *and then you have all those stairs*—as if they were maintained just for the workers' abuse.

All the professional ambition I arrived with in Southern California has been siphoned off to the repair and maintenance of this house and my one indulgence, the garden. The more I find lacking in the immediate surrounding community, and the greater my frustration with writing outlets, editors, and assignments, the more I have poured my energies and attentions into the house and garden. The more I pour into them, the more they demand of me. In lieu of a career, or a child, or children, I have been consumed by this decrepit house and the enchanted, demanding garden with which I've surrounded it.

I return to the bottom of the stairs and hand the bee man his check. He takes it and writes down all my identifying numbers— the license, the phone, everything he can think of. I thank him. He leaves. I scan the front planter beds for the aftermath of his efforts. There are only two crushed primroses at the edge of the retaining wall, but a number of abutilon branches are broken, and the eight-foot-tall pencil plant I started from a six-inch pot is now four feet tall, busted in half on the bee man's way to spraying the upper corner of the house.

I go back inside and call Somebody on his cell phone.

"The credit card has been cut off," I say.

"I know," he says. "I'm sorry. I found the bill in my briefcase on the way to the airport. I just dropped it in the mail."

"Last month you lost it altogether. And the month before that we had to pay late fees. Do I have to take care of that, too?"

"I'm sorry for the inconvenience," he says.

"What do you mean by that—'sorry for the inconvenience'? You just humiliated me in public with a cut-off card, I've still got shopping to do and nothing to do it with, and you're sorry for the inconvenience? You sound like a customer service rep. Are you about to put me on hold and make me listen to bad AM radio?"

"No, I'm about to board my plane," he says. "Can we talk about this later?" He says nothing and I say nothing, and I hear the airport boarding calls in the background. "I love you," he says finally, as if that explains everything, as if that were enough, before he's gone and the line goes dead.

*T*he newborn, the third child, Howard, a question stopped in its tracks before fully posed, was hungry. Lenore stood at the kitchen sink, rinsing his bottle, when she looked up and saw the donkey lady in the window. She couldn't speak. Her mind stalled. She felt stupid and slow. The moment lasted for months. The baby's demands drove her further away.

At least she wasn't her cousin Helene, the shattered vase, her sorrow forever spilled, everyone said, from a failed romance. Her life destroyed by a man. She was a spinster living with her parents, an invisible woman.

At least Lenore had a husband. At least she had children. Surrounded by the bodies of those she had created, those she cared for, she was visible—she wouldn't disappear. She was protected; her future was secure. Or so she'd always believed. But finding herself the mother of three children, alone in a place so surprisingly and unrelentingly strange, she wondered if anything was secure. She wondered how the world could worship mothers while at the same time grinding them to a pulp.

Lenore opened the front door one afternoon to find a man and woman standing on her porch. They said they were surveying the neighborhood for the government's Census Bureau. She let them in, a welcome break in the day, some adult conversation. They were from the government—what did they think of that atomic bomb test in the Nevada desert? What if a radioactive cloud poisoned the air and water? What did they think? What *could* be done?

The woman asked to stick a needle in Lenore's shoulder. Before she could utter a protest her thoughts were clipped from their strings, like a wall of helium balloons. The couple guided her out the door toward their waiting car as she begged to put on lipstick, get her gloves. "I don't want to go out looking like riffraff," she said. They assured her the children would be taken care of. She wouldn't worry, Lenore promised them, ever again.

In the back of the car she rolled her head onto the woman's shoulder and shut her eyes, disappearing into a merciful and quiet dark.

My mother's head rolled onto my shoulder. Her eyes drifted closed. I saw the pink of her translucent scalp through the wisps of thinning white hair brushed back from her brow. Her skin smelled clean and indifferent.

This was her second day in the hospital she had come to by ambulance in the middle of the night because she couldn't breathe. Fluid on her lungs. This fluid buildup, the doctor explained, was from her previous hospital stay for what he believed was a mild heart attack. But it has always been hard to know with her. She doesn't like to tell anyone what is going on, for fear, it seems, they will want to do something about it. She has always distrusted doctors. She has always preferred to keep to herself.

"It happens," he said. "We'll get the fluid out of there and then she can go home."

Her home is a board and care facility. The home in which I grew up, the house in which my mother lived for some fifty years, nearly thirty of them by herself, was sold the month prior. Its contents were evacuated by Hunter, acting with hurricane force, frantically sorting and trucking to landfills, scattering a few boxes of saved items amongst Mother's children's homes—cardboard containers filled with photograph albums, serving dishes, chipped teacups and saucers, a pair of mother-of-pearl opera glasses. Items that seemed important at the time, but now I can't imagine ever wanting to look at them again. When I see these boxes stacked in the back of my garage, I wonder if this is what will happen to the contents of my life when my time is up. This is what happens when things are kept close and people remain distant.

Mother now claims to have no memory of that house and its contents, of our lives together there. The place Mother refers to as home, when she sits in her board and care room with the red geraniums cascading outside the sliding glass door, is the Burlingame home in which she grew up with her now long-dead parents and a brother, my uncle Garland, who went for decades without contacting her before he himself died. That house was sold years ago by my uncle Garland and torn down to build apartments; still, it is what she refers to when she talks about going home, as if it still exists, as if she has only stepped out the door for a moment and now it is time to go back inside.

I moved my chair next to the one in which Mother sat while taking her hospital dinner. I did this when she said she couldn't finish the meal, she was too tired, and she began to nod her head as if she wanted to sleep. She accepted the invitation of my body as her pillow. I was surprised by the intimacy of the moment, that she acquiesced without protest or complaint.

I attributed this willingness to exhaustion—thorough, debili-tating, crippling. She was too tired for a single syllable or gesture of refusal, and for a moment the distance she worked so vigilantly to maintain during the course of our lives collapsed. The soft weight of her head against my shoulder illuminated me like a nighttime re-flection in a window. I felt more visible, if only to her, to her touch, aware that my flesh was supporting her, holding her up. My own existence felt less in doubt, if only for that moment, a doubt I wasn't fully aware of until my shoulder cradled her head.

I left the hospital after helping her into bed, turning off her room lights. My last sight was of her upturned face bathed in eerie green light from the ceiling-suspended television screen. I drove to the nearby motel where I was staying while she recovered. I lay on a too-firm mattress, an unfamiliar pillow beneath my head, staring at the stained, acoustic ceiling and thinking of how long I had waited to feel the soft weight of my mother's head resting against my shoulder. I heard the distant basso rumble of trucks shifting gears on the interstate, a familiar childhood sound. I would lie awake in my bedroom then, imagining the big rigs rumbling down the distant highway with loads of cattle, tomatoes, and logs. Now I had driven that road countless times to see her, to see who she would be when I arrived: comforted by or resentful of her daughter's presence. Eventually she always became the latter, and adding to the drudgery of my constant driving up and down the length of the state was the realization, experienced barreling along in the middle of the night at seventy-five miles an hour, that I needed her more than she needed me.

*H*unter and Hailey believed their mother was recovering from an injured back—maybe that was why she was so angry, because her back hurt—and would be gone for a few months. Their father hired Mrs. Yacksloff to cook and clean and help with baby Howard. She talked softly and combed their hair gently and wiped the jam from their faces and understood it was hard to get your hands as clean as they should be when you couldn't reach the sink without a step stool, and that fingerprints do wipe off woodwork. At the end of the day, when she left for her own family, when their father came home from his job, they always felt sad.

"It's not her back," Gertrude Abbott said to Beverly Watts. Beverly had just been leaving the Castro Village Variety Store, with glue, pinecones, and construction paper for her daughter Tina's third-grade Thanksgiving centerpiece project, when her neighbor in the court had tapped on her driver's window.

"Where do you think she is?" Beverly asked Gertrude.

"Napa," Gertrude said.

"She looked like a zombie those last few weeks," Beverly said. "I thought it was the pain."

"The kids were bruised," Gertrude said. "Hunter came to my house hungry after school."

"I never knew," Beverly said, shaking her head. Hunter's wrist was bruised; she said it was from a fall. She was always climbing trees and jumping off fences. A real wild child. Maybe it was more than that.

"We heard the shouting," Gertrude said.

"Where was he?"

"Men never know."

*G*eorgie, Georgie, pumpkin eater, had a wife and couldn't keep her. It was none of their business. Bad back, long rest, enough said. Lovely weather, isn't it?

No, he hadn't asked too much. Maybe not enough. Maybe she needed more to keep her mind from wandering. He knew some things—floor refinishing and kitchen cabinet hardware and the importance of lubricating the lawn mower, and how best to grout tile versus bricks—but he didn't know what was wrong with her. He wanted her fixed, but he couldn't do it. The doctors couldn't, either. What was there to discuss?

People, they like to ask questions.

He was in his workshop garage to finish a chest of drawers, a child's desk, a bookcase, a step stool. He measured and cut wood, fit pieces together, sanded and beveled and turned legs in the lathe, and nailed and primed and sanded and gave a final coat. Only the work. A troubled mind, he thought in the midst of his midnight projects, wasn't such a terrible thing as long as it produced results. Results. High-priced doctors and still no results. That was the real problem.

Lenore's father called her to say that her mother had died several days before. She'd been ill, but not seriously, so of course, he said, Ellie had asked him not to bother her.

Gone, like a feather launched from a bird's wing. A sudden amputation and cauterization of multiple limbs and vital organs. Something ripped from deep within, singed shut and tossed out, an unspeakable violation. A fluttering veil shredded with grief.

Lenore was underwater, drowning. Howard cried in his wet diaper, with no bottle anywhere near. Hailey and Hunter stayed away from the house until suppertime. No one called for them or came looking.

Lenore lay on the couch, staring at the ceiling until it was dark out and dinner needed to be made. She heard her mother's voice and looked over to see her standing in the kitchen. When she rose to meet her, she was gone.

She told the doctors everything because they told her it would do her good.

Liars.

Dirty bastard liars.

They dug it all out of her, like a grapefruit spoon scraping plaster, and here she was again, emptied onto the couch, immobile. There was nothing left inside her; she couldn't even roll onto the carpet to crawl across it to the door. Her limbs were limp and useless. Her bones were jelly threaded through pudding. All that digging had done this to her.

Her mother floated by again. Still wearing that paisley wool belted dress with the beige jacket she had worn that last day they were together in the City, the gardenia boutonniere Lenore had bought for her lapel still fragrant. Lenore laughed. How absurd that she was dead.

And why was folding laundry so hard? Why did it refuse to lie flat so that the drawer could close? Why did she have to use her good scissors to cut it into flat lengths so that the drawer slid closed?

Gertrude was shocked at the sight of her pregnant neighbor standing unannounced in the middle of her bedroom, holding a pair of scissors and a shredded child's garment.

"Hailey's shirts won't fit," Lenore said in a voice on the edge of flight.

"Honey, you shouldn't do that."

Gertrude put her arm around Lenore, who cringed at her touch.

"Let's put the scissors away, sweetie," Gertrude said. They walked back to Lenore's house. George came home when Gertrude called. He thanked her for her help.

"She called me sweetie," Lenore told him after Gertrude had left. "I just wanted to talk."

"Don't do that again," he said.

"I'm not her sweetie."

As far as he could tell, there was no real harm done. No need to call the doctor. The money they'd save would pay to replace the boy's clothes.

*T*he next baby was due at Christmas, and Lenore was gathering the things necessary for its arrival. She'd had sufficient practice now to do it by rote, if not as well as she liked. Then she noticed the front page of the day's *San Francisco Chronicle*. It was December 12; tomorrow would be the first anniversary of her mother's death. She remembered last Christmas, the first after her mother's death, the flat blank days. Lighting candles and decorating trees and wrapping presents could not lift the gray veil. She had barely been able to speak—that again, infantile paralysis of the tongue—and her limbs had felt leaden. Still, she had managed to do all the things that needed to be done. A whole year now since her mother had passed, and here was Christmas again, with a new life on the way. She was a vessel, but not a Lalique vase like her cousin—she was a crude pot made of clay ropes jammed together and worked over until the edges disappeared, solidified, smoothed away, with nothing but the rough fingerprints of the potter marking its sides, emptied out by sorrow only to be filled again.

The contractions began that day, each stabbing pain a reminder of her loss, a warning of what was to come. The baby, a girl, was born the next morning. A hired nurse cared for the infant while Lenore spent the first three months of the new year in the sanitarium, unable to sleep, eat, or talk.

"*L*eave her," Fiona hissed.
       "Don't tell me . . ."
"Start over."
"She'll recover."
"I won't have anything to do with her."
"The doctors say it's postpartum depression."
"I've never heard of such a thing."
"It happens."
"Not in this family."
"It's happening."
"It's more than that."
"She'll be fine in another month or two."
"She doesn't belong in this family."
"It's not your business."
"You know what I think."

George agreed this time to shock treatments, was told it was their last, best hope. Lenore came home after three months, her waist-length hair shot through with gray as if a ghost were entangled in it, a fugitive escaping the incessant onslaught of voltage. The touch of her mother's hand drew her to the other side with each jolt, extracting the life force from the very hairs on her head. The cure would kill her, she believed. She wouldn't survive another stay.

"*S*he's too young for gray hair all at once like that."
       "That's how the Russo woman came back from Napa."
"*Shock treatments*," Mrs. Russo told anyone who asked, when she came back with hair the color of dirty dishwater. "He signed the papers," she fumed. "A husband isn't supposed to do that to his wife."

A recognizable sign of the times in the suburbs of the '50s, the hair—like a distress banner, a flag of warning or surrender. The heraldry of the harried housewife. Shock treatment–gray tresses. If you colored your hair, according to the ad, only your hairdresser knew. If you had shock treatments, everyone knew. That's how the neighbors knew, finally, what was wrong with Lenore, the woman at the end of the court.

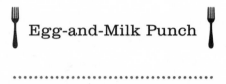

Egg-and-Milk Punch

1 egg beaten with 2 tsp. sugar

1 tumbler of milk

2 tbsp. best brandy

Stir egg and brandy into milk. Add more sugar to taste.

This adapted from the "Sick Room" section of *Common Sense in the Household: A Manual of Practical Housewifery*, by Marion Harland: "I have known very sick patients to be kept alive for days at a time by this mixture, and nothing else, until Nature could rally her forces," the author wrote, adding, "Give very cold with ice."

Chapter 14

TRAIL'S END CAFE

When I was a child, I believed men with difficult wives and unhappy marriages invented Melmac. It was the same kind of thinking that produced the neutron bomb: The dishes would be saved, but the women would disintegrate. Once Melmac came to the suburbs, crazy women had to find other ways of venting their rage, ways that were less satisfying but more public. Like Mrs. Russo, Robert's mother, who lived two courts down, running down the street naked. I never saw it but everyone, including Robert, talked about it for years afterward. Mr. Russo sent her to the state mental hospital in Napa, where she earned credits for good behavior by sweeping floors and cleaning bathrooms. She spent her credits on weekend visits home, where she swept floors and cleaned bathrooms.

Mother broke dishes when words failed her. When she got to the end of her powers of speech, she picked up a plate and let fly. China exploded into a glorious spray of geometric shards; gravy, meatloaf, potatoes, and peas fled across the linoleum, under the hutch, and out toward the living room.

Then Father brought home a set of Melmac from the discount store. He took a plate from the kitchen cabinet and showed us how it could be dropped to the floor and wouldn't break. He let us try it, amused by the earnest enthusiasm of our efforts, our delight with the results. A scientific miracle at work! We showed our friends, pulling the step stool over to the cabinet, taking a plate out, and throwing it with both hands as hard as we could directly, bravely, onto the floor, just as Mother had done at the dinner table.

It didn't break.

Problem solved.

One morning I woke to Mother yelling at Father. He didn't yell back. I got up to see him in the driveway, carrying cardboard boxes leaking cat yowls. It was a midnight graveyard sound, deep and guttural and angry as a loon, angry as my mother was now as she yelled at my father as he took the cats away.

He shoved the boxes into the back of the station wagon.

"Get in the house," he said, waving me away. "Your pajamas are ripped." He didn't want the neighbors to see me standing in rags. We'd had too many cats before several females gave birth to their litters.

"Either they go or I do," he said.

"Then go," Mother said.

She slammed their bedroom door. I stood with my hand on the wall of our tract home and I could feel it shake.

Seventeen adult cats went into the car in boxes, along with the two litters.

Father said he found good homes for them.

Hunter said he took them to the pound to be killed.

"They gas them there," she said. "They think it's fun."

*M*other went to the sanitarium.

We went to play on the trampolines, fifty cents an hour to jump until we were dizzy and thought our stomachs would bounce out of our mouths. For a delicious moment at the top of each jump, we hung in the air above the sky-blue rubber surface stretched below, weightless as astronauts, most alive in that second before we fell back to Earth.

Then we ate hot dogs at Casper's, where the hairnetted old lady behind the counter shook salt from a metal canister and jammed red tomato grins into the steamed bun alongside the skinny dog, and topped it with diced onions that looked like loose teeth. We ate our wax paper-wrapped dogs at a plastic-topped table, ripped open the cellophane bags of potato chips with our teeth, like animals, and sipped Cokes through stiff white straws.

When Father pulled the station wagon into the court, Mother's head was sticking out the front window of the house, like a character in a pop-up book. "You can't do this to me," she yelled. "I'll divorce you! I'll kill you in your sleep!"

"Stay in the car," he said.

"Don't look," Hunter said.

Father came back to sit in the car with us, wiping something from the side of his face with a handkerchief. Mother struggled against the two attendants, a man and a woman, all the way out to their waiting car. I stood as if suspended above the earth, unable to turn away, watching the fear flicker up through the anger in her face.

The man attendant put his open hand on top of my mother's head and pushed her down into the backseat of the car. Like a chicken or a sheep or a cat shoved into a crate.

The woman held on to her as my mother thrust forward and yelled at the man driving. She kept shouting as they drove out of the court.

Quack, quack, quack.

Moo, said the cow.

Meow, said the cat.

Then the car was gone and there was silence. The other houses looked empty, like all our neighbors were gone. Inside our house, no one spoke. I heard breathing. It was quieter than it had been in a long time.

My brothers went to their rooms. Hunter went to Brenda's house. I went to the TV Room and stared at the dead charcoal screen. I heard my father's table saw chewing through wood in his workshop.

A dark weight left the house with my mother. I felt bad because it felt good. Like the day Father got rid of the cats.

I sweep the bees up from the living room floor, where they lie dead or are staggering toward their fate. I dump them into a brown paper grocery bag and spray them with insecticide to end their misery and ensure that they won't colonize the garbage can, then walk them down the five flights of stairs to deposit them on the street.

Saturday night's squab need to be marinated for two days before grilling, a project I must start today. Because I can no longer use the credit card, I stop at the bank for cash to pay for the birds at Whole Foods, where I ordered them last week for pickup today. I could shop with the debit card, but we had one too many overdrafts on the account due to our poor balancing skills. Bank of America now has us on probation. Whenever I hear social workers describe checkbook balancing as a fundamental survival skill necessary for mainstreaming the developmentally disabled or mentally ill back into society, I wonder, *Where can I sign up for their class?*

"I ordered ten fresh squab last week," I tell the butcher, who stands looking down at me from behind the glass counter. "I told them I had to pick them up today."

"I'm sorry, I don't see any back there," he says, wiping his hands on his blood-smeared apron. "Our last poultry delivery was Tuesday. If they came in, they've flown the coop. All we have is what's in the case."

There are four frozen squab huddled next to a pile of frozen duck breasts. At least they're organic. I come to Whole Foods for the organic products, even though I rarely find them there. My growing obsession with organic food has become an organizing principle in my life. I believe organic not only tastes better, but also *is* better for people and the environment. Most important, it simplifies my life. Supermarket choices have been edited down drastically. I can't control what goes on the plate in restaurants, but I can control what is served in my home. And for at least the past decade I've enjoyed a self-prescribed daily salad made of organic lettuce from a bag. There have been days when I've subsisted on nothing but canned organic soup and organic brown-rice cakes, for lack of fresh organic produce. So what if it was recently announced that the lettuce I live for comes from fields irrigated with rocket fuel-polluted water from the Colorado River? If the rocket fuel doesn't eventually kill me, I'm sure the irony will. At least I won't spend my life dithering over which of the hundreds of varieties of fruits and vegetables flown in from all over the planet to buy. If it isn't organic, I pass. I throw the squab into my cart. I call Fish King on my way to the checkout counter.

"We have six squab," he says, "but they're frozen."

"Are they organic?"

"Are you kidding?"

I don't have all day to scour Glendale and its environs for squab, nor do I have a gun, which would feel great right now, to go hunt my own game. It's time, therefore, to compromise my high ideals.

"Fine," I say. "Don't let them out of your sight."

A dank gray fog hung in the light of streetlamps on a mid-February night as we drove to the sanitarium to visit Mother. The hospital's bisque-colored buildings were isolated at the edge of a valley of ranches and farms soon to become a freeway-laced carpet of tract homes and shopping malls. A squat field of dusk-blue vegetables halted its rows at the edge of the hospital grounds, as if it knew better than to go any farther. I thought of the low cluster of buildings filled with nurses and doctors as an advanced guard, like the Indian scouts in Westerns, marking the path for the pioneers to follow.

The housekeeper who took care of us while Mother was there had a small face with a knob nose that looked like it had been caught in a net of red veins. Her eyes were watery gray and she had more than one chin. She drank coffee at the dining room table and coughed delicately between puffs of her filtered menthol cigarettes. She didn't break plates. She wore slacks, a single pair at a time that she changed daily, not several pairs of pants at once, all month long, then a dress over those like my mother had started to do. My father said she did this because she couldn't make up her mind about what to wear.

Even better, the housekeeper cooked casseroles with canned cream soup, noodles from cellophane packages, not homemade, and ground beef, like they said on TV to do. The housekeeper was a working model of what my mother was supposed to be—would be, I hoped, when she returned home.

We walked down the sanitarium's long corridor toward my mother's room as fluorescent lights twitched and buzzed overhead. She waited outside her door, sitting in a folding metal chair, white-gloved hands clasped in her lap. Her hair was braided and looped in an outdated style, a style seen only in the movies, on young girls living in the Alps. Loretta Young might have worn her hair this way to play a virtuous blind girl. Mother's smile was faint, tentative, as her eyes went wide at the sight of me.

"You look like a ragamuffin," she said, her mouth shifting into a grim set.

I didn't understand. I was wearing my new quilted red nylon jacket that Father had bought at the discount store. It made me feel like I was Chinese, eating rice with chopsticks on a square-sailed junk gliding down the yellow Yangtze waters. Maybe the ragamuffin part was my toe poking through the hole in my sneakers and the grass stains streaking my corduroy pants. Or maybe it was my hair my sister pulled into a ponytail but I wouldn't let her slick back with Crisco,[3] so it was falling around my face. Or maybe it was my missing tooth. I wasn't sure what a ragamuffin was, but Mother made it sound like a fundamental human failing.

The three of us drove to Pleasanton, the nearby ranch town, for dinner at the Trail's End Cafe. The chrome-edged tables were dull from being wiped with greasy rags, and the red vinyl booths were streaked from spray cleaner. The waitress's name, Fran, was pinned to her blouse like she might forget it or come out of the kitchen as someone else.

"I'll have the New York steak dinner and french-fried potatoes instead of baked," Mother told her. My father chomped his pipe stem and winced. Mother was on a diet, and steak was the most expensive thing on the plastic-covered menu. My father and I had eaten the pot pies the housekeeper heated for us for dinner before we came, because he hated spending money in restaurants.

"The sanitarium food is horrible," Mother said. "It's salty and overcooked. They serve *canned* vegetables." She once let me sample the obsidian green coil of spinach served with her lunch; it tasted metallic and looked to me like the damp taffeta dress of a drowned party girl.

Fran set down the chocolate cake slice Father let me order. Its icing looked silky and forgiving in its revolving display case, but it was like cardboard, each bite grainy and cold from the refrigerator. It hung in lumps at the back of my throat, and I had to work hard to swallow.

"When are you coming home?" I asked Mother.

She looked at my father, then at me, then, after pausing to take another bite of steak, offered, "When the doctors say I can." She

....

3   This is what she uses when she runs out of the clear, green-tinged goop that holds my hair stiff like dried shellac.

finished all her french fries and devoured the steak down to its gristle and bone. Then she picked up the bone and began gnawing on it. Father said nothing.

Mother ordered apple pie "à la mode," as Fran cleared her plate and Father's teeth clamped down on the mouthpiece of his pipe as he puffed in sputtering bursts.

"Could you bring the check with that?" he asked Fran.

He put the money on the table with the bill and said, "Let's go."

"I'm not finished," Mother said, taking the first bite of her pie and ice cream.

"I am," he said. I started to scoot out of the booth. Mother grabbed my arm and held me back.

She held on to my arm the whole time she ate. She did this quickly, with frantic little bites, humming softly to herself. When the pie was gone, she used her spoon to scoop the melted ice-cream puddle like it was soup. Then she took the last two bread rolls and all the individually wrapped pats of butter, gathered them in a paper napkin, and tucked them into the large patch pocket of her coat.

"That was delicious," she said in an enthusiastic stage whisper, letting go, at last, of my arm. There were red marks on my skin where her hand had been. Father waited in the car. She sat in the front passenger seat, took the rolls from her pocket, smeared one with a pat of butter, and began to chew.

"Don't," he said.

"Don't tell *me*," she said.

He looked away and started the car. I thought of the little red hen that grew the wheat and ground the flour and baked the bread all by herself. We stood beneath the single light of the sanitarium door, and Mother cupped her hand on the back of my head like a prayer cap. I smelled White Shoulders perfume and restaurant bread.

Father craned his head forward to briefly touch his lips to hers. They both pulled away as if repelled, like magnets, like those shuffling, bobble-headed dolls, tugged along by stringed weights, tumbling off a tabletop to the floor.

It was the only time I ever saw them kiss.

*M*y hands are fragrant with the rosemary and garlic I am dicing for the birds' marinade bath when Somebody calls from New York.

"I promise," he says, "I won't forget to mail the credit card bill again."

"You always promise," I say. "You make promises while I'm still stuck dealing with all the problems. All of them. I'm sick of it."

"Me too," he says.

"What do you mean?"

"Your problems."

"My problems?"

"You complain about everything."

"Like what?"

"You couldn't stand working in an office, so now you work at home. Then you complain about the neighborhood nonstop."

"I don't."

"You do, you do, you do."

"You're always traveling and I've got to take care of everything here and this place is falling apart."

"If I turn down any travel for work, I could be out of a job. We can't afford to live off what you make freelance food writing."

"I'm canceling the dinner party."

"Don't be ridiculous," he says.

"Don't call me ridiculous," I say. "You won't be here and Hunter will. That's ridiculous. I'm canceling." I hang up. I shove the birds into the rosemary-and-garlic bath I've divided between two oversize Tupperware containers. I put the lids on without even listening for the goddamn burp. I leave them out on the counter to hasten their thaw.

*H*e needed to tighten the jib lines and head for a new spot on the horizon. When she got home from the sanitarium, he would leave. He couldn't live like this. Four children and her mind gone. He was a good husband and a good father. He only wanted the best for all of them.

Correct his course. They needed a mother. Maybe if he left, she'd come out of the bedroom, take care of them.

Maybe they should never have married. Maybe they should never have had kids. A bad match, if not bad faith, like his mother said. That was all. Never meant to be. Like in one of those songs.

Kids are tough; they'd get along. Everyone would.

He felt the wind rising. Time to lift anchor, adjust his course, find a new spot on the horizon.

*M*other came home from the sanitarium and Father moved out of the house.

"Your mother and I are going to try to live apart for a while," he said. At least that's what I remember. It *is* the kind of thing people in movies and television say to children when they are done with a marriage. I might have picked up the memory there. Sometimes I don't remember him saying anything at all; I just see sunlight from the front door framing the dark silhouette of a man with a suitcase. To see this, I would have had to be across the living room, standing in the doorway of the TV Room. Afterward I would have gone back to the television, which was on all the time by then. That's why I might have seen it there, instead of for real.

My father rented a duplex apartment at the other end of town, off the main boulevard, near the freeway on-ramp to Oakland and San Francisco. The walls were the color of a coffee-stained cup, and the cracked tiles and sinks were streaked a rusty yellow. Outside, instead of a yard there was a buzz-cut patch of straw that was supposed to be a lawn, a magnet for hamburger wrappers from the new McDonald's across the street, the first McDonald's we'd ever seen.

Sometimes Mrs. Yvonne Yacksloff, a divorce from up our street, was there when we came to visit. She drank coffee and smoked menthols and made yellow cheese sandwiches with Miracle Spread, as if she were interested in us. When my mother was still in the sanitarium, my father told me more than once to go to Mrs. Yacksloff's house after school, when the housekeeper couldn't come. She lived up the street in one of the small, flat-roofed buildings with the tiny yards and cement floors.

Her two teenage boys lived the next town over with their father. Their tinted school photos sat in brass frames on top of a blond television console that looked like what contestants won on TV game shows. In real life her sons' skin was pinker than the milky-blue, rubber-smooth faces in their pictures.

One day at her house, Yvonne, as she asked me to call her, showed me how to make angel food cake, a cake full of air and beaten egg whites, a cake that had no flavor, no color, no weight, a cake that barely existed on the plate and was forgotten before the last bite. Angel food cake needed something on top of it, like strawberries or chocolate sauce or ice cream; otherwise, it was hard to know it was even there.

While the angel food cake baked, we sat down at the kitchen dinette to look at her cosmetics catalogs, items she sold door to door, perfumes and soaps and lotions. Her favorite scent was Peaches 'n' Cream. It smelled like stewed fruit, and her house, Hunter said, "reeked" of it. I wondered if Mrs. Yacksloff didn't use these cosmetics whether she'd smell like anything at all.

*N*ot long after my mother returned from the sanitarium and my father left, our neighbor from the next court down, Mrs. Allen, the one who did charity work, paid a call. Mrs. Allen was in the habit of greeting my mother with a rush-up hug and a lean-in-close, calling her "Len" or "hon" or "darlin'." Mother always recoiled at this—she hated being touched or having people come too close.

This time Mrs. Allen stopped short of her usual, overly familiar greeting. This time she stood on the porch with her mouth dropped open, a home-baked cake about to slide off the platter she gripped with both hands. "Lee-Nore," she said, both syllables drawn out slow.

She set her offering on the table and announced, "It's lemon," as if she were tamping down what she most wanted to say. The top of the cake was dusted with a lacy pattern of powdered sugar. "I filtered it through a doily," she continued. "The instructions were in *Good Housekeeping*."

Mother insisted on making coffee. Mrs. Allen clutched the strap of the purse that she held on her lap, and sat rigid in the dining room chair as we both listened to the percolator. The cups rattled in their saucers as Mother carried them the few steps from the kitchen. "Oh, please, let me do that," Mrs. Allen insisted, rising from her chair and stepping in to take the knife from Mother's hand as she was about to cut the cake. Its feathery design disintegrated beneath the recently sharpened blade.

"You look tired, Lenore," Mrs. Allen said. "Are you getting enough rest?"

"My husband signed papers for shock treatments," Mother said, delicately licking the powdered sugar from the back of her fork. Her hair was grayer than it had been before she went to the hospital, and deep bags were beginning to sag beneath her eyes. "I could barely remember his name when they were done. That was the only good to come of it."

Mrs. Allen didn't retrieve her plate. A few months after the last yellow crumbs were deposited on a tongue, the plate washed and dried and set on the sideboard waiting to be returned, Mother saw Mrs. Allen pulling out of a parking space at East Hills Market. Mother knocked on the driver's side window.

"Oh, please, keep the plate," Mrs. Allen said as she continued to back up her car and drove away. Mother held her white-gloved hand in the air as if she were about to speak, but no words came out. She started rummaging through her purse, couldn't find what she was looking for—*the words?* I thought—as she pulled me by the hand into the grocery store. When we were done doing the week's shopping, Hunter picked us up in the Tempest.

The smashed cake plate shards went into the wet kitchen garbage Mother dug into the backyard. The former flower bed soon looked like an abandoned archaeological dig, jagged bits of pottery hinting at a lost civilization.

Lace-Topped Lemon Pound Cake

All ingredients should be at room temperature.

1 cup cake or pastry flour

1 tbsp. baking powder

3 large eggs

1 cup plus 2 tbsp. sugar

¼ cup plus 2 tbsp. heavy cream

6 tbsp. melted butter

½ tsp. salt

Grated zest from 2 lemons

Juice from ½ lemon

Powdered sugar

Paper doily

Melt the butter on low heat and set aside to cool.

Preheat oven to 350 degrees F (325 degrees if using convection oven). Prepare a 9-inch springform pan or 8½ x 4½ x 2½–inch loaf pan (4 cups), or a 6-cup loaf pan, by greasing it, then lining the bottom with parchment or wax paper, and then greasing again and flouring it.

Sift the flour with baking powder.

In a mixing bowl, beat the eggs with a whisk and gradually add the sugar and salt. At low speed with an electric mixer, mix in the lemon zest, the flour and baking powder, and the heavy cream. When butter is cool, add it to the flour mixture and mix until just combined. Pour into prepared pan. Bake at 350 or 325 degrees (if using a convection oven) for 30–40 minutes, if using the springform pan, or 40–50 minutes if using a loaf pan. Cake is done when a toothpick inserted into the center comes out clean or cake comes away from the sides of the pan easily. Cool on a rack, and when completely cooled and out of pan, place paper doily on top and gently sift powdered sugar over it to create a lace pattern on top of the cake. You can also use the juice from half a lemon and mix it with sufficient powdered sugar, as much as ¼ to ½ cup, depending on consistency desired, and drizzle that over the warm cake. When done, transfer to serving plate.

Chapter 15

REFUGEES' COOK BOOK

I stand at the kitchen counter, turning the birds in their marinade, contemplate canceling Saturday night's dinner, compose and rehearse in my head the excuse I'll leave on each guest's answering machine, when I feel a bump at the back of my leg. It is Dalai, tail swaying aloft and wide obsidian eyes filled with the hope of dinner. The kitchen clocks all say it is five, the time each day when she comes to me for her meal, as if she can read them, as if she has a watch hidden in her fur. If only all relationships in my life were this simple, clear, and consistently satisfying.

I spoon up her portion of canned food and kibble, which she inhales. Then she heads for the door, tail thwacking, eyes glued to me, an invitation to our evening walk. I grab a bag and a house key, attach her expand-a-leash, and we're off.

Together we tromp down the wooden stairs, cross beneath the elegant sweep of the deodar cedar tree, and hit the sidewalkless street. I know people who take pride in the absence of sidewalks in their Los Angeles neighborhoods, pointing to it as proof of some rural charm they enjoy in the midst of the city. These people do not have dogs in need of regular walks. Without sidewalks, dog and walker must traverse a grim layer of urban sludge composed of oil leaks, food remnants and wrappers, dirt, plastic detritus, and expectorant, in both fresh-puddle and dehydrated-stain form.

Some litter has remained in place long enough to earn landmark status, like the disposable plastic flossing bow next to the front left tire of an aging, possibly abandoned Chevy that signals the last hundred yards before our first set of stairs. And when the streets are as narrow as ours, and crowded with cars that cannot be parked in garages because those are being used for storage or an income-supplementing rental unit, dog and walker must constantly dodge passing vehicles that rarely proceed with appropriate caution.

As Dalai and I step off our brief stretch of curb into the unknown of our nightly neighborhood adventure, I consider the damage canceling Saturday night might do. I'll be stuck with ten intensely marinated, previously frozen squab that will benefit not one wit from a return to an iced state. These are not arctic birds. I'll have to cook everything I'd bought fresh and find room for it in the freezer, amongst the containers from other abandoned entertaining projects.

That said, could I cancel and still save face? What excuse could I give? I couldn't claim my back has gone out; anyone who knows me knows that I exercise religiously in an effort to avoid back problems and have never had any. Claiming the flu is too clichéd. West Nile

Virus is more original, but a stretch. Might I contract salmonella poisoning from improper handling of poultry? Or maybe I have the rash, fever, and crippling lethargy of Lyme disease from a tick infestation in the garden? No one would set foot on the property again without a certificate proving eradication from a licensed exterminator and clearance from county vector control.

Dalai and I make our loop through the winding streets. We arrive back at our doorstep and she still hasn't done her business. I open the gate and we head up the stairs.

I will claim the safe, predictable, universally vague and amorphous flu as my excuse for canceling, and gird myself to make the necessary calls. Kathleen is first on the list. I am poised at the den phone to punch in her number when Dalai scratches with a familiar urgency at the back door, demanding to be let out. I swing it open and she trots up the steps to the wall at the top of the garden, an anxious spot, as I never know what might be waiting for her there—maybe a coyote.

She begins barking, then screeches in agony, and I am out the door and running up the stairs. Before I see her I smell what she was barking at. She's been skunked. I find her in the pergola, wiping her snout on the chaise cushion and whimpering in pain. She's taken a direct hit in the face. This is bad enough, but even worse is her wiping her snout on the chaise cushion. I can't have it skunked for Saturday night.

Not if I'm going to do Saturday night.

I resolve on the spot, skunk fumes swirling about me, that I'm not giving up my garden to this skunk. I'm forging ahead full force. If I weren't already in the midst of planning a dinner party I would start to plan one, if only to prove to the skunk just who owns the place.

I go back to the house, grab a towel, and wrap Dalai in it. I carry her into the bathroom, where I poor an entire bottle of Skunk-Off down the length of her body, add a dose of dog shampoo, and work up a lather.

We keep a supply of Skunk-Off in the upstairs linen closet for just such occasions, which happen with surprising frequency. It is the most effective product we've encountered, better than tomato juice or Massengill powder douche, but it's hard to find. Considering the skunk population in this town, it should be sold alongside lottery tickets at the front counter of every gas station and 7-Eleven. Once bathed and dried, there is only a faint scent of skunk, the signature note being rotting onions, lingering on the dog's coat.

Dalai shakes herself free of excess water, spraying the bathroom walls and me, before I wrap her in a towel for a drying rubdown. Then I set her atop a folding wooden table and begin to dry her with the blow dryer. She dances around on the table, putting up with it only because she knows she won't get down until she's dry.

Canceling plans, I consider as the dryer flattens her fur to reveal the taut landscape of her square terrier body, might be why I don't feel a deeper connection to the larger world. I replaced the solid satisfaction of doing with the evanescent relief of foregoing. I did this because nothing mattered, nothing led to somewhere else, a better or different place inhabited by people I felt closer to or cared for more.

Dalai holds her head high, as if taking pride in having survived the dryer encounter or trying to rise above its indignity, then does a full body shake hard enough for me to fear the table's collapse. Her fur feels dry enough. I set her down on the floor and let her tear down the stairs to the living room.

The chaise cushion will now have to be shampooed and sun dried. But first I have to call Derek, the skunk trapper. It will be his season-opening visit. Derek is our skunk man because he claims he sets trapped skunks free in the San Gabriel Mountains, up behind the Jet Propulsion Laboratory in Pasadena. I can't handle the guilt of euthanizing them, so I leave it to the rocket scientists to figure out what to do with the little darlings. Maybe a space launch is the only permanent solution.

And yes, we have a professional trapper for our backyard, along with the bee man, a rodent wrangler, and two different termite companies on annual retainer, one for wood-eating termites and another for subterraneans. I handle the numerous ant invasions myself.

I do wonder if Derek really just lets the skunks go at the end of our street for the repeat trapping business. It seems as if they reestablish residency in our backyard in the amount of time it takes to walk a few blocks.

Derek insists they are different skunks. It is possible that when a den is vacated, another skunk family jumps on it. Such are the population pressures, human and non, in Southern California.

Derek says he'll be by tomorrow morning at about eleven o'clock. I know he'll call at eleven ten to say he's running late, and I won't see him before one thirty. He'll have only one day to trap the skunks, but that's better than no days. I go up to the garden with another bottle of Skunk-Off to relieve the lounge cushion of its new perfume. I consider that going through with the dinner party may help alleviate my personal stench of failure.

My mother knit a black woolen shawl while she was at the sanitarium. Row upon row of purl and knit stitches, not a single snag or run or slip of the needles. It looked like a well-plowed field on a moonless night. The shawl was at least fourteen feet long, much too long to be worn by any reasonable person. It was a shawl that didn't know when to stop.

She brought the shawl home from her last trip to the sanitarium. When Father left, she began to unravel it. She said it was so she could start another project, which she never did. It remained on a shelf in the hall closet, warm to hands inserted between its folds, until it was consumed loop by loop, disappearing by rows, taking its spongy dark comfort with it. Its space on the shelf was soon filled with the empty chow mein cans and family-size cereal boxes and egg cartons Mother took back to the grocery store.

She was obsessed with the fate of every object entering the house, and took all the packaging back to the store from which it came. I wondered if she wished she could take us back.

"Mother is nothing but a burned-out schizophrenic," Hunter said, as if it were common knowledge. It was the first time I'd ever heard it. We were driving to get her giant pink plastic curlers for making loose, floppy waves, instead of the tight, flippy kind. She said orange juice cans slipped off her head and the spike-covered store-boughts grabbed her hair and didn't let go. "Reach Out I'll Be There" was on the AM radio.

"Who says?"

"I heard a nurse talking."

Hunter heard all the most important stuff.

*T*hick bursts of bottle-green palms punctuated the delicate tracing of ferns that lined Steinhart Aquarium's alligator grotto. Coins shimmered up from the murk on the pond's black bottom as ashen light streamed through high windows.

My father gave me a penny. "Make a wish," he said. I tossed the coin into the pond and wished that Hunter, Hailey, and Mother were there. They weren't, and it was like something bad had happened but no one would talk about it. It was an invisible, secret bad, a bad that I couldn't see and feared might happen to me: Someday I wouldn't be here, either; I would be absent and unseen. The coin landed on the scored back of an alligator, its pudgy legs sticking out from its sides like one creature trapped in another, trying to escape.

"Your mother and I are getting a divorce," my father said.

A turtle swam up to the alligator's razor-toothed jaw. I wanted it to snap at the turtle and shake my coin off the alligator's back so it could fall into the pond with the other wishes. But the alligator didn't move. They never moved. I wrapped my hands around the grotto's black railing and stuck my tongue out to see if I could taste alligator in the thick, moist air.

"Did you hear me?"

"Yes," I said.

Howard said nothing.

We walked into the night depths of the aquarium and stopped at the lungfish display to watch their undulating bodies quiver in a silt-bottomed tank. I'd heard of lungfish at school. They buried themselves in the African mud and breathed oxygen through a tube that was part of their body, waiting out the drought until the rains returned to free them. Gurgling sounds came from wall speakers—

the language of fish, clicks and whirs, a language of assessment, like radar mapping the emptiness.

The sign above their case said they protected their territory, their eggs, and their offspring fiercely. But their tubular rubber bodies looked like they'd be easily torn.

I wondered, as I stared at these ancient remains in their putty-colored universe, who protected the protectors.

Physics defines a parent as a radioactive particle that must disintegrate to create a new particle. This new particle, called a nuclide, joins other nuclides as members of a radioactive decay series. These decaying particles emit energy, a form of familial warmth.

According to the chaos theory, members of a decay series soon begin to spin farther apart, losing energy as time and distance increase, entropy finally cooling them off as they settle into their far-flung places in the universe, a dark expanse dividing them from each other and what was once a vital part of themselves.

The dog's leash was coming undone and Mother's anger was rising from her belly, like steam from a blubbery cauldron, her expanded waist a monument to pregnancy and food. Mother held the dog's leash in her plump, white-gloved hand. She always wore gloves, as if to remain separate, untouched by her surroundings. She shook the leash at the shoe repairman's face.

"Why so much for just a few inches of stitching?" she demanded. "I stitch and no one pays me a cent!"

Wolf, my dog, and I stood on the sidewalk. Wolf was a Pekinese/dachshund mix, built like a padded footrest. His eyes bulged and he struggled to keep his chest off the ground when he walked. When he stood still, he panted and his pink tongue lapped at the side of his mouth like a tidepool flower. Hunter called him pathetic, said I should put a bag over his head. "It doesn't have to be plastic," she said. "Paper will do."

"If you don't like the price, throw it away," the shoe repairman said.

Castoffs would be charged to Mother's tax bill. Everything had a price, coming and going, when you bought and when you discarded.

"It's not right," she said, shaking the leash, her voice scraping at the shop's edges.

"Lady," the man said, stepping toward her, arms folded over his chest, "maybe you should take it someplace else."

Wolf growled and raised the dark slick of fur on his back.

"You can't do this," Mother said. Suddenly she was Susan Hayward pleading for her life. She jerked her arm from the man's touch and held her palms in the air as if her gloves were a surrender flag, as if she were under arrest.

Wolf started to bark and test his leash.

"My husband," Mother said, her face flushing red, "left me after *twenty years* of marriage and *four children*." Every conversation with a stranger ended up here. She said "four" accusingly, as if each successive child added to the insult. The fact was, Hailey moved out with Father. Mother was left with only three. I never mentioned this.

Her face looked like the dried plums we sucked while walking through Chinatown, their sweet ocean saltiness in the rising squall of her voice.

Wolf exploded in a rabid machine-gun volley of barks, snarling each time he stopped for air. I had to hold him with both hands.

There were no uniformed people with calming words to escort Mother to a waiting car. My father wasn't taking us to bounce on trampolines until this woman was gone, safely removed from the house, off for another long rest. Now it was just Mother and me, standing in front of the repair shop with Wolf, the odd dog, barking.

The man flung his arms, as if to push her away, and disappeared into the back of his shop. It smelled of leather, polish, sweat, and the gum he chewed.

"Go to hell," she said. "And tell my husband who sent you."

She clipped the fraying leash to Wolf's collar and folded my hand into hers. I felt her heat through the smooth cotton fibers of her glove. We walked to the bakery at the end of the row of shops, tied Wolf to a pillar, and went inside. The sign over the counter, its red painted letters carved into a white wood board, boasted they used REAL WHIPPED CREAM in all their baked goods, as if this were important and other bakeries lied.

We bought two authentic whipped cream and chocolate éclairs and ate them sitting on the bench across from the shop window, which was filled with meringue swans and buttercream tiered wedding cakes. Those cakes looked too good to be true. I thought they must be fakes, since the same ones had been in the window ever since I could remember. Or maybe someone might buy them if the bakery took the dead fly off the one's bottom ruffle of icing. "It's just sleeping," Mother said.

Mother peeled back the white pleated paper that kept chocolate from soiling her gloves and severed the pastry neatly with her teeth.

We ate our éclairs filled with real whipped cream in silence, then threw our trash in the bin like good citizens and set out for home. Wolf tugged on his leash, his chest dragging on the pavement. I reached for Mother's hand and the game began: She tapped my palm with her fingers, pattycake-style, for a ways, then finally slapped my hand away.

I decide I need an early taste of Saturday night and break open one of the evening's designated bottles. I give the wine thirty seconds to breathe before I take my first sip. The pinot noir is as lovely as the wine salesman said it would be—currants, raspberries, with an overlay of ripe plums. I settle in with a fresh baguette and a wedge of organic blue gouda cheese from Holland, a rare treat discovered in Whole Foods' cheese section, a delightful tangle of sweet fermented cream and silvery veins of aged mold, an exquisitely pungent molecular thicket. I sip the wine; I take a bite of the crisp-crusted bread and cheese. The setting sun casts the hill opposite our home in an amber glow. The sky darkens into the indigo of night; the lights of the houses across the way begin to sparkle.

I think of the first dinner party Somebody and I did together. We'd just started dating. It was April, and I proposed a dinner to commemorate the anniversary of the 1906 San Francisco earthquake. He was surviving a divorce, and I was surviving a crash landing back in California at the end of the long-term relationship that took me from college in San Francisco to New York.

The evening's menu came from *The Refugees' Cook Book*, published originally in 1906 to provide instruction for San Francisco residents turned refugees by the quake, many of whom lost their cookbooks in the disaster. My copy of *The Joy of Cooking*, an encyclopedic account of middle-class American gastronomy, had stayed with me throughout my postdisaster wanderings. That April I was back on my feet, tackling my first staff job on a newspaper, living in a modest Palo Alto apartment, and ready to crack open *The Joy* again.

I invited curly-haired Ted, another feature writer at the newspaper, and Elena, his exotic-looking new bride with the radiant smile; and Rafe, a lifestyle columnist for the paper, and his wife, Sheila, whose youthful charms were fading into a bittersweet middle age. He often wrote about her, as it was his first marriage and her second. She had an adolescent daughter always on the fringes of his concern and at the center of hers.

I served Spanish bean soup—a substantial concoction of beans, vegetables, and "a knuckle of ham about three pounds"— which was cooked, then strained to a velvet potage, finished with Madeira, and served with a classic touch of thinly sliced lemon and crouton. Next came oyster cocktails served in rakish green pepper cups. The main entrée was refugee stew, which I tweaked with red wine, garlic, and tomatoes and, for special effect, cooked in an institutional-size tin can over a charcoal grill on my apartment balcony. Dessert was peach crumble cooked in a Dutch oven over the same charcoal fire, with coals added to the lid to create the desired oven effect. I transformed my Palo Alto ledge into a postapocalyptic culinary adventure.

I remember the warm peach in its juices beneath the cinnamon sweet of the crumble, and that everyone, as far as I know, had a good time. Rafe and Sheila were heard to have words on their way out to the car; still, we all managed to get together for a Lake Tahoe ski weekend and I think at least one hiking adventure, before Ted left the paper for a corporate public relations job and Rafe was reassigned, shortly after a column graphically describing his vasectomy, to doing obituaries and the TV listings. Thanks to his vivid powers of description, I will forever see him sitting naked from the waist down on a stainless steel table with the fate of his family jewels literally in the doctor's hands. I have lost track of Ted and Elena. They probably have children in their late teenage years by now. I do know that Rafe eventually divorced Sheila, but I don't know if he's still in journalism, or even writing.

I considered it my unsinkable meal.

As Somebody stood by my side in the kitchen, scrubbing pots, I told him of my personal earthquake, how I'd returned to California from New York for a book project I thought would save my life as a writer, but that nearly ended it instead. I spared him most of the details.

*I*t was in the emergency room of a hospital outside Salt Lake City, Utah, when they asked me to sign the papers to be admitted for psychiatric observation, that I considered the possibility that this had been Mother's fundamental mistake—once a mental patient, always a mental patient. Somewhere along the line, she'd signed the papers. And her gift to me at that moment: Don't trust doctors.

Yes, there were bruises on my torso, just below my breasts, that came from I didn't know where. Yes, I'd just woken in the middle of the night in a motel room and witnessed, or so I thought—because really, you can never be sure of these things just because you've personally witnessed them—that my soul had left my body. It hovered in the corner of the room with the cottage cheese ceiling and the print of a painting of Little Bo Peep (or someone who looked suspiciously like her) and some sheep (and who would bother to make a print of such a thing, or paint it in the first place, for that matter?), and then it came back to where it, my soul, belonged, inhabiting my body. And yes, I didn't tell the doctors that because they were so busy—and that was back in the day, before doctors were as impossibly busy as they are now (why, now you can writhe on the emergency room floor in agony, begging for attention while a janitor mops around you, and no one will come near you except the police, and then only to run your name through the system to discover you're wanted for traffic tickets, so they'll handcuff you and lead you out to the patrol car to take you downtown for booking, only you die before they can shut the door, and still no doctors have come to deal with the pain that, surprise, surprise, just killed you)—even if they had heard me correctly, what could they possibly have done? Mother had taught me that. What could the doctors possibly do? Get me a shaman, a midwife, a wet nurse, an appliance repairman. These were only, after all, doctors, and there really was only so much they could do.

Yes, there was the young man who'd been driving me to Montana to see my friends, the poet and the writer, because I was in no condition to fly, as I was losing track, was off track, or had jumped the tracks. All I knew for sure was that doctors weren't the only thing I couldn't trust; suddenly I couldn't trust my senses, anything I saw, smelled, or tasted. And everything held great meaning and portent: the numbers on the motel room door, the hawk wheeling circles in the sky above me as I lay on the grass, all held the key to the universe in that exact moment. Then the phones stopped working. I could no longer summon familiar voices, my fingers couldn't punch the buttons, I'd forgotten the mechanics, I couldn't find the right combination of levers and lifting to even get a dial tone.

I had been working on a book about the Jonestown suicides, the story of a Bay Area family that drank the poisoned Kool-Aid with the rest of the cult. I mean, who wasn't writing a book about that? That was, after all, what writers did: write books about mass insanity followed by group suicide. That's a writer's job, to make sense of that stuff. I was only doing my job. Then, suddenly, I was driving to Montana with a young man I'd only just met, drinking straight from a tequila bottle—a lovely parting gift from the author I'd been assisting, who had started to bounce my paychecks before my senses gave out—and singing, "Que sera, sera, whatever will be, will be."

I told the doctors in the emergency room in Utah, just outside Salt Lake City, in the middle of the night on my way to Montana, that I was a writer. I would keep my stories for the page.

They gave me Thorazine and Haldol for the rest of the ride. I watched a Three Stooges film on the emergency room television as I waited for the prescriptions to be filled. Curly, Mo, and Larry's inability to move a ladder across a room without hitting each other seemed shockingly profound.

In Montana I checked into the town's lone hospital, a place where all the workers were wearing costumes. A parade of space aliens, cats, and witches walked past my bed. I'd never stayed in a hospital before, and I considered these conditions normal. Then I remembered it was Halloween. I stayed just one night.

My friends hosted me through Thanksgiving. I stayed in the guest room of their shotgun shack, the room they dubbed, in my honor, the Bug House Suite, the room with the bullet holes in the hollow-core door. We cooked a turkey according to Julia Child's instructions. I got back to the Bay Area, got off the Haldol and Thorazine, got a staff job on a newspaper where the deadlines and paychecks just flowed.

And yes, *yes*, que sera, sera.

I pour the last of Saturday night's pinot noir into the proper balloon glass for red wine and admire the bell's clarity, take pleasure in the starry glint of kitchen light off its curves, its ruby coloration. I finger-ping a crystal *clink*. All seems right with the world. I am a solo sybarite spinning gleefully in my private universe of pleasure.

If Somebody doesn't arrive until Saturday, Carlotta and I can get the evening off the ground. We are survivors.

I see the empty bottle on the counter and realize I will need to buy another, maybe tomorrow, after the skunk trapper comes. This perfect moment could be improved only with a Jacuzzi before bed. I carry the last glass of wine into the bathroom. My foot catches on the bunched-up corner of the throw rug and I lurch violently toward the tub. The delicate wine glass becomes a high-speed projectile spewing red across the bathroom's wood-paneled walls. I consider the challenges of getting the stain out in the instant before my left hand lands on the Jacuzzi spout. When my body comes to rest, I feel the gash across my wrist before I see the busted-off spigot in my hand. I grab a washcloth and wrap my arm in it to stop the blood's flow. Dalai stands with her tail wagging tentatively at the door. She cares enough to come see what's happened, but puts her head down to make it clear there's nothing she can do about it.

The spigot has permanently parted company with its base. I see the jagged and rusty metal protrusion that slashed my wrist. I get out a roll of gauze and dress my wound, then take spray cleaner and a sponge to the paneling. When I'm done there's only a faint pink, an abstract expressionist trace left of the spectacularly plummy wine's final stand. I carefully pick up the largest pieces of the shattered glass and get the rest with a brush and dustpan. Dalai maintains her position at the bathroom door, greeting my passage with a tail wag and a sniff, but never entering the room itself, as if content to supervise.

I reach for a last consoling bite of bread and cheese from the dining room table. Lula, the cat, has beaten me to it. I carry the remaining dishes into the kitchen, where I leave them for the morning, a last ignoble act of irresponsibility.

I stand at the upstairs bathroom sink and look at myself in the mirror. The accident has had a sobering effect. I now regret the last three glasses of wine. My right eyelid has started to sag and my face looks puffy and swollen from the alcohol, an increasing hazard of overindulging with advancing age. I'll be foggy-headed, splotchy-skinned, red-eyed, and paying for this in the morning.

But it was such a complex, sophisticated, and delicious wine—a raspberry poem in a bottle! Or maybe, just possibly, it was a raspberry of the Bronx appellation. An excuse, a glorious escape and deliverance from the daily trials of the world in which we live, a loud, honking, finger-flapping, thumb-to-nose momentary pause to refresh; a full-bodied, well-balanced reboot of my system. I would sleep perchance to dream and see if I couldn't figure it out from there.

Refugee Stew[1]

(from *The Refugees' Cook Book,* Compiled by One of Them, 1906)

Take 3 pounds of round of beef cut in medium-size pieces; take 2 good sized onions and fry brown in beef drippings; fry meat, after sprinkling with flour, in the onions very brown, turning frequently; put it in a stew kettle and cover with boiling water; let cook very slowly 3 hours, adding boiling water as it cooks down; an hour before serving add 3 carrots, 3 turnips, potatoes, parsnip, parsley, bay leaf; thicken it with ½ cup of flour and a teaspoon of caramel; be very careful not to burn; don't use cold water or too much grease.

---

1 This is a fine, traditional beef stew recipe lacking only in the basic seasonings of salt and pepper. I don't know if that's because those were lost in the rubble or One of Them was sufficiently distracted by the challenge of rebuilding San Francisco and compiling a cookbook, that they forgot to put it in. Either way, you will want to salt this to taste and pepper it too, if so inclined.

Chapter 16

SARGASSO SEA

"If anything happens to Mother," Hunter said, as cars made left turns in front of us on the green arrow while we waited to cross the intersection, "Uncle Garland and Aunt Hennie won't have anything to do with us."

"So?" I didn't know what else to say. I never thought anything would happen to Mother. She didn't leave her room or the house often enough to let anything happen to her.

"Yeah, *soo*."

"How do you know?"

"I heard them talking."

She had a knack for hearing all the best stuff, or maybe it was a talent, like perfect pitch or drawing a straight line without using a ruler.

A skinny lady in a dark hat and close-fitting suit came to take Shirley Temple away from the blind grandfather, who let her sleep in a loft filled with hay that looked out onto the snow-covered Alps. Last time it was a tap-dancing black man she couldn't live with anymore. This woman said an orphanage was the best place for a young lady to grow up. Shirley Temple started crying and tugging to get away from the woman, but the woman didn't let go. If that woman ever knocked on our door, I was going to pull real hard like Shirley Temple, but I wouldn't cry. I just wanted to see what it felt like to not be let go.

"Then what?"

"What what?"

"What happens if Aunt Hennie and Uncle Garland won't have anything to do with us?"

"How am I supposed to know?"

M other's voice bubbled up, light as a French schoolgirl's, from behind her closed bedroom door. "*Entrez*," she said.

She was propped against bed pillows as she lay beneath a frayed patchwork quilt, her head wreathed in cigarette smoke. She looked up from the *Ladies' Home Journal* that lay across her lap like an anchor pinning her to the bed.

"*Bon soir*," she said.

I'd come to visit the baby clothes—the quilted satin jacket, knit cap, and booties Mother kept folded in the top dresser drawer. At least, she said they were baby clothes, but they were so clean and spotless, and babies were so messy. I thought of them as Mother's doll clothes, even though she had no dolls. They were hand-stitched by one of the grandmothers—the dead one, the living one . . . it was always a different story. They were folded and polite on top of each other, waiting to be worn, maybe by the children who would arrive with the right life.

I put the peach-colored satin jacket on my baby doll, something I could only do in Mother's room while she was watching, because she was afraid someone was going to ruin the few nice things she had left. I imagined the jacket's snug reassurance around my shoulders, how the lavender-scented satin would feel on my arms.

Mother kept a cedar chest, which she had once called a hope chest, next to her bed, where she kept her wedding gown and a rumpled clutch of thin summer dresses. These were made of diaphanous floral prints that fluttered beneath my breath, with rolled, hand-stitched hems, made-to-order dresses. My fingers felt ugly and thick when I held them by their delicate shoulder straps and tried to imagine Mother wearing anything so slim, light, and unfettered.

I couldn't get fat like Mother because I wanted to wear these dresses when I was old enough, so she could be happy to see her daughter succeed where she'd failed. She never said she wanted me to wear them, but didn't every mother want that for her daughter? Why else would she keep them? And if she'd kept them because she was crazy, I'd ignore her; I'd save the clothes from her craziness by wearing them, even if I couldn't save her.

A two-story, peaked-roof doll's house the dead grandfather built sat on top of the chest. Its outer walls were missing, like on a house ripped apart and torn off its foundation by a tornado. Mother stored junk in it. Balled-up socks to darn were stuffed in the upstairs bedrooms, and a pair of scissors protected the dog biscuits and tortoiseshell comb on the living room floor. A box of gold-edged thank-you cards crowded the dining room, untouched since Mother had stopped going anywhere, writing anyone, or saying thank you. The house looked like the place Alice fled after she began to grow big and had to escape before being crushed.

"It's time you went to bed," Mother said.

I slipped the satin jacket off my doll, put it back in the drawer, thought of the lungfish suspended in the jellied earth, and said good night before I closed the door.

We lived in a bedroom community. I thought that was the reason Mother slept so much and encouraged us to do the same. If I didn't wake in time for school, she didn't bother me and I went late or not at all.

At school they said to listen to your dreams. If you listened to your dreams and set your mind to it, you could be anything you wanted to be; you could even grow up to be president. I thought this was easier to do in a bedroom community, where we had more dreams to listen to. It was okay when I didn't go to school, as long as I listened to my dreams while I was at home. It was easier to listen to my dreams at home. It was quieter there and I could hear them better. I liked best of all to sit up in the apricot tree, watch the light filtered through the lime-colored leaves, and swing my feet high above the scabby remains of our lawn while I dreamed my dreams of fixing Mother.

"Don't ever eat fruit cocktail again," Hunter warned ominously when she came home from her second and last day working at the Del Monte canning factory in Hayward. "You have no idea what goes into it!" she said, pulling a hairnet out of her purse and throwing it in the wastebasket. "And believe me, you don't want to know."

She dreamed of becoming a model, and used her only Del Monte paycheck to pay for a portfolio of photographs of herself in different poses. There were shots of her in thigh-high boots and a miniskirt with her hands on her hips, her right leg straight, left leg forward, like she was in charge and about to take a big step. She looked like a female executive in another, dressed in a houndstooth-check pantsuit. There were close-up photos of her freckled face where she sucked in her cheeks to look gaunt, and the ends of her batwing eyeliner lined up perfectly with the swing of her geometric haircut. She got hired to model underwear during lunchtime fashion shows in the golf course restaurant at the edge of town.

"It's the edge closest to San Francisco," she said. "So it's a start."

"I'm not going," Howard said.

He was still in his pajamas. Cartoons were on. We had fallen asleep on the TV Room couches. There were two, fanning out like gurneys from a low table wedged into the corner.

I'd lain down on the couch the night before while I waited for the pan of penuche fudge I'd made to set. I didn't know what penuche fudge was, except that it didn't require chocolate, which we didn't have—only brown sugar, which we had too much of. I'd cooked the brown sugar and butter until the soft-ball stage, like the cookbook said, then poured it into the cake pan I used for chocolate fudge. It tasted like brown sugar, raw and too sweet, and I hoped that when it set it would taste better, closer to caramel if it couldn't be chocolate fudge.

Howard and I had watched *Sing Along with Mitch*.

Both of us, without looking at each other, joined in on "You Are My Sunshine" and a couple of other, even cornier songs. We didn't want to but we couldn't help it, and it made me feel kind of sick and good at the same time while we did it. Then we fell asleep.

Mitch was gone when I woke up. It was still dark out, and there was a test pattern on the black-and-white TV screen and the painful sound of a high, piercing hum. I turned it off and went to bed. Howard slept all night on the couch. I tested my penuche fudge when I got up, and it still tasted like cold, cooked brown sugar and congealed butter, far from caramel and not even remotely akin to chocolate. Wherever penuche came from, it was a land of permanently lowered expectations and chronic making do. The recipe should have come with a warning to only make it if desperate for a sweet and there were no better ingredients on hand. Next time I'd know better. I'd march to the store for the chocolate and make the right kind of fudge. That was my penuche lesson.

"He's taking us both," I said.

"I'm not going."

"What'll I tell him?"

"I'm working on my pond."

Howard was digging a hole in the backyard. He'd started it after we got back from the aquarium. He said he was going to fill it with water and stock it with trout and charge the neighbor kids to go fishing. He said he wanted to make enough money to buy locks for his bedroom door. "So I can keep my crummy sisters out." We'd already broken the lock on his desk drawer. That was how we found his stash of bodybuilding magazines. On a notepad he wrote out what his measurements were and what he wanted them to be, and how many push-ups and sit-ups and jumping jacks he had to do to get there. We kidded him about it until he got mad and broke my plastic palomino horse, the one I built from a kit I bought at the five-and-dime in the Shopping Village. He grabbed it off the shelf, where it was prancing with the others, and smashed it on the TV Room's linoleum floor.

"You tell him," I said.

"I hate sailing," he said, rolling off the couch. The way he said it sounded as if he might cry.

*I*n school I was writing a report on the Sargasso Sea. It was a sea within the Caribbean Sea, defined by unusually calm waters and the presence of a weed. According to the encyclopedia, it stretched toward Europe and south to Latin America and was considered within but separate from the Atlantic Ocean. I couldn't imagine the Caribbean or the Atlantic, let alone the Sargasso Sea. The Caribbean was warm, but I couldn't conceive of a warm ocean. All I knew was an expanse of slate blue wild with chop, a chill mist stinging my cheeks, the San Francisco Bay from my father's sailboat.

The Sargasso kelp weeds, bits torn from kelp forests along the coasts of the land and carried there by the currents, made this "pooling place" a sea. Along with the weeds came the creatures clinging to them when they were ripped from the shore. These animals hung on for their lives, suspended miles above the ocean floor, unable to swim home. If they let go, they would sink until they were crushed by the pressure of the water above.

They adapted, grew stronger and more intricate claws for grasping. The crabs are the most extreme. They changed their color from pink to brown-green and their bodies became pointed and ribbed like the Sargasso leaves. Even their eyes changed, stretching out on tubular lengths to imitate the air-filled bulbs that kept the Sargasso weeds afloat.

I thought of the crabs with their stem-and-balloon eyes watching for food and predators, a rippled, glassine layer of water surging overhead. They clung to almond flat leaves the color of burnt butter and mildew on glass. Everything familiar was no longer within reach. No shifting, sandy bottom for footing. One could know the swell of the current but lose touch with the pull of the tide, the sure sweep of the day's rhythms, anything close to solid land. You could find yourself in a sea within a sea, surrounded by a vast ocean, with nothing to hold you aloft save for a loose knit of flesh and weed. You could only sense the sea bottom, littered with splintered skeletons. Light passed through the water, but there was nothing to catch a reflection. In this pooling place, fear was the only thing that kept them afloat.

"Come about," my father shouted, and Howard and I pulled on the jib line as we ducked under the swinging boom. It was Sunday on the San Francisco Bay and the sailboat was heeling hard, the frigid spray slapping my cheeks red and slick. With each smash of the bow, the cabin's front windows sunk underwater. Mrs. Yacksloff sat below, trying to concentrate on her *Reader's Digest*. I was scared the waves would punch the windows open, flood the cabin, and sink the boat, drowning us all.

"Geo-*urge!*" she called out to my father.

"Ah, geez," he said, before letting the tension out of the sails. The boat stopped leaning so hard; the windows rose, as if by some miracle, from the water; and we could all sit normally again, without standing up, our legs stiff and backs braced against the side of the boat. We glided over instead of punched through the waves.

My father let me steer because Howard didn't want to. "Just fix the tip of the bow on a point on the horizon and head straight for it," he told me. The tiller tugged and wanted to leap from my hands, then I relaxed into the rhythmic pull and release of the waves and wind. I thought of things I wanted to say to him, but I didn't because I knew he wouldn't hear me above the wind.

We dropped anchor in Angel Island's Hospital Cove.

Mrs. Yacksloff passed around the tuna sandwiches she'd made. They were good, thick with mayonnaise and flecked with sweet bits of pickle relish. It made me think about calling her Yvonne.

"Don't sail like such a wild man," she told my father.

"That's the fun."

"It frightens the children," she said.

"It's good for them," he said.

"I don't like it," she said.

"Then I'll take it easy when you're along," he said.

She gave a puckered smile and passed around a box of Safeway powdered-sugar donuts. Seagulls dove for the loose sugar and crumbs that fell like snow as I held the empty box to the breeze. It was like winter in summer. People waved hello from the deck of a passing cabin cruiser. Howard flailed his arms back at them crazily, as if signaling for help.

It wasn't until I started to fall asleep on the drive home that I remembered what it was I wanted to ask my father when we were on the boat. I wanted to ask him if I could come live with him. Just for a while. Or if that was too long, maybe for just a few nights. We could sit at the dinette table in his apartment kitchen and play Rock, Paper, Scissors, like we used to. I'd be the rock and hope that he'd be paper, so I could feel his hand wrap around my fist.

But then I wondered if I asked him the wrong thing, maybe I'd never see him again. The car's window was cool against my cheek as I let the drowsiness seep in. I didn't wake until my head bumped against the door as we crossed the court's drainage ditch. My father pulled up in front of the house and let us out. He didn't walk us to the door because Mother got mad if she saw him. Howard tore up the walkway without saying goodbye. I stood on the ratty front lawn and waved at the back of the car carrying my father and Yvonne— Mrs. Yacksloff—as it disappeared around the corner.

Hunter hated Mrs. Yacksloff. She said she would never call her Yvonne.

"She drinks beer from a can," she sniffed. "Whores drink beer from a can."

I slather night cream on in preparation for bed when the phone rings. I smooth the last white slick of cream into my gleaming, responsibly moisturized cheek and stand staring at the phone. I let the machine pick up.

"Hellooooooaaaaaahhhhh!" It's Hunter.

I interrupt the message she's in the midst of leaving.

"It's eleven o'clock," I say.

"Is it? I'm sorry."

"Is something wrong with Mother?" I hiccup violently.

"Mother? No. Have you been drinking?"

"No," I say, sucking in air in an attempt to make the hiccups stop.

"You've been drinking."

"I've got the hiccups. Why did you call?"

"Where's your husband?"

"He's wo—*hic*—oorking—*cup*."

I sit down to stop the room from swaying and hold my breath to stop hiccuping. I press my fingers to the bandage on my wrist to stop the pain of my wound.

"I called to say I was coming by about two on Saturday. If that doesn't work for you, I'll just leave your 'present' on the deck." I cringe at the way she says "present" with amused, ironic quotes around it. Could she be bringing a Hickory Farms cheddar cheese ball Mother saved from some mid-'60s holiday gift basket? Or maybe it's a lifetime supply of well-worn, yellowed-with-age white cotton gloves.

"Teeeerrrific," I say.

"I don't have to come," she says.

"Nooooooooo, I want you to!" I laugh at this. Nothing has struck me as this funny in a very long time.

"I'll see you Saturday. Get some coffee."

She hangs up.

"Then you won't be staying for dinner?" I say into the dead line.

*T*he world stops reeling after a double shot of espresso and half an extra-dark chocolate bar. The phone rings. It's now midnight.

"Don't cancel the dinner party."

Somebody is calling from New York.

"It's 3:00 AM. Go to sleep."

"I can't."

"Take an Ambien."

"I did. It didn't help. I'm too upset."

"About the dinner party? You didn't want to have it anyway."

"I want you to be happy. I want you to do the dinner party. You've put all this effort into it."

I realize he is possibly the only person on Earth concerned with my happiness, especially at 3:00 AM in New York. If it were earlier and I weren't so exhausted, I'd consider it sweet. I wonder if our marriage exists outside these moments of concern. I wonder if it can.

"I haven't canceled. No sirree!"

"Are you drunk?"

"I had a lovely pinot noir and I am *soooo* very fine."

"I'm coming home early."

"The skunks are back."

"What happened?"

"They got Dalai."

"How's she doing?"

"One bottle of Skunk-Off down, and she's resting comfortably."
I check the blood blossoming on the gauze over my wrist wound.

"And Hunter?"

"Saturday afternoon ETA."

"I'll try to be home Friday evening."

"I'll see you when you get here."

"I love you."

"Get some sleep."

I had the *McCall's* cookbook open on the tiled kitchen countertop and was following directions for making cream puffs. I had cooked a dough of milk, sugar, butter, and flour in the double boiler and was now beating in one egg at a time. The oven was heating as I worked. While the puffs were baking I would whip a container of heavy cream and make a chocolate glaze to drizzle over the top.

"Guess what I heard," Hunter said, in that teasing tone that meant the answer was going to cost me something. She dipped a finger into the chocolate I had melted for the glaze in an upside-down lid over hot water in another saucepan. We only had one double boiler and this called for two, so I improvised.

"I don't know," I said. If I acted like I didn't care, maybe she'd get bored and tell me without my getting into debt, but I doubted it. I kept stirring in the eggs, one at a time, with a wooden spoon, watching the dough develop a satiny sheen and a warm yellow color from the yolks.

"Guess!"

"I don't want to."

"It's about Dad."

"Is he sick?" She'd gotten me to guess. I stopped beating.

"It'll cost you."

"Was he in an accident?" I couldn't stop guessing. I had to know. My dough started to brown and stick to the side of the double boiler.

"Give me a book of stamps and I'll tell you."

I had almost enough Blue Chip Savings Stamps to get the Sunbeam electric skillet I wanted for braising inexpensive cuts of meat in until they were fork-tender. If I gave her a book it would take another month of trips to East Hills Market until I had enough books for the skillet. Still, I had to know. There was no escape with Hunter. I turned off the heat under my dough and went to my room to fish a book out from the stash I kept in the drawer under my bed.

She was licking a spoon dipped in the melted chocolate and rolling her eyes ecstatically up into her head when I returned to the kitchen and handed her the book. "Thanks," she said. "Now I've got enough for my bonnet hair dryer." She wanted the one that, according to the TV commercials, was quiet enough to talk to your boyfriend on the phone while you dried your hair. "I'll let you use it," she said. "If you're lucky."

"Tell me what you heard," I said.

"Dad married the whore," she said, thumbing through the book to check that all the pages were full.

"Who?"

"Mrs. Yacksloff."

"Who told you?"

"Brenda. She heard at school."

The cream puffs came out flat and rubbery instead of puffed and filled with air. I should never have stopped beating in the eggs or turned off the heat to get Hunter the book of stamps.

I wanted my stamps back; I didn't want to know what she had heard.

*T*he accident and espresso have canceled the wine's soporific promise. I lie awake in bed, staring at the peeling clapboard ceiling cross-laid with sloppily stained beams that no painter will touch for less than several thousand dollars and a week's worth of sanding in the middle of our bedroom. I wonder why all my social efforts involve so many complications and extenuating circumstances. Why can't I just press a button and have a few people come over, commune, and go home? Why can't life be like TV? Why can't there be a script—or at least known rules, an identifiable social hierarchy, dynastic protocols, or visible community requirements—to force attendance at a social event, at *my* social event?

Everyone in this day and age has got an airtight alibi, a legitimate and perfectly plausible excuse, even a lie, if need be. It's all legal when it comes to arranging one's social life. Ours is a duty-free civilization. Pity the poor hostess such as I, trying to fill a room. One must be clever and calculating from the outset, extending invitations that reveal a tantalizing tease of information designed to hook a reluctant guest. Less is more when inviting. Keep it mysterious, casual; start your dance with seven veils and drop them at a deliberate pace. Never state the obvious: "We're hoping to validate our continued existence on the planet with proof that we still have a few friends."

Why can't we be like the Javanese? All adult male villagers in Java are required to attend what is called a *slametan*. An invitation comes without warning—there is no time to find something better to do or conjure excuses why one can't go. A host doesn't even issue a summons until the food is on the table. The men must drop whatever they are doing and help the host achieve *slamet*, a kind of spiritual equilibrium. Women stay in the kitchen cooking, experiencing what I imagine to be their own form of grace.

The host calls a *slametan* for any reason—a death in the family, a wedding, a birth, or even just a bad dream. Guests come, the host tells them his problem, they pray, they eat for five minutes. Then they leave, taking leftover food back to their families. The party's over before it began, and everyone's needs are met—the host's to celebrate, the guests' to barely be there.

In my next life I want to return as a Javanese man.

Sayur Lodeh
(Indonesian Vegetables in Coconut Curry)

3 tbsp. oil

2–3 cloves garlic, minced

2 tsp. minced fresh gingerroot

1–3 chili peppers, sliced

1 stalk lemongrass (white part only), minced

1 tsp. ground coriander

½ tsp. turmeric

2 cups coconut milk

1 potato, peeled and diced

1 carrot, peeled and sliced

1 cup green beans

1 onion, thinly sliced

1 cup chopped Chinese or Napa cabbage

2–3 scallions, cut in 1-inch pieces

Salt and pepper to taste

Heat the oil in a large saucepan or wok over a medium flame. Toss into this the garlic, ginger, chili pepper, lemongrass, coriander, and turmeric and stir-fry for a few minutes. Pour in the coconut milk and bring to a boil. Add the potato, carrot, green beans, and onion to the pan and mix it all together. Cover the pan and lower the heat to a simmer, cooking about 10 minutes, until the potatoes are almost cooked. Add cabbage, scallions, and salt and pepper and continue to simmer another 2–3 minutes until the cabbage is tender. Be inventive with the kinds of vegetables you use and add some cubed firm tofu, cubed cooked chicken, or shrimp (at the end, with the cabbage) for protein. Serve the curry with traditional Javanese yellow rice (rice cooked in coconut milk, turmeric, and lemongrass) or a white rice, like jasmine or basmati.

Chapter 17

AN ARMY OF GINGERBREAD MEN

Stuffing tumbled out of the turkey's cavity like kapok from a slashed mattress. "Never again!" Mother hissed. Melting ice crystals dripped from beneath the turkey's wings. Uncle Garland and Aunt Hennie were coming for the last Thanksgiving that Mother would cook, the last Thanksgiving we celebrated as a family. Hunter had Thanksgiving with Brenda's family. She disliked Garland and Hennie.

"They're so middle-class," she said, rolling her eyes. There was no greater sin in Hunter's book, unless it was being boring. Hunter considered Garland and Hennie to be both.

Dried bread and celery bits clung to Mother's fingers, jammed into the wedding ring she refused to take off. The center diamond, the size of a spring hailstone, had yet to disappear into the garden, where she worked with her bare hands, kneading the raw garbage into the soil to amend it with beneficial nutrients, or so she claimed. As far as we could tell, it most benefited the garbage man, who rarely had anything to haul out of our can on his weekly rounds. Mother would wear the ring long after the largest diamonds had disappeared, until arthritis's swelling forced a technician to cut it off her finger in the emergency room when she suffered her first heart attack.

"Where's my trussing kit?" she groused. "If you were playing with it, I'll slap you silly."

Mother always threatened to slap us silly. We imagined this meant until we started acting goofy, like cartoon characters. If it weren't such a ridiculous idea, we might have been afraid. I went back to watching the Macy's parade on TV. The Snoopy balloon was snagged in a streetlight, and all the people trying to pull him free looked like Lilliputians from *Gulliver's Travels*.

We had bought the turkey, frozen and big as a toddler, two days before at East Hills Market. The butcher had warned us it wouldn't defrost by Thanksgiving, but the fresh birds cost more. Mother wrestled the biggest bird she could find to the top of the pile and dropped it into the basket with such a thud, I looked to see if it had bent the wire bottom. She held the shopping list in her hand, as if she feared it might disappear like the lost parts of her mind. We walked with a heaping basket of bagged groceries out to the car, where Hunter sat flipping through the December issue of *Glamour* magazine, and Mother had to go back in to get "the damned celery."

*W*e all sat at the table Mother had set first thing Thanksgiving morning with her good white damask cloth and all the wedding gift china, the etched crystal goblets, and the silver, too. With a flickering smile of accomplishment, Mother brought to the table the bird, roasted to a golden-mahogany sheen. "I think it should be done," she said, but when Uncle Garland sliced into the turkey's breast, the juices ran red with turkey blood.

Mother's face fell into a tightened mask of disappointment as she shoved the platter back into the rapidly cooling oven. We ate the other dishes, had our pie—pumpkin or mincemeat, as always—and soon stood in the driveway, waving at Garland and Hennie's departing car.

In the morning I discovered where Mother had dug the turkey into the dark clumps of soil near the fence in the far corner of the yard. Neighborhood cats, tails twitching as they scratched at the pink and bloody carcass, marked the site. A carving fork was still embedded in its congealed breast. The shattered white Haviland china serving platter with the gold painted rim, the centerpiece of the wedding set, bubbled up from the ground as if regurgitated by the earth.

*M*other answered the phone in the musical voice of a young girl, only more so than usual, as if bursting with energy, as if running to catch the phone on the fly. She'd just had the most *mar*-velous meal—turkey—and what is that sauce you have with it? Yes, cranberry. And the stuffing was so good, she took bites from the plates of others who left the table without finishing it all. Can you imagine not finishing it all? And dessert was some kind of pie with sauce. "Delicious!" she said with a grand flourish.

She no longer remembered the names of the dishes whose recipes were once etched in her mind, along with the shopping list of required ingredients—only how much she'd enjoyed the meal, whatever it was. She was ebullient, thankful to be alive, having sat at the table with the other five residents of the board and care home—"the girls," she called them, all of them older, most in their nineties. She was only eighty-five and the sole resident still capable of producing coherent sentences, though that ability was beginning to slide. I said good night—she never cares to talk long—and I had my own holiday meal to make: braised pork tenderloin in pomegranate sauce.

I don't eat turkey. Not because they're so dumb that when it rains, the entire flock looks up to see where the water is coming from and drowns. And not because modern turkeys are forced to grow so fast and big that their huge breasts and weak legs prevent them from moving. I don't eat turkey because the L-tryptophan in their meat puts me to sleep.

The Average American, I recently read, is eating more turkey now than ever before. According to the U.S. Census Bureau, the Typical American consumed 13.7 pounds of this mildly sedating meat in 2003. This is a 69 percent rise from the 8.1 pounds consumed in 1980, a fact I take to mean that the country as a whole has an increasingly greater need for tranquilization during the holidays. Who wouldn't want another nice slice of L-tryptophan-laced white meat when you find yourself every year, on the fourth Thursday of November, sitting around a table filled with relatives because you believe family is all you've got? L-tryptophan is a requirement, along with alcohol, at any properly laden holiday table, a way to get some distance from the close confines of the familial embrace.

While I don't do Thanksgiving myself, I do like to shop the day before. It's one of the finest days of the year for clamorous crowds, a splendid opportunity for making one feel useful and connected to the world, even if it is to strangers and only in passing. I push my cart through the store, enjoying the physical contact of glancing off other shoppers, apologizing all the while even if I have done it on purpose. Then I plant myself next to the potato bins, specifically to aid neophytes puzzling over the best tubers for mashing (I prefer Yukon gold with the peels on, but tradition dictates peeled russets, if you're a slave to those things). Next, I scout the store for trussing kits so I can rescue lost souls in search of them. No one ever knows where to find the trussing kits.

"And don't forget the miniature marshmallows for your baked sweet potatoes," I'll urge after they speed their baskets down the aisle. They'll look back with a nod and a wave, as if thankful for the tip, when truth is, it's my way of taunting them for their cowlike observation of tradition.

I do this in lieu of an actual family encounter, or pulling together a group of friends, an impossible proposition for the noncelebrity, a member of the disconnected minions, in L.A. One of the many clichés and fundamental beliefs about Los Angeles is that everyone is really an actor, whether they're waiting tables, parking cars, or teaching students. This is the one day a year for my greatest public performance: as the happy homemaker who enjoys helping people, a foodie action figure, savior to confused cooks and paralyzed palates. It's all the social fix I need to get me through the holiday. I will braise a pork loin in pomegranate sauce for Somebody and me.

We'll have a nice salad, some couscous. Watch a little TV. Go to sleep early and check another major holiday off the annual list.

"*I* won't be doing Christmas this year," Mother said.

Only dead people didn't do Christmas, and even then they came back from the grave to show the living how it should be done, like in Dickens's *A Christmas Carol*, the old black-and-white film with the British people in it I watched every year on TV. So only extra-especially dead, completely and totally nonexistent people, didn't do Christmas. If you didn't have money, you made gifts; if you were separated from your family you left the battlefront, ignored the snow, escaped the collapsed coal mine, and crawled bleeding on your hands and knees to commune by the fire with children who were crippled or terminally ill, and you did it because these children might not be around next year. You held hands and counted blessings and gathered strength to face the future.

"So don't get me any gifts," Mother said.

I baked an army of gingerbread men in retaliation. I mounted the assault to lure her back to her senses with a warm embrace of ginger, cinnamon, and molasses. The recipe came from the *McCall's* cookbook with the tired green cloth cover, faded with age, spotted from use, its spine cracked in multiple places, separating from its binding far enough for a finger to slip in and feel the rough edges of failed glue and thread that had once held it together.

I struggled to get the dough's consistency right, the proper ratio of wet to dry ingredients so it didn't stick to my hands, the board, the rolling pin. I discovered the power of flattening things, the satisfaction of reducing a softball-size lump of dough into a thin, circular expanse to cut into the shape of my desires. I left the oven light on and watched the men rise and plump and come to be.

I spread my army across cooling racks on the dining room table, where I outlined their limbs with red and green icing. Multicolored, ruffled cuffs and collars made some Caribbean, others wore button-down business suits and ties, while spotted animal skins draped the fronts of my wild men from Borneo. I thought of cannibals as I ate them, how they dined on their warrior victims to gain their strength; or hunters who believed they ate the bear's and the tiger's courage when they dined on their flesh. The cookies smelled and tasted to me of Christmas, and I would have my Christmas by eating them.

*I*f Mother tasted my army she didn't tell me. And she didn't change her mind about Christmas.

I ate them until I was sick, until my stomach was full to bursting, my head was spinning, and my eyes rolled up in their sockets from the sugar. I ate them while watching every Christmas special on television and reading every Christmas story I found at school or in the newspaper or in magazines. Sometimes I cried over these stories and television specials, thinking at the time it was from the deep longing I felt for the sweet-and-sticky-as-molasses endings they offered. I wonder now if my tears weren't actually from sugar shock, my brain turning to candy, my emotions stretched and wrapped around me like a taffy straitjacket.

"*Mother*, look who's here!" Aunt Constance said, as if surprised to find us on her doorstep, even though Hunter had called ahead several days before to suggest and schedule the visit. Aunt Constance and Grandma Kerry lived together in a house of beige rooms, satin brocade furniture, and light filtered through sheer curtains. It looked like something out of a movie where the rich people lived, only smaller, like a waiting room for heaven.

"I'd hug you darlings, but I've got a cold." Aunt Constance held a linen handkerchief monogrammed in gold threads to her nose, and kept the other arm out straight to prevent our approach. She always had a cold when we came to visit, which by now we only did at Christmas. Aunt Constance was my father's sister. She didn't have any children, only ex-husbands, but she always did Christmas. She checked the bottoms of all our shoes for dirt or gum. "People spit the most awful things out on the sidewalks these days," she said before leading us into the living room, our footsteps hushed by the thick pile of the ivory wall-to-wall carpeting.

An artificial aluminum Christmas tree decorated with red glass ornaments the size of jawbreakers stood on a side table in the corner of the room. Its branches were puffy, like the poodle dogs Aunt Constance always talked about but never owned for fear of the mess they'd make. There were piles of colorfully wrapped packages at its base, and the nearby fireplace had plastic logs that glowed red with electricity.

"Look, Mother, they've brought us gifts," Aunt Constance said. "I hope it's one of your mother's fruitcakes."

It wasn't. Mother didn't make fruitcakes anymore. I'd packed a tin with my gingerbread men, a collection that included a few of the Caribbean men, but mostly the suited men and none of the wild men—I'd already eaten all of those.

"My, my," Grandma Kerry said, eyeing the container, decorated with a picture of a horse-drawn sleigh in a snow-covered landscape. She offered her limp hand for each of us to grasp by her fingertips, as if in greeting but without the certain presence of a handshake.

We sat on the celadon empire couch and listened to the faint electrical hum of the logs while I wondered which of the beribboned boxes was meant for me. Aunt Constance bowed ceremoniously in front of us each to offer a poinsettia-decorated platter of "hors d'oeuvres": crustless squares of white bread topped with slices of waxy yellow cheese. There were cut crystal tumblers of 7UP to drink, even though we preferred Coke. The 7UP bottles were the color of emeralds, but when it poured out, it was invisible. Coke came in a clear glass bottle and brought its dark, honeyed-caramel color with it to the glass. Hunter and I ate the way Aunt Constance taught us that ladies do: with our little fingers sticking into the air, like bird perches or a landing strip for the unnamed rewards to come from practicing perfect manners.

Grandma Kerry reached behind the pile of festive boxes beneath the artificial tree and pulled out a stack of envelopes, handing each of us the one with our name typed on its front.

"Well, it's been lovely to see you," Aunt Constance said. This signaled the end of our visit. Grandma Kerry yawned. "It's time for Mother's nap."

We opened our envelopes when we got back to the car, since cards weren't really like presents, Hunter said, so you didn't really have to wait until Christmas to open them. Hunter got $10—I guess because she was older and her stuff cost more—and Howard and I each got $5, a dollar of which we ended up giving to Hunter, who said she needed it for gas to get us home.

*A*wake in the middle of the night, bleary eyed and cotton tongued, contemplating the lingering scraps of a dream involving sin eaters. I once did a feature on them for an international food syndicate, and it left me with a book's worth of research, though I'd forgotten most of it until now. Sin eaters were hired to attend funerals and eat food symbolic of the deceased's sins. The practice started in ancient times, continued in Europe until the twentieth century, and was popular in America during the nineteenth.

The sin eater was a stranger to the dead and had to be desperately hungry and/or poor to do this unappetizing job—food was usually eaten directly off the dead body. The prospect is even less appetizing considering that embalming wasn't invented until the American Civil War, as a way to ship bodies home from the battlefront, and prior to that corpses got ripe rather quickly. The deceased left money to pay for the service, in hopes of shortening their stay in purgatory. The sin eater's own stay in eternity's middle ground was lengthened by the act.

In my dream I am lapping like a dog at a bowl of oatmeal and gnawing on a hunk of stale bread over a body that is cold to my touch. At first I think it's a stranger. I don't recognize any of the faces of the mourners who've come to pay their last respects. I don't feel that I know anyone here. The room is lit by candlelight, with daylight leaking through the edges of dark brocade drapes. The people in the room are dressed in black. The face on the corpse is my mother's. When my bowl is empty, the mourners bring me more.

I shudder at the dream's memory, go to the bathroom, turn on the light, confirm that my eyes are as bloodshot as they feel. I brush the previous night's excess from my mouth with minty-fresh paste and return to bed.

As I lie there in hopes of claiming a few more hours of sleep, I am filled with terror that I hate the people coming to dinner Saturday night. I fear their anxiety, their dis-ease at being in my home, their self-loathing for being too weak to refuse my invitation, their sense of failure for not having something better to do, a more prestigious event to attend.

I see their blank expressions and wan smiles, their failed attempts at covering raw disappointment as they arrive at the top of my garden. Rather than savor the view of mauve mountains in the twilight and the sparkling warmth of civilization below, they shiver at the thought of Forest Lawn at their backs, wondering, possibly, how much longer until they are invited over the wall to a permanent place next door.

I imagine, as I note the blue light of dawn through the muslin curtains, they will see my garden as seedy, too overgrown for their tastes. The view won't face in the right direction, toward the vast Los Angeles basin, a sizzling reflection pool of lights, its glare ignited by the unquenchable longing of its populace, a longing surpassed only by their need to rise above and look down upon.

No one will share my fondness for the simplicity and humble beauty of this place. "Nice," they'll say. *Odd*, they'll think.

Not that I'd invited shallow people. They were good, interesting, solid people. But they were like everyone else I knew: uniformly infected with the need to doubt their place on the planet. Professionally. Personally. Socioeconomically. They reeked of anxiety and insecurity, and I invariably caught it from them.

The cool sheets and down comforter feel good against my skin, much better than the thought of getting up and going downstairs to begin yet another anxious day devoted to preparation for yet another potentially disastrous dinner party.

I consider how women doubt themselves more than men, how they are childlike well into adulthood in this sense, constantly seeking the approval of other adults, of men and women alike. I consider how the bookstores are filled with polemical harangues dictating what women should and shouldn't do, scraping at every aspect of their lives, whether it's eating or child rearing or relationships or the work they do inside or outside the home, and what they are wearing while they're doing it. I consider how such heroic measures of self-doubt make women prime candidates for madness. I consider the possibility that if I do write a book about this dinner party and it doesn't help me conquer my fear of going mad in the midst of one, or the urge to give one, maybe an accurately charted romp through my own doubt-filled swamp will help others to find higher, drier, and safer ground.

I throw off the covers and go downstairs to make my morning espresso.

Thanksgiving Braised Pomegranate Pork Tenderloin

. . . .

2 pork tenderloins (2 lbs. total)

Juice of 1–2 lemons

½ cup pomegranate juice

2 tbsp. honey

2 cloves garlic, minced

1 tsp. minced rosemary

¼ cup olive oil

Salt and pepper to taste

3 tbsp. butter, preferably ghee (a clarified butter available in specialty stores)

1 onion, cut into chunks

1 cup baby carrots

12 baby potatoes, halved

14 oz. chicken broth

2–3 tbsp. pomegranate molasses

Cut tenderloins in 3 pieces each crosswise. Marinate overnight in a whisked emulsion of lemon juice, ¼ cup of pomegranate juice, 1 tbsp. honey, garlic, rosemary, olive oil, salt, and pepper. In large braising pan, heat butter or ghee; sauté onion in it for a few minutes. Add pork pieces and brown on all sides. Add baby carrots, potatoes, marinade, and broth. Bring to a boil. Cover and simmer on medium low until pork is cooked through (about 10 minutes). Remove pork; keep warm. Continue cooking vegetables until tender and sauce is slightly reduced. Remove vegetables. Strain sauce through a sieve, return to braising dish, and stir in an additional 2 tbsp. of butter. Return vegetables to sauce and keep warm. Cut pork into ½-inch slices and serve with sauce and vegetables.

Chapter 18

FROG STEW

*T*here was frog skin on my lips, and the weight of a rain-filled cloud was crushing my chest. We were playing African Lungfish in my backyard. Susan was shoveling the mud we'd made from Howard's excavation dirt onto my body as I lay across the dandelions and crabgrass that used to be our lawn. The slime on my lips and seeping onto my tongue made me think of how the Indians in the Amazon made a stew of boiled live frogs, cooking them into a mushy gray murk that must have tasted like this. I saw the sun filtering through the heart-shaped, lime-green apricot leaves until I had to close my eyes so Susan could bury my face. Two drinking straws saved from the school cafeteria were shoved into my nostrils so I could breathe.

Lungfish could exist like this for years, suspended in damp soil and a jelly of their own making. It was as if they were not really fish at all, but some kind of animal in situ, waiting for their chance to attain land. Hold a lungfish beneath the water's surface and it would drown, as a bird might, or a snake or an unwanted dog.

Muck slid off my skin like motor oil.

Susan mixed in more dirt until the mud became the consistency of canned pudding. She dropped flat cow pies of it onto my thighs and stomach. The cats printed on my swimsuit began to disappear and ooze crept between its shirred wrinkles, soaking the fabric until it felt cold and gritty, like a sea sponge.

People took mud baths. I heard it was supposed to suck out the dirt clean through to your bones. I was losing myself in it. How did lungfish keep from sprouting roots, becoming plants? Why did they become fish instead of grass or trees?

Mud smothered me, invaded my ears, tried to penetrate my clamped mouth and flood my nostrils. I wanted it to dry, encase me in its shell, so that I could sit out the approaching drought with its choking dust and cracked earth and skin. I wanted to go back to the dark moisture of the beginning until the rains freed me to swim again.

Queen for a Day was on our black-and-white Zenith television. Hunter said it was the show where "the biggest loser always wins." Listening to other people's troubles made me feel lucky my family had none of its own. Three women told their tales of woe as I pasted Blue Chip Savings Stamps into blank books. Hunter promised to drive me to the Blue Chip Stamp Redemption Center out on Niles Boulevard, past the cemetery, to cash the books in for my Sunbeam electric skillet.

I smoothed the wet sponge over the stamps' shiny backs until their mint mucilage was sticky and fragrant—ready to lie down on the pages' faint grids.

The scrawny blond lady with the toasted skin and the daughter dying of leukemia won. She was widowed, with six children, and her skin reflected the television lights as she stood in an ermine-edged cape so big, it made her look like a bird captured beneath a throw rug. A rhinestone crown bobbled on her head like it might fall off, and I wondered if the cloak was thick enough to protect her from the stickery sheaf of roses laid across her arms.

Her face clenched like a fist and mascara leaked down her cheeks as her prize was wheeled out. It was a popcorn wagon with a mechanical clown on top. Her wish was to support her family by selling cups of popcorn at rodeos and fairs. The balding, mustachioed host made light of her speechlessness as he teased her and hugged her close. She swiped with the edge of the cloak at the mascara scrawls running down her cheeks and tried to be brave. I counted up my stamp books and discovered I was just one short for my skillet.

"Why don't you drive Mother to see a psychiatrist anymore?" I asked, dipping a fry into a catsup puddle at the edge of the white paper sack Hunter had dumped the fries onto. We were having cheeseburgers, Cokes, and fries at the Foster Freeze on our way to the Shopping Village variety store so Hunter could buy cork balls to paint for earrings she would wear to Frenchy's Night Club. It felt good to be sitting at an outdoor table in front of Foster's and eating with her. Almost every other car that went by honked and waved at her—people she knew from school and around.

"She doesn't need it," Hunter said.

"She's still crazy," I said.

"She's not crazy," Hunter said. "She's eccentric."

"What's the difference?"

"Money. Mother has enough to be eccentric. If she kept seeing a psychiatrist, she wouldn't have any money left—*then* she'd be crazy."

*M*rs. Albrecht was crazy. She looked crazier than Mother, always wearing a long gray skirt and a cardigan sweater too warm for the weather, ankle socks, and saddle oxfords. Her gray hair matched her skirt and looked like she cut it herself. She had less money than Mother—I knew this because she came by the house to sell us canned peas, spinach, and beans she said her relatives gave her, but she needed cash more. We refused to eat the food Mother bought from her, because the sweet corn and sliced carrots tasted as gloomy to us as Mrs. Albrecht looked.

One day Naomi paid a call with her mother. While Mrs. Albrecht was in the house with Mother, Naomi helped me plant my vegetable garden. Naomi and her mother lived up the street, near where Mrs. Yacksloff had lived before she married our father, in the flat-roofed houses that were smaller and less ambitious than the houses on our street. Naomi's father lived in San Leandro, a place Hunter said no one in Castro Valley ever wanted to have to go to.

Naomi was the opposite of her mother: light and giddy, her hair a dark mass of tangled curls thick as matted garden vines. She wore Evening in Paris, a perfume that came in a laundry box. She laughed a lot, making me wonder if it was because she found something funny or because she was just practicing not being sad.

My garden was a hardpack triangle of clay at the far corner of our backyard. The soil here was obstinate and salt encrusted. I had to stand on the shovel blade and rock it back and forth with my full weight to get a single slice of dirt. Naomi dug alongside me, making straight furrows for the vegetable seeds. We measured the depth and spacing for the seeds with a wooden ruler, following the written instructions exactly. I believed then in written directions—that if you followed them and something bad happened, then it wasn't your fault. And as long as you could follow directions, you knew you weren't crazy.

We planted popcorn. I wanted its exploding puffs of pleasure rising in generous mounds in my electric skillet, the skillet I would get with my Blue Chip Stamp books. I would share the popped corn that I grew and popped in the skillet that I purchased with the stamps that I pasted into the books with anyone who cared to join me in beating back the gloom.

I studied the back of Naomi's head while we worked, to see if there was any way to spot, in her dark tangle of hair, or her hands with their chipped nail polish, or her laugh, a sign that someday she might go crazy, like her mother. If something was planted just below the surface, something invisible at birth but eventually pushing through, like an all-consuming vine of trumpet flowers and depression fruit that would seize Naomi's life. It would fell her with its weight and she'd be left on the ground to rot, a source of nutrients for her own demise.

Strong green shoots emerged in the garden, pushing through the difficult soil, rising in neat rows that amazed me with their generosity. When the corn was shoulder high and the tomatoes still green, I took my father's work shirt and khaki slacks from the back porch where he left them, impaled them on a bamboo stick, and used them for a scarecrow.

Mother put Mrs. Albrecht's beans, fruit cocktail, and tomato soup in the hope chests she was keeping for us in the bottom of her closet. She packed Salvo detergent boxes with tins of pâté, smoked oysters, mock turtle soup, and jars of supermarket caviar. There was one for each of us, even Hailey, even though he'd moved out.

Mother said we couldn't touch them until our weddings. I studied the can labels for the names of countries I could move to when I turned eighteen. The chocolate-covered ants were from Senegal, the sugarcoated honeybees from Tonga. I imagined I could go to one of these countries and work in a candied-insect factory to pay my way through college. I didn't want to get married as much as I wanted to go to college. Most of the contents would be spoiled or stale by the time I got to taste them.

The boxes were orange, like flames. "Salvo" meant a military attack or a salute, a volley of bombs dropped from an airplane's bays. The soap powder came shaped like giant aspirin pills, like they were meant for a fatal headache.

Mother called these our dowries, the property we'd bring to a marriage, what I assumed she meant to be the ammo with which we'd waylay a spouse. My husband was going to look like Gardner McKay; we were going to have an Adventure in Paradise, and on our wedding night we would toast our future with spoonfuls of supermarket caviar daubed on Ritz crackers (more sophisticated than Wheat Thins, more solid than a Triscuit), celebrating our vows of eternal love with pink-foiled bottles of Cold Duck. Sometimes I wondered, though, if these delicacy-filled soap boxes were my mother's hopes that her children would say, "Fire!" or "Charge!" instead of the doomed and useless words "I do."

Howard's digging was furious, mechanical; he reminded me of Wolf when he gnawed his tail to stop an itch but only made it raw and worse. Howard said the hole was going to be a pond.

"Stop it," I said from my perch in the apricot tree. "You're messing up the yard."

"It's already messed up," he said.

I watched him work as I sat on a thick branch, chewing the tart flesh of green apricots. He dug in the private, fenced-off part of the yard, near our empty woodshed, an interior corner at the bottom of a downslope, bordered by other people's yards, opposite the rise in the yard by the street where I planted my garden. The woodshed was empty because our father had stopped stocking the structure months before he left and Mother had burned all the wood that remained.

The hole was at least six feet across and more than six feet deep. Howard could stand inside or lie down and disappear from sight. When he tried to fill it, the water leaked out. If he could get it to stay, he could swim from edge to edge.

Howard's hair made him different from the other sixth graders. Our father used to make him sit in a chair on the patio for a buzz cut so short and rough, you could see the nicks on his scalp for days. If he opened his mouth to complain, hair fell into it, so he had to shut up. Now his hair grew long and wild like the dandelions in our garbage-filled yard. He walked across the schoolyard pushing the long, stringy locks back from his face, like they bothered him, only I knew they didn't. His mouth turned down as he did this and he held his head at an arrogant height, his chest puffed out, swinging his arms like an ape. No one talked to him and that seemed to be what he wanted. We didn't talk anymore, not like we used to, not like the year before Father left, when we were still friends. When he wasn't watching television, he stayed in his room now, reading bodybuilding magazines.

Hailey beat Howard up all the time before he left. He was a wrestler in high school and he'd put Howard in a headlock, twist his head around until he cried, then slam his head on the floor until he cried even louder. I watched them and cried, too. I believed Howard read the bodybuilding magazines so he could fight back if Hailey ever tried that again.

Howard liked to practice mean stuff on me. He didn't beat me up, maybe because I was a girl, but he tore the heads off my stuffed animals and broke horses from my collection on the TV Room shelf. That's why I snuck into his room and stole his stuff. That's why I knew he had bodybuilding magazines. That's why he wanted to buy locks for his door.

A thick branch of the apple tree behind the pyracantha hedge bordering the patio lay on the ground, broken by the weight of its apples. No one pruned the fruit trees when they were in flower, so when they fruited now the branches just broke and fell off before the fruit ever got a chance to ripen. I always wondered why my father had to prune the branches back each winter. Now I knew.

Howard's face got hard as Hunter cut his hair while he sat in a patio chair. It was not as short as Father would have made it; still, it was shorter than Howard wanted it. But he had gotten a note from school saying he couldn't come back until it was a proper length. When Hunter was done, Howard looked smaller than he did before.

"Will you phone Tod and tell him I can't go out with him tonight?" Hunter asked. She was dressed to go dancing at Frenchy's with her girlfriends. She looked like an Egyptian goddess in an ankle-length orange silk caftan with a hood that draped across her shoulders. High-heeled leather sandals with straps that wrapped around her legs up to the knees gave her a regal height and posture. The cork balls she'd painted in orange and blue stripes hung from gold chains clipped to her earlobes and swayed with the slightest motion of her head. She met boys at Frenchy's who bought her Singapore Slings. She'd met Tod, her boyfriend who raced old cars, at the garage where she took the Tempest when it wouldn't start. Now it ran fine. Now he bored her. I called him Toad behind his back because he liked to stomp his work boots at Wolf to scare him.

"Tell him I've got cramps," she said.

"I don't want to lie," I said.

"After all the places I drive you to," she said, "all the things I do for you."

"Have Brenda call him," I said.

"Brenda's not family," she said. "That's what family is for."

Hunter was the only one who ever talked about family, which made me feel I only had a family when Hunter was talking. We weren't like TV families because Hunter was playing the part of the parent, as if Princess were Margaret, the mother, and Margaret, the mother, was really Kitten, the youngest girl. I didn't know who I was because I looked like Kitten but felt like Margaret, acting grown-up and thinking I was supposed to know stuff I didn't.

Hunter said Howard was adopted and I believed her. He didn't fit in. Bud, the TV son, was still being played by Hailey, even though he'd moved out with Jim, played by Father. It was like Bud was absent for a season, like when an actor is sick and his character is writing letters from somewhere, only he's really recovering from a near-fatal car accident. Howard was like a character visiting from another show, guesting for just a couple of episodes. I would have been happy if he were gone by the next season. And Mrs. Yacksloff, she wasn't even on the same network. She was like one of those actresses in a commercial who beams a toothsome smile because she's finally using the right dishwashing liquid and her hands have gone back to normal from being giant red lobster claws.

"I won't ever give you a ride in the Tempest again," Hunter said. The Tempest was the family car, and she'd promised she was going to take me in it to the Blue Chip Stamp Redemption Center to get my electric skillet.

I told Tod that Hunter couldn't go out with him that night because she had cramps, even though they'd taught us in school that the truth was as important as listening to one's dreams, and that on television liars were always getting caught.

Before she left for Frenchy's, Hunter made me up on the "Evening" setting of her three-way makeup mirror.

"Dating is so tedious," she said while she smoothed foundation onto my face with her fingertips. "Just wait." Then came blush and next mascara, black and clotted. To give me batwing lines at the end of my eyeliner, just like hers, she spit into the eyeliner cake and swirled the brush around until it worked into a thick liquid. Then she outlined my lips in pencil and slathered on a creamy, iridescent pink lipstick with another special brush. There was a special brush for every application. At the end we held our faces side by side in the mirror and sucked in our cheeks for a gaunt model look.

Then she let me sip blackberry schnapps from the flask she kept in her purse. It tasted like liquid jam and made me feel good, like everything was falling into place, like something great was going to happen because I believed it was going to (even if I did lie to Toad), like the people on TV talk shows who said they always knew they'd be a star. I sat on the couch in front of the TV with my face freshly painted in foundation, blush, eyeliner, and lipstick, the sweet essence of blackberry schnapps coating my tongue and throat, and dreaming of the night when I could dress like my big sister and go to Frenchy's.

"Que sera, sera, whatever will be, will be." Susan and I sang this in her living room to her mother's Doris Day record. When I sang it, I sang real loud in hopes that someone would hear me, that I'd be discovered and the whole world would fall in love with my voice and want me to sing, sing, sing.

The future's not ours to see, que sera, sera.

*H*unter came back early from Frenchy's. She sat on the edge of the couch in the TV Room. She never lay down on the couch like Howard and I always did. She liked to keep moving. She always sat on the edge. When she was going somewhere she always said, "I've got to jet." Like in an airplane, like jet-setters do. That night she sat on the edge of the couch for a minute before the phone rang. "I've got to jet," she said after she answered it, and then she was gone.

I watched some more TV, and during a commercial I snuck into Hunter's room to look at myself in her makeup mirror. I tried it on all the different settings, on the blue white of Daytime, the greenish tint of Office, and the warm yellow of Evening, which I still thought was the best. I thought about the legend I'd read in school about a Greek princess who was so beautiful that she made the gods jealous. I decided they were probably looking at her in the light of Evening. They were so jealous, the legend claimed, they turned her into the world's first artichoke, all her tight, nubby leaves closed like a shield of armor, her secret sweetness hidden, waiting to be discovered. I wondered if when the first artichoke became a lavender-colored flower like the ones in our yard, it just made the gods more jealous still, jealous enough to tell the mortals how to cook and eat the artichokes before they had a chance to flower.

I sat in the highest branch I could reach on the apricot tree and picked a few of the still-firm fruits. A golden blush rose through their outside's green tint, but they were sweet and ripe inside. I saw the awning of the roof off the garage and the empty bottles from Hunter's weekend—beer, wine, and clear square ones with black-and-white labels I knew were Jack Daniel's. Hunter stashed her empties there. When they started to fall out of the boxes onto the corrugated tin roof and rolled onto what was left of the lawn, she tossed them in the Dumpster at the Wishing Well Trailer Park down the road at the Boulevard, even if they had deposit refunds, because Hunter liked to be done with things and get on with stuff.

My Three Sons was on TV. The father, Fred MacMurray, used to be a famous movie star, and now he was the father of three boys on television. Their mother was dead, but because their father was Fred MacMurray, a famous movie star, everything would be all right, even if their show was still in black and white when every other show was starting to be in color. His voice had a gentle, velvet quality; his face registered concern and interest; and he held his head high and alert, not aloof, as if he knew something and was about to share it, like the way attentive dogs do. He was a good father.

The families on TV were happier, it seemed, when the mothers were dead. I didn't know anybody whose mother was dead, not yet, so I didn't know if that was true. I did know a lot of people who were unhappy or sad because of their mothers, but I didn't know if that meant they'd be less sad if their mothers were dead.

Amazon Frog Stew

Basically, get a pile of frogs (at least half a dozen), boil up an Amazonian court bouillon of roots, leaves, and bark—more than enough to cover, maybe ½ quart of liquid per frog—then toss in the live frogs all at once, put a lid on the pot or they'll get out, and keep the lid on for at least 15 minutes, until they're sure to be dead and you don't have to witness their suffering anymore. Then remove lid, add a cup of full-bodied red wine, and continue to boil down until half the liquid is gone and the frogs begin to break down into their basic elements of green, skin, innards, and eyes for an hour or more. Season to taste with salt and pepper. While stew cooks, finish drinking the bottle of wine—you'll need it to help you forget what you're eating. Prepare to dine alone, as no one is going to join you for this dish, even if you do sprinkle parsley on top.

Chapter 19
REDEMPTION CENTER

*L*annie Marsh and I sat on her back stoop, eating the mayonnaise on white bread sandwiches we'd made on the worn pine counter in her kitchen, with its peeling linoleum floor and the curtain instead of a cabinet door under the sink to hide the plumbing. I never made these at home, because they didn't taste as good as they did at Lannie's house, even though she used the same brands of bread and mayonnaise. I liked to pull off chunks of bread and squish them into dense white pellets, my fingers heating them so they smelled and tasted even stronger of mayonnaise and yeast.

We held our faces to the sun and looked out on her mother's garden as we ate. Butterflies flitted among the huge green rows of tomato plants, bush beans, green bell peppers, zucchini the size of fire logs that spilled out from beneath expansive frond leaves;

pumpkins for carving in the fall; fruit trees heavy with apples, lemons, and peaches; and flowers. There were bushes of marigolds and daisies, upright wands of giant blue delphiniums, and dahlias Lannie said were called dinner plates because that was the size of their flowers. Beyond this garden, which sustained Lannie's family throughout the year with food and bright colors and smells, was their family property, filled with wild grasses and eucalyptus trees, the few acres that remained of what used to be a farm, and it felt like we'd escaped to a place far out in the country, even though the school and my house and all the other houses were close by.

The three black labs they kept chained to a tree near the house barked like crazy when we first sat down. Each got tossed a torn chunk of sandwich and then went back to sleep. Curious chickens came over and pecked at the ground near our feet. One of the dogs had once broken free and killed a chicken. Lannie's brother Larry, who was the same age as Hailey and a friend of his, had tied the dead chicken around the dog's neck to teach it a lesson. It never went near another chicken again.

Stacks of empty wire cages for minks lined the back of a shed across from the house. Lannie's father was going to raise minks for the cash he could get for their pelts. When he told his daughters the minks were killed by electrocution to preserve their pelts, the girls snuck out one night and let them go from their cages.

"We told Pop we thought a raccoon got 'em," she said. "He was mad as heck. He's thinking about goats now. Says their milk is the best thing going. Says they can stand up to raccoons."

*W*e'd spent the afternoon asking her Ouija board how long we were going to live, whom we'd marry, how many kids we'd have, all the most important stuff. We didn't watch television at Lannie's house because the reception was bad ever since a windstorm had knocked the antenna off the roof. It was still lying in their front yard. Their TV was a dead, dark box in the corner of their living room, with a ruby-eyed ceramic panther stretched across the top, as if ready to strike anyone who tried to turn the TV on.

We put the Ouija board away when Lannie's mother was due home, because she thought it was the devil's plaything. Lannie climbed on a stool and tucked the board behind the boxes of dolls on the upper shelf of her wardrobe. Lannie saved all the dolls she ever got, in their original boxes, for the three children the Ouija board said she would have someday. The wardrobe was made of cardboard, and she and her sister Lena used it instead of a closet. The two sisters only ever shopped at the Goodwill and discount stores, which was why Hunter, who was the same age as Lena and used to be her friend, wasn't anymore. She said Lena "dressed like a ragpicker."

We finished our sandwiches and headed for the abandoned car that was deep in the middle of the dry grass field behind their house to play Make Out. Not with each other—just with ourselves. We lay on the car's rusting hood with its missing tires and grass as tall as the windows. There was a woman's black bra across the open trunk and lacy panties hanging off the door handle and bullet holes in the metal doors, like some gangster and his moll had run it into the ground. We rolled around, acting like we were making out with boys. I always thought about Gardner McKay and wrapped my arms around myself, like Lannie showed me, kissing the inside of my arms because that was the part, Lannie said, that was as soft as a boy's lips. It felt good on the warm metal hood to kiss the inside of my arm and hold myself close.

We went back to the house for bowls of peppermint-stick ice cream. The flecks of peppermint candy made the ice cream seem colder, so cold it got close to a kind of heat, and sweeter than it already was. I walked home as slowly as I could, remembering the feel of hugging myself on the hood of the car, and how peppermint ice cream might become my favorite flavor.

I heard my mother laughing to herself from behind her closed bedroom door. It was a deep, guttural laugh, as if someone were tickling her hard, only I knew she was alone. I would have asked her what was so funny, but she only ever laughed at nothing. The laughing was creepy, like Laughing Sal at San Francisco's Playland at the Beach, an unstoppable, strangling laugh that rolled out like a car without brakes, pausing only to gasp for air before continuing on its driverless ride. Sometimes I fell asleep to the sound of her laughter coming through the wall between our two rooms, and woke to the same sound. Sometimes I wondered if she was laughing at me.

I found a can of vegetable soup in the kitchen. It wasn't Campbell's, or even Safeway's; it was from a market we didn't shop at and it was probably a Mrs. Albrecht can. I was too hungry to care. I brought it to a boil in a pan, watched the lacy, rust-colored scum form at the edges, then took the pan with a spoon into the TV Room to watch *Combat*.

The soup didn't taste so bad, even if there were more chunks of potato in it than anything else. It helped that I pretended I was a GI in Italy, eating K rations out of my helmet in a foxhole. I liked *Combat* because I knew the war had ended almost twenty years before and the GIs had won, so everything that happened to them, even though it was pretty scary, wasn't the end of the world. Even if someone got killed, it was usually only that week's guest star, an actor who would show up on another series. They always did.

I laid across my bed and rolled up the sleeve of my shirt to suck the inside of my arm, to give myself a hickey like Lannie had showed me how to do. She said that was a good thing to know because boys liked how it left a bruised mark on their skin.

While I did this I heard my mother's laughter through our shared bedroom wall and it reminded me of one of those laugh tracks they used on every TV show, only the recording was made in the 1930s and a lot of the people on it were dead. After Hunter told me that, the shows were less funny, not that I had ever laughed at them in the first place. I sucked hard on my arm, my lips humid and slithery, and my arm felt solid to the point that I could imagine someone else in the room with me. I sucked until specks of blood appeared just below the surface of my skin, as if they wanted to leak through and make a burgundy oval patch. No matter how hard I sucked and how loud the roar of blood rushing through my head got, I still heard Mother's laughter.

*D*eep-sea prawns are colored in vivid reds, scarlet, and purple. At the depths at which they dwell, they look black because all the red and blue rays of light have been strained by the water far above. No one knows the reason for this coloring; no one can see or appreciate it until the prawns are brought to the surface.

When I was a child I imagined I was one of these creatures, my pulsating body a vibrant purple, the color of blood and oxygen coursing through a transparent shell, feeding on the drifting flakes of matter that fell from above like a constant snow. The more I consumed, the more vivid and intense became my secret coloring.

Mother said when they gave her electric shock treatments, they put wires in her head and shot it through with electricity and it made her vomit and forget everything she knew. She said the wires were still inside her head. Sometimes while she was watching TV, she claimed she had just gotten a big shock.

"Shut up!" Howard would say. "Stop talking like you're crazy. I don't want to hear any more of that crazy shit." But it didn't stop her.

I didn't want anyone poking around inside my head with electric wires, so I acted as normal as I could. Hunter told me the crazy things people did, and I added them to a list in my head. Like when Tod's sister slapped her purse against a picture window to kill a fly and broke the window instead. Hunter had always thought Tod's sister was crazy, and breaking that window proved it.

I wondered if Mother got to be the way she was by listening to her dreams. I decided to stop listening to mine. I was only good for a couple of days. Then I was back in class, dreaming about things I could do to get away from there, how I'd fall into something or jump ship, or my ship would come in or something, and I'd land somewhere else. I wondered if Mother started thinking her crazy thoughts because she wanted to get away from somewhere, too. But I can't imagine that our house was the place she wanted to be.

I had just enough books for the Sunbeam electric skillet. Tuesday after school, Hunter drove me to the redemption center. It was all the way out Niles Boulevard in Hayward, past the cemetery dotted with statues of people looking sad but peaceful, like I felt when I was pasting stamp sheets into books. At the redemption center, I waited in line behind all the other people with all their books of stamps until it was my turn to hand mine to the lady with the thin, red-lipped smile. She thumbed through all my books to make sure I hadn't missed any stamps, then tamped them on the counter like they were a deck of cards that needed to be set right, and said, "Wait here and I'll see if we have your skillet in stock." She made it sound like she'd been forced to disappoint others who'd driven all the way out past the cemetery, had to tell them to come back in weeks or months, until more of what they desired was waiting on the stockroom shelves. Or maybe that cautionary tone was from her own surprise by some ugly life disappointment, and she wanted to save others from her fate.

"Please wait over there," Tight Red Lips said, "until your number is called." "There" was a glass counter lined with strapped-down catalogs and merchandise displays. I couldn't concentrate on anything, though, thinking about Hunter waiting in the car. I knew if I didn't get my skillet fast enough, she'd drag me back to the car to drive home because she had better things to do with the rest of her day. And if they didn't have it at all, it would cost me plenty to get her to drive out here again.

Finally, the woman brought my box to the counter. I rode home with it on my lap in the passenger seat of the Tempest, dreaming of all the inexpensive cuts of meat I would soon be braising.

*T*hat night I watched *The Twilight Zone* on television. It was a rerun, an episode I'd seen before, in which a girl discovers she can reach through her bedroom wall into another world. First her hand goes in, then her arm; then her dog's ball rolls through and her dog disappears into the wall, chasing after it. She goes in after her dog, gets trapped in this other world, and starts crying for help. Her father hears her cries from the other side of the wall and discovers he can go through the wall as well. Only he just looks in far enough to see his daughter, then comes back out, ties himself with a safety rope to the bed frame, and goes back in after them. He scoops them up in his arms and pulls on the rope until they're all safe and back in the bedroom together.

I thought about that *Twilight Zone* episode when I heard my mother laughing on the other side of my bedroom wall. I wished I could reach my arm through into that other world of her room and save her. Or that my father would do it. He'd once tied himself to the bumper of a car and walked into deep mud to rescue a lamb that got stuck on a farm out in the canyon. It was like something heroes did in movies or on television. He was good with knots; he had boards filled with all the fancy knots that sailors learn to tie. He could tie a knot strong enough to rescue me if I went through the wall to stop Mother from laughing, if he really wanted to.

Only now that he lived two hours away with Yvonne, Mrs. Yacksloff, he probably couldn't get here fast enough. That's why I slept on the far side of my bed that night, away from the wall. I didn't want to accidentally roll up against it and wake up to find myself on the other side with no one to rescue me.

*S*unday bells rang as we pulled up to Lannie's grandmother's house on San Francisco's Church Street. Her grandmother had said she could bring a friend, and I was the one she'd asked. I could smell the garlic from the front door when we entered; it was in the meat Lannie's grandmother was slow-simmering for dinner: a dish called osso buco—veal shanks cooked in red wine, garlic, and tomatoes—with garlic bread like my mother used to make, buttered and larded with garlic slices.

Lannie's grandmother fussed over the clutch of blooms I'd brought. I'd gathered them from our garden, where Mother said nothing grew. I'd found grape hyacinth, pale yellow daisies, and pink Jupiter's beard, which Mother called a weed, and dandelions, which everyone called a weed. Lannie's grandmother put them in a vase she set in the middle of the table.

The tender meat fell from the bone in velvet strings. Lannie showed me how to scoop out the marrow from the veal shanks and spread it onto the bread. The marrow brought out all the gravy's flavors and more. I mopped up the gravy with the rest of the bread. It was all so good, I nearly swooned. I wanted to eat more, but I wasn't used to sitting at a table full of people and I didn't want to look like I was too hungry.

"You must give me the recipe," I said to Lannie's grandmother. That's what people said on TV when they thought something was delicious.

Lannie's grandmother gave a delighted laugh. "I will," she said. "Do you cook?"

"No, but my mother does," I said. I hated lying to Lannie's grandmother, but I didn't want to shame my mother by making anyone think she couldn't care for her own children, that she wasn't the little red hen who could grow the wheat and grind the flour and bake the bread. I didn't tell Lannie's grandmother about the electric skillet I'd just gotten, and how I wanted to make osso buco in it. "I think she'd like to try this."

When I said that, a piece of bread went down my windpipe and I began to choke. I coughed hard but still couldn't breathe. Lannie's father jumped up from his seat, wrapped his arms around me from behind, and pushed up under my rib cage a couple of times until what was stuck in my throat came up and I could breathe again.

"Are you all right?" Lannie's mother asked, leaning over me, her face so close to mine that I could see myself reflected in her glasses. A weight settled into my stomach and it began to ache. I asked to lie down on the couch. Lannie's mother arranged the pillows for me, covered me with a throw, and smoothed her hand across my back before she returned to the dinner table. I fell asleep, and then it was time to go home. Before we went, Lannie's grandmother made a fuss all over again about the flowers I'd brought and handed me an index card on which she'd written out, in her own hand, her recipe for osso buco.

As we pulled away from the curb, Lannie's grandmother waved at us from her doorway. Her house was wedged between other houses, a whole block of houses without yards and distances between, like at home. They looked as if they were huddled together, as if each house knew where it stood on the sidewalk because it could feel the other houses touching its sides.

Osso Buco

....

8–10 large veal shanks (or the equivalent in
   bison shanks if you prefer not to eat veal.
   Either way, you are looking at about 5–8
   pounds of meat)

Flour for dredging shanks

8 tbsp. (one stick) butter

¼ cup olive oil

1½ cups dry white wine

1 large onion

3 carrots, diced

3 ribs celery, diced

1 tsp. minced garlic

3–4 cups chicken broth or beef broth

1½ cups peeled, seeded, and chopped tomato,
   or 1 28-oz can plum tomatoes, drained and
   chopped

sprigs of fresh parsley, thyme, and a bay leaf in a
cheescloth bag

salt and pepper to taste

Gremolata:

> ½ cup minced fresh parsley
>
> Grated zest of 1 lemon
>
> 3–4 cloves garlic, minced

If using veal shanks, tie them with kitchen string to keep the meat on the bone during cooking. Bison shanks won't require this string step. Rinse shanks and pat them dry, then season with salt and pepper. Put a sufficient amount of flour on a plate and dredge the meat in the flour, shaking off any excess. In a heavy skillet or large brazing pan, heat a half stick of the butter and the olive oil over medium high heat. Brown the shanks in the fat in batches, adding extra butter and oil if needed. Transfer the browned shanks to a platter. Add the wine to the pan and boil it while scraping the brown bits from the pan, until the liquid is reduced to about ⅓ cup. Set the wine mixture aside in a bowl.

In a flameproof casserole dish or large brazing pan, either of which needs to be just large enough to hold the shanks in one layer, add the remaining butter and cook the onion, carrots, celery, and garlic over medium low heat, stirring a few times, until the vegetables are soft. Add the shanks, their platter juices, the reduced wine, and broth just to cover the shanks. If you are using bison shanks, which are huge, you may need to divide the ingredients between two pans to cook the shanks in one layer. Top the shanks with the tomatoes in an even layer; add the cheesecloth bag (make up 2 if you are using 2 pans), season with salt and pepper to taste, and heat until simmering over a medium flame. Cover the mixture and braise in a preheated 325-degree F oven until the meat is tender, about 2 hours. With a slotted spoon, remove shanks to an ovenproof dish for serving. Discard the strings from the veal.

Pour the pan juices through a strainer into a saucepan, squishing the solids hard to extract as much liquid as possible, and try to skim off as much fat as you can. Boil these juices until they are reduced to about 3 cups.

Baste the shanks in their ovenproof serving dish or brazing pan with a cup or more of the reduced juices, then return them to the 325-degree F oven to bake for 15 minutes, basting them several times until they are glazed.

While the meat is baking, stir together the parsley, zest, and garlic in a bowl to make the gremolata.

Sprinkle the gremolata over and ladle a generous amount of the juices around the shanks, offering the rest in a separate dish.

Serve with a basket of sourdough bread with butter to soak up the juices. Delicious!

Chapter 20

HOW TO MAKE A PIE

I open the refrigerator door for the container of coffee and flip on the espresso machine to wait for its go-ahead green light. I see the tub of crumbled blue cheese I want to use for Saturday's salad and remember to check the expiration date. BEST IF USED BY—I turn the container in my hands, searching for the words. I don't want it to be any bluer than it should safely be, so I don a pair of reading glasses to see if that helps me locate the official claims of its continued viability.

If the government can require manufacturers to include this data on packaging, why can't it also make them put it in the same place on every package, and do so in lettering that is large enough to be read without the aid of glasses? IS THAT TOO MUCH TO ASK? By the time of my own expiration date, I will have spent several months, if not years, standing in the market aisles, scanning labels for this basic information.

I now live by expiration dates. If I can find the latest expiration date for every product that needs one, my next trip to the store can be staved off that much longer. If time spent in the company of others at the table is bonus time on Earth, then shopping and reading labels in the market is time begrudgingly spent. I detest shopping, with its rude crowds, annoying music, and long checkout lines. I worship youth as much as everyone else, only I apply it to perishables instead of people.

Then Somebody comes home and blows my whole system. He can barely be bothered to open the refrigerator door to see if there's anything inside to eat, let alone look for an expiration date. If so moved to actually investigate the interior of what he calls the "large cold cabinet in which you hide things," he immediately ignores the refrigerator's consumption timeline and invariably eats the item with the latest expiration date first or, even worse, takes something from the freezer, where expiration dates have little if any bearing, while fresh stuff decays before his eyes. He's *supposed* to take whatever item whose number is up next. He's supposed to know these things and pay as close attention to them as I do. But as far as Somebody's concerned, expiration dates are my problem. I'm the designated concerned party in this alliance because I'm the one who goes to the store.

My diligence is born of an awareness of my own expiration date. According to insurance actuarial tables and accepted wisdom, I've reached my half-life. Time is now as officially limited a resource for me as it is for that tub of cottage cheese. Shopping is a theft of time, one I seek to arrest and contain.

My husband takes the opposite approach. He'll dash off to a full-blown major supermarket, the scary kind with a large bank of checkout stands like cattle chutes at the rodeo, for just one or two things he suddenly feels we need. I think he does this in an effort to deny time's passing. It's as if the more trips, stops, and distractions he crams into a day are proof positive of his access to a youthful fountain of disposable time.

He is a Catholic—lapsed, yes, but still raised in the Church and educated at its schools. Catholicism is a mystery religion. I need full disclosure; I want to see my options and know clearly what they are. Yes, that wine may be the blood of Christ and that wafer may be his body, but that wine's eventually going to turn to vinegar and that cracker's not going to stay crisp forever, despite what Catherine of Siena claimed.

Unlike my mother, who refused to throw anything out, I am happy to relinquish; I just demand to know when the appropriate time for tossing has arrived.

I finally find the expiration date on the blue cheese. It's a relief to know it's good for another week. I make my espresso, sweeten it with a demitasse spoon of raw brown sugar, and take it back upstairs. The room spins gently from my pinot noir idyll until I lie back down on the bed, *A Brief History of Time* in one hand (176 pages to go), coffee in the other, hoping to read myself back together and rescue this day, the last full one to fill with angst before my dinner party.

*L*annie and I sat in a flat-roofed shack at the edge of her property, not far from the gangster car where we used to roll around and play Make Out. From that distance it made me think of Cinderella's coach, only I didn't mention it because it might have made me sound immature. Lannie was starting seventh grade at the end of summer. She'd be making out with boys now for real. I'd be in fifth and I still wanted us to be friends, even though we wouldn't be going to the same school. Now Lannie'd be too busy making out with real boys to have anything to do with me. She'd be living her life instead of just dreaming about it.

The sun was in the middle of the sky and it was almost too hot to stay inside the shack, where it was dark and stifling, even with the glass of the two small windows punched out, but it was worse outside. Lannie's mother's tomatoes and zucchini looked limp and begging to be picked, while the wild field grasses appeared bleached from the intense light. A fence at the edge of the yard leaned gregariously toward the neighboring property, as if telling it a secret. We spread our kitchen towel across a wood crate, turning it into a proper table on which to set the plums from Lannie's yard and an apricot tart I'd made from our backyard fruit. All the apricots had become ripe in the last few days and they'd all be gone in a few more, between what we picked and what the birds ate. We piled everything in the middle of the towel, and it looked to me like a still-life painting I'd seen once on a field trip to the museum in San Francisco.

In the half-light of the shack's noon shade, I savored the sound of Lannie's high, raspy laugh and noticed how her collarbone at the base of her throat looked blue-white and carved out, as if from marble, like she wasn't a girl anymore. I saw the outline of her breasts beneath her shirt and the pale image of the white cotton bra she now wore.

"Boys don't like fat girls," she said, taking the knife and halving the slice of tart I gave her. Then she took a bite. "Mmmm," she said, reaching for the other half of the slice. It was like we were doing something we shouldn't, finishing off the pastry with eager, almost frantic delight. When we were done, we each had a plum. Then we threw the pits out the door, thinking they might start new trees.

*T*he foul odor coming from the kitchen hit me as I stepped into the house after weeding my vegetable garden. I lifted the lid on the Sunbeam electric skillet and saw my plastic palomino stallion, the one I'd glued back together after Howard smashed it, in melted tan globs of hooves and hair, floating in the osso buco I'd made from Lannie's grandmother's recipe.

This was the skillet I'd dreamed of having, the skillet with which I would take care of myself. I could set it on low heat, leave a meal to cook in it, and work on other things, like my garden. I'd never imagined anyone would mess with my plans.

"I don't know what you're talking about," Howard said when I accused him of the crime while he sat on the couch, watching television. "But it sounds crazy to me."

"I never go near that stove," Hunter said.

Mother's door was closed and I heard her laughing on the other side. I didn't think she was laughing at me, but still, she was no use and took no interest in what was going on.

The plastic had fused to the skillet's metal and wouldn't come off. Hard as I scrubbed, there was still the outline of the melted horse, its hooves reaching toward the side of the pan. The skillet was ruined and I had to throw it out.

I knew Lannie was dead even before Hunter told me about her brother Larry's call. I'd had a dream the night before of a young woman laid out in a funeral bier, a table draped in linen and white roses. When I woke, the thought came to me calmly that it had been Lannie and that she was dead.

At Lannie's funeral I knelt at the end of the pew before I took a seat, and I crossed myself, not because I knew what I was doing, but because everyone else was doing it. It felt good that we were all doing the same thing, all these strangers and I. Her funeral was held in a Catholic church built of cinder blocks on the far edge of Castro Valley Boulevard, at the east end, where it started heading toward the canyons where Lannie's family had moved a few years earlier, to a ranch property her father bought. They had a barn and some animals, and her father ordered more minks but still couldn't fill all the cages or make a profit from their skins.

We stayed friends, despite our age difference, and I used to visit her on the ranch. Then she got her driver's license and took a curve too fast out in the canyon on her way into town. She was driving the old family car we'd ridden in that Sunday to visit her grandmother in San Francisco. It had no seat belts. She was thrown from the car and crushed when it rolled on top of her.

I smelled the incense and looked at the closed casket covered in white roses and thought about the dolls Lannie's children would never take out of their boxes, and how those children would now never be born, and how much, if she had lived, she looked forward to having them. Maybe she'd have them wherever it was she'd gone to, or when she came back as another someone. How lucky they'd be. They'd be certain to ask, as all children do, how babies are born, never imagining in their innocence to ask about all those who never are.

I thought about that apricot tart and how it was so good, we cleaned the plate by pressing the last crumbs with our fingertips and then to our tongues.

I must have dozed off for a minute, because I am suddenly awoken by the sound of pans banging downstairs. I can smell the scent of coffee coming up from the kitchen. I go below to see if Somebody has changed his schedule yet again, was here after all.

I am surprised to see that it is my mother in my kitchen. The board and care home in which she now lives is five hundred miles north of here, a distance she would never willingly travel, even if she were not now too frail to make a car trip to the store. But here she is, standing at my kitchen counter, rummaging through my drawers.

"Measuring cups?" she asks.

I'm speechless. She looks like she did when she was younger than I am today, instead of the paper-skinned, white-haired woman perpetually dressed in a jogging suit whom I sat on the patio with in December, both of us bundled against the Northern California winter air as we enjoyed the feeling of the sun on our faces, her eyes bright when she turned to me and said with genuine delight and curiosity, "Now, tell me again: What is your name and why have you come?"

Before I left her that day, she looked at me with a sweet smile and asked, "Did you have children?"

"No," I said.

"Then who will take care of you?" she asked.

"I will," I said.

Here she is, a younger version, collecting tools from my kitchen drawers and pulling a flour bag and a Crisco can down from the top shelf of the cupboard.

"Just where they always are," she says. I keep these in the same place she did. Did her mother and grandmother arrange their shelves the same way? Am I genetically incapable of arranging mine otherwise?

Mother, her skin richly colored and firm in contrast to that of the pale, wrinkled woman I last visited, fills my glass measuring cup to the one-cup mark, then spoons in dollops of Crisco and watches the water level rise. This is the backwards way of measuring she taught me in her kitchen when I was young, a method based on the laws of liquid displacement I considered then to be clever, advanced, and scientific.

"What are you making?" I ask.

"A piecrust," she says.

I know how to make piecrust—she taught me, I've even written about it, and still, at this moment, I recall none of it. The steps escape me; the theories and hopes and assumptions the seemingly simple ritual of mixing flour and shortening and liquid has always engaged in me are now completely and utterly unavailable to my conscious mind.

"Show me," I say, forced to step back as she brushes by, swinging a rolling pin, in search of a pie pan. I smell her White Shoulders powder, and a faint odor of cigarette smoke clings to her muumuu.

Her *muumuu*! This woman, who prided herself on looking fashionable in the latest tailored suits and chicest dresses before moving to the suburbs and having children, wore muumuus when she was too fat to feel comfortable in clothes. Muumuus were what the missionaries dressed the Polynesian natives in when they conquered their souls. Muumuus marked a transition in my mother's sense of herself, a capitulation, a giving in to not what she dreamt of becoming, but what others considered her to be. I haven't seen her in a muumuu in thirty years, and she quit smoking years ago, after her first heart attack. She quit to live, proving she was more in control of her mind than anyone gave her credit for. And while she wasn't living a life we could participate in, she was living a life she cared enough about to want to extend it.

She doesn't respond to my request.

"I said show me how to make a pie, Mother," I repeat.

"You have better things to do," she says. Her hair is in a bun atop her head, salt and pepper, like it was then—not the pure, thin white it is now, with her pink scalp showing through.

"Go practice your dance lesson. And I haven't heard the piano for days."

"I don't want to," I say, as if I were still a child practicing the unknown. "Please show me how to make a piecrust."

She stands at the sink and looks at me, as if tallying every inch of my person, and I can't tell if she is trying to memorize me in this moment or if she has suddenly, again, like she did in December, forgotten who I am.

"What happened to your wrist?" she asks, alarm clouding her face as she pulls my arm close to examine the blood stained gauze. Her damp fingertips leave moisture on my skin.

"An accidental scrape," I say, not wanting to explain that I fell onto the bath spigot after an evening spent with a bottle of wine.

She lets go of my wrist. The moist pressure of her plump fingertips lingers for a moment after she lets go. Her touch is like a balm lifting the dull, diverting pain at my wound's site.

"I'll show you how to make a pie," she sighs.

Was this really my mother or only, as she often suggested, wishful thinking on my part?

She continues spooning out the bobbing bergs of Crisco until the water level rises to indicate the amount needed for a two-crust pie. She pours the water out, then puts the shortening aside. Next, she measures loose spoonfuls of flour into a one-cup dry measuring cup. When the flour mounds above the rim, she slides the excess off with the back edge of a table knife. She dumps the flour into the sifter, then adds a fraction of a teaspoon of salt.

She works at a cutting board like the wooden board she used in my childhood home, a wooden board that slipped out from beneath the lip of the tiled countertop as needed. She works here with a confidence I witnessed only as a child when she was baking. Odd thing is, I don't have a pullout cutting board. This day, however, I do.

I've always wanted one. Oftentimes I've gone absentmindedly to that section of the counter and pawed at the tile edge where such a board belongs. My mother, or some version of her, arrives in my kitchen and reaches out to the same spot and there it is, waiting to be extracted, from where—the Clause? Are we standing together in this moment in the Clause?

She sifts the flour into the big yellow mixing bowl I bought because it looked exactly like the one she had when I was a child. Next, she dumps the Crisco on top of the flour, then takes two everyday flatware knives and shows me how to cut the shortening into the flour with back-and-forth slicing motions, like two loose scissor blades, until the flour and shortening are mixed together into pea-size lumps.

"For biscuits," she says, "you would keep cutting in until the shortening is the size of cornmeal."

I nod as if I am hearing from her for the first time how to make something out of nothing.

She adds a few tablespoons of milk to the flour and shortening mixture, enough to pull it together into a dough. She mixes this with her hands into a ball and pats all the loose bits together until it is the size of a small melon, which she slices in half, then pats each half into a ball. I notice that her wedding ring is still on, the large stone is still in place, and her fingers aren't yet swollen from arthritis or age. They look like my hands now, middle-aged, slim, but sculpted by muscles gained through experience.

My muumuu-clad mother sprinkles a generous amount of flour on the cutting board, then smoothes some onto her rolling pin and begins to flatten a dough ball, pushing the roller in alternating directions, forming a circle, reaching out from the center, lifting the pin and slapping it down and rolling it outward in a familiar rhythm.

Her hands are swift and sure as she works the rolling pin and I think of the hands of the two local women, both *nonnas*, grandmothers, at the cooking school in Umbria. They visited our villa's kitchen to mix pasta dough with flour and water in a graceful swirling of hands. They rolled the dough with their palms into long, stout ropes, a shape indigenous to their native region, a pasta called *ombricchelli*. They spoke only Italian, and there was no recipe to be written down—it could only be shown, learned by doing. Their hands were as thick as the dough and moved deftly as they shared with us their pasta intelligence: a pile of flour, local flour, that was most important to them, and that it was grown and ground nearby, and some water, that was all, and mixing with the hands until the consistency felt right.

They bought fresh anchovies that morning for the sauce. The older woman instructed me on splitting their plump silver bellies open with my finger, then scooping out the spine and guts. My hands became pleasantly sticky with bloody entrails as I developed a rhythm, and it all went very fast.

I can't think about them now, though. I must concentrate on Mother. When her pie dough is an even circle and thin as a kitchen towel, she pulls it gently from the board and, with both hands splayed for support, swings it over the pie pan and drapes it across the bottom and comes up the sides, leaving a rough, ragtag margin hanging over the edge.

Next she pulls a bowl of fresh apricots from the refrigerator.

"Where did you get those?" I ask.

"The yard," she says.

"Whose?"

"Ours," she says. "This is the moment. For months they swell up green, and in a blink they're ripe and ready for eating or making pies or jam. And then they're gone," she says. "And you have to wait a whole year before you can have them again."

She cuts the apricots into a bowl, then sprinkles sugar and cinnamon over all and squeezes a lemon on top of that. She mixes the fruit and sugar and spices with a wooden spoon and then pours the filling into the middle of the dough-lined pan. It is a glorious tumble of sweet orange light.

Watching her confident moves within the confines of my kitchen, a place she has never visited before yet appears to know as well as if it were her own, I consider that she never needed to be rescued, that all I ever needed to rescue was myself, that her pain belonged to her and I had to face my own.

"Almost done," she says as she rolls out the second ball into a circle, then eases it across the top of the apricot filling, cuts slits in the top to let steam out, then pinches the edges together, trimming the excess dough and then crimping it with her fingers into an elegant pattern of waves.

The phone rings and I go into the living room to pick it up. It's Walter. He is coming Saturday night, looking forward to it.

"And I'm bringing a date," he says. "An old college friend who's in town for the weekend. Is there still room?"

"Yes," I say, "of course."

"She's a writer from New York," he says. "I think you'll enjoy meeting her."

"I'm sure I will," I say.

Walter makes no mention of Jackson; no concerns are revived about Jackson in the garden, as if the subject has never been raised.

"I told her how wonderful your dinner parties are," he says. "It's been so long since I've been invited to one. I'm looking forward to it."

"Thank you," I say. No one has ever said these things to me before, that my dinner parties were wonderful, that they were looking forward to it. Or maybe they have but I haven't heard it.

"Can I bring anything?" he asks.

"Wine. Bring yourself, your friend, and a bottle of wine," I say.

His voice sounds good. I feel buoyed by it. I hang up the phone and turn back to check on Mother and the pie project. A lovely apricot and cinnamon fragrance fills the house. In the kitchen, there is no cutting board out, no flour on the tiled floor, and the mixing bowls and measuring spoons are in the dish rack, washed and dry. I have no idea how long they have been there. A golden-crusted pie sits on top of the stove, the dough having risen and fallen like miniature mountains as the filling baked and settled into an inviting landscape.

I touch it to make sure it's real.

Mother. I don't say it, only think it at first, in case she is napping, I don't want to wake her. I walk around the corner to see if she is sitting at the dinner table or on the couch. The television is on—maybe she is watching it—but no one is there. I notice that a light rain has begun. There haven't been any predictions of rain for days, and the morning has been bright, the sky clear. Now it is fast becoming a heavy downpour.

"Mother," I say softly. There is no reply. I listen for footsteps above. Is she moving about upstairs? I hear nothing. I go up and walk through the rooms, see no trace of her. I open the den's back door, feel the cold wind on my face and the dampness of the rain beating down. Wind tosses the Augusta rose bursting pale peach in the middle of the garden, the oak tree above sways before the cement wall we share with Forest Lawn, and the rain is coming down.

Mother is gone.

There's a pie on the stove—of that I am certain.

Apricot Pie

There are many good recipes out there for apricot pie. I encourage
you to find your own. I cannot provide one for you here, as I'm not
sure myself how this one was made. All I know is that it was, and
it smells delicious, and I look forward to sharing it with my guests.
I will recommend that you seek out Blenheim apricots; ask for
them by name. I know at least one grower at the farmers market
who was selling Blenheims but not advertising it. His sign only
said APRICOTS. And they were organic to boot. I was shocked. But
he was a troubled man. And who knows—you may find another
variety out there that you prefer more. Or maybe peach is your pie.
If so, I encourage you to find a recipe and a variety that you love
above all else. And then, when you have the time and the season is
right, make it for yourself to share with others.

Chapter 21

HANDS FRAGRANT WITH ROSEMARY

It is ten fifty-six on Friday night. The skunk trapper came this afternoon, set the cage baited with canned tuna at the base of the backyard palm, and left instructions for me to call if anything lands in the trap. I went back to the wine shop and got a replacement bottle of pinot noir. Kathleen called this evening to say her father is improving and she's looking forward to joining us. The plumber is coming Monday to repair the Jacuzzi. My squab are marinating in the refrigerator, plump and cozy in their pungent bath. Somebody is lying beside me in bed, having arrived just after 9:00 PM. Dalai is stretched out at our feet, on top of the comforter. Our bodies are touching enough to be aware of each other's presence, yet we are not crowded; there is enough room to feel separate and relaxed. I hear them breathing. Dalai snorts in her sleep. Somebody turns and murmurs in his. I switch off the bedside lamp, pull up the covers, and close my eyes to join them in our dark and quiet place.

I wake in the morning to a bright flood of sunlight through the bedroom windows, the hum of the basement washing machine, and the smell of coffee on the tray Somebody is bringing up the stairs. He swings through the door, two full cups and a cluster of orange wedges crowded onto a purple plate.

"*Signora?*" he says, offering a cup.

"*Grazie,*" I say.

"How else can I help?" he asks.

"Besides coffee and laundry?"

"Besides all the countless things I've done for you today and the day before and the years leading up to today, but who's counting? I'm not, and I trust that you're not—but yes, how else might I be of assistance?"

"A lounge cushion," I say. "The skunk smell refused to vacate the last one."

"And so the good knight rode off to the lounge cushion store," he says.

"Find one," I say, "and your reward will be the grilling tools!"

"The keys to my kingdom!"

"Our kingdom," I say.

I'm rotating the squab in their marinade, enjoying the earthy scent of juniper berries and garlic, when the phone rings.

"Hi there," Somebody says.

"How is the cushion quest?"

"Success still eludes us, though we need not despair," he says. "One box store remains unturned."

"Keep me posted," I say.

No sooner do I hang up than Dalai begins to bark. I suspect it's Hunter coming up the stairs, and start to take my apron off. Then I stop. If she finds my domestic pursuits a horror, so be it. This is who I am.

I hear her clomping up the stairs, see the curly red top of her head, and then she is there, standing outside my French door. She looks familiar, as young as the last time I saw her all those years ago. Her instincts at self-preservation and lessons learned at the Chateau du Charm have served her well.

"Helloooooaaaaah!" She lurches forward for a tentative hug, an un-Hunter-like gesture I wonder if she's practiced just for this day. The old Hunter was allergic to touch. Or maybe the hug is offered out of the same desire I feel as I throw my arms around her shoulders—not fondness, but a need to absorb the shock of her presence. I feel her bird-thin bones beneath her linen jacket.

"How are you?" she says, her voice strong save for an underlying wobble of nerves.

"Good, and you?" I say, vamping for time to take her in fully.

She eyes my apron, T-shirt, jeans, and running shoes.

"Still shopping the garage sale piles?" she says. It's the old Hunter after all. I can almost relax.

Dalai jumps up and bounces off Hunter's legs, then stands on her hind legs, pawing the air as she does a 360-degree turn, testing this newcomer to gauge the ease with which she gives biscuits. She throws in a yodel for good measure.

"I must give her a biscuit," Hunter says, diving for the treat jar she spots on the counter. Dalai has found an easy mark. And so has Hunter.

"That's enough," I say as Hunter gives her a third biscuit. "Biscuits are just for training."

"What are you training her to do?" she says. "Clean house?"

"It's so nice of you to drop by once every ten years," I say.

"I'd come more often," she says, "but the parking in this neighborhood is terrible! Is my Benz safe?"

"They key them here every chance they get," I say.

Her car was always getting keyed. I didn't know anyone else who had ever had a car vandalized this way. I had always wondered if it was done by people whom she'd so enraged that they couldn't think of any response besides dragging a key the length of her car body, permanently etching a thin white expletive in the enamel that required the entire side of the car to be repainted to delete it. Keying Hunter's car seemed to be one of the few ways to get through to her.

"They'd better noooooaaaaat," she says in a dragged-out, needling tone that indicates any misfortune this day will be my fault for having moved to this neighborhood, for attempting to have a life—a sign of ingratitude for all she has ever done for me, a threat that will hang over my head the entire length of my span on Earth.

"Do you like my hair?" she asks, running her French-manicured fingers through it. "It grew in all curly after the chemo."

"How is that going?" I ask. She hadn't left any further details in any of her phone messages. I didn't know whether she was still in treatment or cured, or if she'd come to tell me her days were numbered.

"I'm still here," she says. "I'm getting my energy back."

My own energy flags as I consider all that has not been said, that I thought to say in the decades that have passed—the territory not mapped, the time lost, and interest required to attempt reconstruction of two lives lived separately for so long. She is still alive and physically here, something I thought I always wanted, but in her physical presence my heart remains dormant, as if cauterized long ago and covered now by a healing layer of scar tissue.

"I've got a lot to do," I say. "I've got friends coming over tonight."

"How nice," she says, her voice filled with a familiar condescension. She's never approved of my friends. They were "skanky" when I was a child and "boring" when I was an adult.

"I see you still cook," she says.

"I enjoy it," I say.

"I've never understood how anyone can spend hours on something that people will devour in minutes," she says.

"I write about it," I snap. I feel foolish about the defensive tone, yet justified. She's never given me credit for my professional pursuits, unless she's found a way for them to benefit her.

"Really," she says. "For who?"

"Magazines, newspapers," I say.

"Well, if it wasn't in *Vanity Fair*," she says, "I haven't seen it."

I am reminded of Hunter's fondness for sensational stories of mayhem in the lives of the celebrated and well-to-do, wild stories so distant from her own, it made me think of the ancient Greeks and their need for myths of chaos amongst their gods to lift them above the muck of their collective, primitive past.

She takes a seat and sets her bag on the counter, as if settling in for a real visit. I don't know how much more of her I can take.

"Can I offer you something to drink—before you go?" I ask. I won't invite her up to see the garden. Even if I had the time, I don't want to submit myself to her reaction.

"Just a glass," she says, pulling a bottle of expensive water named after a Polynesian island out of her bag.

"How are things in Las Vegas?" I ask, handing her the glass.

"Good," she says, wiping it out with a tissue, also pulled from her bag. "I've been incredibly busy."

"Doing what?"

"I have my dealings," she says.

"Dad says you're selling used cars."

"Luxury pre-owned. Certified. That and other *projects*," she says.

"Such as?" I ask.

"I'd rather not say," she says. "I don't want to jinx anything."

"And you came here because?" I ask.

"I wanted to bring you this." She pulls a lumpen package wrapped in packers' newsprint out of her handbag and sets it down unceremoniously on the counter.

I don't touch it. It could be anything—Mother's potato masher, Wolf's skull, a clutch of Christmas ornaments to remind me of all the holidays we never had. No, scratch that. She would never bring anything so deeply personal, anything that would ever suggest that she had given me any actual thought, unless it was something that indicated her wish that I were more like her. Something that she herself would wear or use. Like a wacky joke, a rubber chicken to throw around or maybe a squirting camera that soaked the person you were pretending to take a picture of. Or a garish piece of clothing—a sequined top—or a pair of feathered earrings. Something she knew I'd never wear, but if I ever did it would make me look like a tawdry imitation of her. At the moment I don't care to see any of it. All I can think about is the comforting distraction of everything that must be done before a crowd gathers at my table tonight.

"What is it?" I ask.

"If this is a bad time . . ." she says.

"It's not great," I say, "but if you ever called anything other than my cell phone and actually tried to talk to me, I might have been able to tell you."

A flood of anger takes me by surprise as I remember all the years she has stayed away, how she has never been to this house, the decades of distance, and now she breezes in with a gift and spoils the dog with her biscuit tricks. I pick up a plate and raise it above my head and smash it on the floor with a satisfying crash. The pieces go skittering into all the corners of the kitchen. Dalai flees to the other room, which I feel bad about, except that the farther away from Hunter she is, the safer she is.

"You're acting like Mother," Hunter hisses.

"So what?" I demand. "What's wrong with that? What's wrong with acting like Mother? Because she was crazy? She wasn't crazy. She was mad. Mad as hell. She was mad because her family fucked her over," I say, and feel more solid in saying it than I have about anything I've ever said before to Hunter or anyone else in my family.

"Fucked her over," I repeat. "Her mind failed her and everybody turned their backs on her. They left her to rot in that house that rotted around her and left her children to rot with her. And they all kept their distance and they only lived across the bay, not across an ocean or across the country, or they moved away and went on with their own lives and kept their distance." I turn away so Hunter can't see the tears tracking down my cheeks. "And that was her family," I say, "and she'd been raised to believe that family was all she had." I go to the sink and run water and splash it on my face and wipe it away with a kitchen towel. I think of the kitchen towels Mother used until they were shredded gray rags, refusing to throw them away even when they became more thread than cloth. Dalai is barking wildly from her post in the living room.

"You know that's not true," Hunter says.

"It is true," I say. "Stop apologizing for them, and stop pretending that you're not one of them. I got mad, and all I've seen since is your back. Why didn't you tell me you had cancer, let me help you? That's what family is for, isn't it? Isn't that what you always said?"

"I didn't come here for a debate," Hunter says, rising from the stool and gathering her things. "Maybe I lied, maybe I was wrong, maybe I just told you what I wanted to believe. Maybe distance is the only thing this family is capable of giving. Maybe it's an immigrant thing—we're wired to leave. Our ancestors left the Old Country and we ran out of places to go; once we hit the Pacific Ocean, all we could do was leave each other. It's tough, but what are you going to do? I didn't call you when I had cancer because I needed to prove to myself that I was strong enough to survive it on my own. That I wasn't like Mother, that I didn't need anybody's help, because if I did need it, it wouldn't be there. That's what I got from being older. I told you family was all you've got because if I couldn't believe it, I needed you to."

"All you had to do was let me know," I say. "And give me an address and a phone number. Other than that, trust me, I would have been there."

"That's history. I got through it. Open the package," she says, blowing her nose in the tissue she used to wipe out the glass.

"What is it?" I ask. "Will it explode? Maybe you should open it." Hunter loved to give exploding gifts. She found them amusing. The most important aspect of a gift, as far as she was concerned, was that it should provide her with a laugh. I tug at the cellophane tape, peel back the packers' newsprint, and recognize from the first glimpse the rolled, pale yellow metal edge, dotted with ancient batter, of Mother's recipe card case.

"I found it in the house in Castro Valley," Hunter says, "behind those Salvo boxes Mother stuffed with all that crap, on her closet floor."

"The hope chests?"

"Yeah. The hope chests."

I open the lid and flip through the cards. There are clips from long-dead magazines, yellowed newsprint, and the recipe cards delicately penned by her mother that Mother used to cook from. Here is the Manhattan clam chowder, not that bland New England gruel—this is Manhattan, vibrant with tomato sauce and crisped bacon softened with a milky base. Here are the oven-baked spare ribs none of us could resist, and the garlic dip, the Garlic Dip—in writing. Her turkey stuffing and the cranberry relish she always insisted on making from fresh, whole berries. I feel their hot skins pop on my tongue. Pinwheel icebox cookies—I'd forgotten about those tender striped rolls of chocolate and vanilla. And the recipe for ginger cookies her mother wrote up for her when she was just embarking on her life. Mother's hope chest.

"Why did you bring this?" I ask.

"There wasn't anything I could do with it," Hunter says. "Maybe you can write about it."

"Maybe," I say.

"Mother would want you to have it," she says. "If she were that kind of mother."

"Somewhere, she still is," I say. "Thanks for bringing it."

"Yeah, well, I have to be going," she says. "I'm meeting friends."

"I'm sorry to hear that," I say, and she knows as well as I do that it is a necessary lie. She pulls a dog biscuit from her jacket pocket and gives it to an eager Dalai before she moves toward the door.

"Byyyyeeeeee," she says to Dalai, clutching her bag's shoulder strap as if to protect it from some impending theft. Then she turns to me with a tight smile and a brief wave from her shoulder, like some desert flower fated to collapse as soon as it blooms.

"Next time, you'll have to come visit *me*," she says.

"Sure," I say. "Just get me that address and a telephone number."

"I will," she says, moving out the door. "I promise."

I watch her red after-chemo curls bounce as she descends the stairs on her high heels, one hand holding tight to the strap of her oversize bag and the other clinging to the wooden railing, her pinky held aloft, as if it's a perch waiting for a bird to land, as Aunt Constance taught us ladies do.

I take the bag of artichokes I bought at Wednesday's market out of the refrigerator to prepare them for this evening. I think of my two nights in Pisa, on my way from Turin to Umbria, to attend the cooking school at which I learned to make the *carciofi alla Romana*. I'd never been to the town made famous by its notorious engineering failure, the Leaning Tower of. It was the day after Halloween, All Saints' Day, a day for honoring saints known and not, those lucky, martyred souls who were believed to have achieved the highest possible level of happiness, along with direct access to God.

I made the required trip to the Piazza dei Miracoli, where I found the wedding cake of a tower more engaging than I'd expected.

I was charmed by its impossibly tall stack of layers. Its serene white marble facade glowed as if lit from within beneath the roiling slate of the Tuscan sky. Steel cables were strung from its sides to prevent further leaning, or even collapse. These were anchored from behind with lead weights, a rig to pull it back and correct its forward angle by a few degrees.

Death in the form of seductive decay seemed everywhere that day in the Orto Botanico di Pisa, the University of Pisa's garden dating back to the sixteenth century—in its cracked and faded stucco walls, etched with skeletal vines strung with scarlet and rust leaves, and in its pond filled with curled ocher remnants of summer's water lily blooms. *The Triumph of Death*, the late medieval fresco on the wall of the Piazza dei Miracoli's Camposanto, is said to commemorate the plague that ravaged the citizens in the fourteenth century. Snakes wound through open coffins. There was no cure for the plague, only a condolence of paint bearing witness. The thought occurred to me that culture was invented by a drowning human, someone going under for the last time and clinging to their creation like a flotation device, like bits of weed in the Sargasso Sea.

I went to dinner that evening of All Saints' Day in Pisa at a restaurant near my hotel: Osteria Mele, Apple Tavern. An elderly gentleman greeted me at the door and escorted me to a seat at a white-clothed table in a stone-lined dining room. Sheaths of grain hung from the ceiling alongside oversize copper pots.

Next to appear was the waiter, a middle-aged version of the man who had seated me. I asked for *minestra di cavolo nero*, what I knew to be black cabbage soup, but still managed to pronounce wrong. *Ca-vo-lo*, he corrected with gentle amusement, not *ca-val-lo*—you don't want a horse, he said.

My black cabbage soup was brought to the table by an adolescent boy whom I took to be the son of the waiter and the grandson of the maître d'. I wondered if maybe this was another miracle, found beyond that of the piazza's leaning tower, that the food here was capable of pulling people back, like the steel cables attached to the tower, to their youth, or an equivalent form of innocence and grace.

That night I stayed up late in my hotel room, alone, trying to get a phone card to work. I'd paid $20 for it before I'd left on my trip, grabbed it in the travel store in the mall in Glendale, trusted that it would connect me to Somebody during my solo travels. But I spent hours talking instead to long-distance operators in Italy and then in the United States, all of them trying to convince me that it would work, should work, if only I dialed this number, and then that number. Finally, a fellow in Tennessee, I believe it was, suggested that it didn't work after all—in Italy, only Italy, for some particular reason—and that I might want to pursue the subject further with the issuing company when I got back from my trip. I gave up on the card and dialed straight through, willing to pay what I was sure would be an exorbitant hotel price just to hear the sound of Somebody's voice. I got the machine. I left a message. I put down the phone and began to sob. I missed him, our home, and our dog, and I couldn't stop thinking about them and the distance that separated us in that moment, unable to imagine in my sorrow that we would be together ever again. It took the unbridgeable separation of an ocean and continents to penetrate the protective layers in which I'd buried myself to make me realize how much I needed them, how much they meant to me. And so, alone in my hotel room in Pisa, I sobbed myself to sleep.

I rinse and dry the artichokes, leave a length of stem, like a handle, on each, and tear off the tough outside petals to expose the tender, pale green inner leaves. I slice off the tops and dig out their insides. Then I dice garlic, parsley, and basil and revel in the lovely cloud of stench that envelops me. I stuff the centers of the artichokes with the diced mixture and then put them top down, stems pointing up, in a large pot. I cover the pot with foil to hold the steam in while they cook. With a twist of the range's knob, I reduce the flame to a shallow blue halo, cover the pot, and set the timer for forty-five minutes.

Osteria Mele. Apple Tavern.

It's Saturday evening. Somebody has returned home triumphant from his lounge cushion hunt, with a forest green number found at not the biggest and cheapest, nor the smallest and most precious, but the sizable and independent and most frequently just right hardware store. On top of that, genius that he is, he has brought home ice cream, vanilla, without even having to be asked—ice cream for the apricot pie that sits protected from the devil cats in a high cupboard. He has earned the grilling tools; I gather them for him on a towel-lined tray.

I wonder if the smell of garlic from the cooked artichokes is too strong, if my guests will find it offensive. I could open some windows, turn on the ceiling fan, get the air moving and out. I could also put on a pot with water and half a lemon and even a stick of cinnamon to freshen the air. But I won't. My guests will like the smell. Together we'll revel in the aroma of garlic and grilled squab and *carciofi alla Romana*.

The garden has dried sufficiently from the previous day's rain for us to dine in it. The sky is clear. A full moon will be out.

Carlotta has arrived and is sweeping the kitchen floor. I set out the champagne flutes. We will have a round of *prosecco* in the garden at the top, enjoying the twilight and the summer air. I take the cheese out of the refrigerator, unwrap it, cover it with a dome to keep the cats away, let it come to room temperature.

I take off my apron and go upstairs to change into my dark slacks and sweater and earrings that I've picked out for the evening. It is dull, I'm sure, compared with anything Hunter might wear. It's a look that favors the understated style of Italian women, who place a greater value on what is experienced within. I look in the mirror of the vanity I brought with me to Los Angeles from San Francisco, the vanity that was my mother's when she was a young girl in the Burlingame house. I see my mother in my slightly upturned eyes, my full, bowed lips and my delicately straightforward nose. I smile at the recognition. She was, after all, a beautiful woman.

I hear Dalai bark—the incessant, rapid-fire, reload-and-fire-again yapping that I once loathed in dogs but now appreciate, even adore. Now she is silent; she's probably trying to jump all over whoever is at the door. I hope they don't mind; it's just her way and she is small, unlikely to knock them over, and there's nothing we care to do to make her stop. We want her to greet us in this way, and so she greets everyone in the same fashion. I hear my husband's rich, deep baritone voice; he is at the door, saying hello to our first guests.

I go down the stairs to see who has arrived.

ACKNOWLEDGEMENTS

I want to thank the following people for helping this novel find its way into the world: Joan Didion, for the seminal and sustaining inspiration of her writing; Kate Braverman, for making literature seem both possible and necessary; the women of Hard Words for their encouragement and friendship, especially Karen Horn, Jody Hauber, Lola Willoughby, Rochelle Low, Candace Pearson, Colleen Burns, Amy Wallen, Mary Rakow, Janet Fitch, Samantha Dunn, and Julianne Cohen; the women of Call of the Wild; the writers' communities of Squaw Valley, the New York State Summer Writers Institute at Skidmore, and UCLA Extension Writers' Program; Jack Shoemaker for letting me breathe again and editors Jane Vandenburgh and Laura Mazer and everyone at Counterpoint for making the rest easy; my agent, Betsy Amster; Mary Ann Aronsohn, Natalie Kirchoff Van Tassel, Susan McBride, Tim Cahill, Harriet Fier, Jeffrey Klein, Charles Perry, Emily Young, Lidia and Luis Diego Parada, Emilia Carrillo, Slow Food, Evan Kleiman for teaching me her carciofi alla Romana recipe, and Sumi Chang of Europane for her lemon pound cake recipe; all the guests at my table, past, present, and future; Brian Malcolm, for not letting me forget; my parents and siblings for making me want to remember and try to understand; my stepsons Nick and Matt for being so understanding; and my husband, Tom Weitzel, and my dog Dalai, for letting me know what it felt like not to be let go.

ABOUT THE AUTHOR

© David Sobel

A third generation native of Nothern California, Nancy Spiller is a writer and artist living in Los Angeles. She has won multiple blue ribbons in agility with her dog, Dalai. *Entertaining Disasters* is her first novel.